FACES OF BETH

CARVER PIKE

Copyright © 2022 by Carver Pike

All rights reserved.

No part of this book may be reproduced in any form or by any electronic or mechanical means, including information storage and retrieval systems, without written permission from the author, except for the use of brief quotations in a book review.

❦ Created with Vellum

NEWSLETTER SIGN-UP

If you're not already a subscriber and you want to keep up with all things Carver Pike, sign up for Carver's Horrific Sunday Paper and get my monthly (or not-so monthly) newsletters straight to your inbox. I promise I'm not a pest, but I'll let you know about new releases, upcoming projects, freebies, events, and all kinds of other cool info. Just go to https://carverpike.substack.com/ or click HERE if you're reading this on ebook and want to go directly to it.

DEDICATION AND AUTHOR'S NOTE

This book is dedicated to everyone out there struggling with any kind of mental or physical illness or injury. Maybe you don't even know what it is that's plaguing you. I've spent most my life trying to figure out how to complete my thousand-piece puzzle when I know I've always been missing a handful of pieces. I'm not the only one. You're not either. If all the rest of the world would only understand that a smile on the outside doesn't always mean things are okay on the inside, maybe we'd all be a little more okay.

A squeegee and some soapy water can do wonders for a window, but it won't wipe up the clutter inside. It might just keep it hidden behind that bright reflective façade. Don't be afraid to let people know the inside needs some work too and that you need a little time and some help getting things back in order. Your real friends will understand and will be there to help.

This book is also dedicated to family. All of it in all its forms. Family is family. Remember that. No matter how crazy things get. Family is family. You're not forced to stick with the ones you share blood with. If they treat you like shit, if they don't understand you, bully, and belittle you, then maybe they don't deserve you.

Real family is love. Distance can't destroy it. Time can't strip it.

Family is always there when you need them. Family can also be the ones you choose or the ones who filled gaps in your life you didn't even know were there. Don't be afraid to let new family in and don't be afraid to blend the old with the new. Family can grow if you nurture it – if you allow it.

My family is my wife who sits right here in this wide reclining chair with me and cuddles up close every night to remind me I'm loved. Jules is my ride or die and will be with me 'til the end. I've seen what true family is with her. What fighting for someone means. What being there means. What a true partnership means. She recently joined me in attending my first ever horror convention and even though she didn't think it was her world, she blended right in. She did that for me because she knew it meant that much to me, and that horror world – my horror family, accepted her. Hell, she probably made more friends than I did. Jules fucking rocks, man. She gets it. She gets me. And I hope she feels I get her.

My family is my kids over in Panama who I hope to have here with me someday. They're far away, but I hope they catch a glimpse of some of this and that I make them proud. I hope they can see me following my dream and working my ass off to make this work. I know at least one of them reads my work sometimes. My family is my kids here in West Virginia who let me come to their ball games and who make me feel included. We're one big ass blended family. It's awesome. My family is my parents, my brothers, my grandma, in-laws, aunts, uncles, cousins, nieces, and nephews spread out all over this country.

My family is the group of horror authors, traditionally and indie published, who continue to lift each other up and inspire authors like myself. I love knowing I can reach out to almost anybody around without fear I'll be ignored or pushed away. I've said before, and I truly believe, that we might write the craziest, sickest shit around, but the horror world has the kindest, gentlest people on the planet.

My family is also my friends and dedicated readers who have stuck by me through all kinds of changes in my life, through my ups and downs, through my crossing literary genres, and who continue to show up for me, share my work, read everything I have to offer, and who are always there to remind me real life comes first and book world comes second. You're the best and I hope you know you're as appreciated as you always make me feel.

Thank you to the other three members of what have become dubbed the Gore Four by our great friend Candace Nola. My three co-hosts on the Written in Red podcast. Aron Beauregard, Daniel J. Volpe, and Rowland Bercy Jr. Having you guys to bounce ideas around, to share book covers, and for constant inspiration has been awesome. We've challenged each other and really pushed each other to be better all-around. Not only as authors but as businessmen as a whole. Thank you for being friends and brothers.

I also want to say a special thanks to my author friend Lucas Mangum. Lucas is an author I've looked up to and have been inspired by over the years. He's not only an outstanding author in the horror world who has a wealth of experience and has co-written books with so many horror greats, but he's also such a genuinely nice guy. I got the pleasure of being on a panel with him during Killercon 2021 and since then we've become good friends. I asked Lucas to read *Faces of Beth* prior to publishing it, and it was his kind words that made me comfortable enough to hand it over to Brian Keene for his introduction. In other words, Lucas helped me make sure I didn't chicken shit out. Ha!

A big, special thank you must go to the group of dedicated friends and readers who helped me clean this story up and make sure it was ready for publication. Thank you to Autumn S., Stephanie A., Fran R., Beverly S., and Mary H. for all your help with this one. You've been with me for so long and I've always been able to count on you. You're the best.

As always thank you to my great author friend and big sister, Faith Gibson, for doing a final read through. You always make me feel comfortable with hitting that "publish" button. If you're reading this and you haven't read Faith's books, you're missing out. She writes some of the baddest gargoyle and gryphon and werewolf mixed with biker and... just... just go check out her shit 'cause she's fuckin' awesome.

Lastly, I want to thank Brian Keene. During virtual Killercon 2021, when I was taking part in one of the panels, I looked over to the right of my screen and saw the chat box. Brian Keene's name came up and he said something about reading my work during the pandemic. I immediately closed the chat box. I didn't want to have a total fanboy moment live on video. After that, we chatted a bit on Twitter and his words of encouragement did a lot for me right when I was going through some self-doubt. That damn imposter syndrome is a beast. Having one of my literary heroes tell me I've got the goods lit a spark under my ass that led to me finishing this book. He didn't have to take the time to talk to me or offer up those words of encouragement. Then, he told me he'd write the introduction for my next book, which happened to be this one. The words he put into the following intro mean more to me than he'll ever know. I'm not kidding when I say they brought tears to my eyes. If I ever again wonder if there's a place for me in this career – in this horror world of ours, I'll re-read this introduction. It'll be framed on my office wall. Thank you, Mr. Keene.

Here's Brian Keene's Introduction to Faces of Beth…

THE MANY FACES OF CARVER: AN INTRODUCTION BY BRIAN KEENE

Way back in the ancient times of 1988, horror fiction found itself divided into two tribes. One side was composed of authors such as Charles L. Grant, Dean Koontz, William F. Nolan, Dennis Etchison, and T.M. Wright, all of whom were proponents of quiet, traditional horror. They often bumped heads with a group of emerging writers who called themselves splatterpunks. The core of this group of writers consisted of David J. Schow, John Skipp, Craig Spector, Richard Christian Matheson, Joe R. Lansdale, and Clive Barker. Unlike traditional horror fiction, splatterpunk depicted graphic violence and sex, and usually addressed socio-political topics and taboo subjects head-on.

These two groups argued a lot, at first, except that the internet and social media didn't exist back then, so they debated the merits of Splatterpunk (as the sub-genre had come to be known) in the letter columns of magazines like *Afraid* and *The Horror Show* and *The Twilight Zone*.

Around this same time, there was another movement happening within horror fiction. Writers such as Edward Lee, Richard Laymon, Jack Ketchum, and Rex Miller were writing works that made Splatterpunk seem tame by comparison. For many years, these works were categorized as Splatterpunk, but what we were really seeing was the birth of Splatterpunk's twin brother – Extreme Horror (a label that would not come along until writers such as myself, Wrath James White, J.F. Gonzalez, Bryan Smith, Ryan Harding, and Monica O'Rourke began to get published in the late-1990s and early 2000s).

But I'm getting ahead of myself. By 1991 (several years before me or any of my friends mentioned above came onto the scene) the horror fiction tribe had pretty much decided to get along, and everybody was happy and welcome again. Splatterpunk and the then-still-unnamed Extreme Horror fit in right alongside Quiet Horror, Cosmic Horror, mainstream Horror, and all of the other sub-category marketing labels that booksellers and publishers use to move product.

Today, younger readers (and some writers) are often not sure what constitutes the difference between Splatterpunk and Extreme Horror, and indeed, the differences can often be as thin as gossamer. The main difference is that Splatterpunk usually has a politically or socially conscious angle to its boundary-pushing graphic content, and extreme horror is about boundary-pushing for its own sake. Both sub-genres are artistically valid, providing they have heart.

And Carver Pike has a big heart.

As I have often said, if you think of Splatterpunk and Extreme Horror as music, then the former is The Sex Pistols, Black Flag, The Misfits, The Ramones, and Green Day, while the latter is Anthrax, Iron Maiden, Gwar, Metallica, and Cannibal Corpse.

Easy analogy, right? But stick with me a second longer. If you are a fan of music, then take a moment to consider Motorhead – a band that comprised both genres, with one foot firmly in punk and the other firmly in heavy metal.

Carver Pike is Motorhead.

He's motherfucking Motorhead, gang.

He is a fourth-generation Splatterpunk and Extreme Horror writer with one foot firmly in each camp. I'm not sure if that's on purpose or just a natural progression. Maybe it's a result of his influences. But I suspect it is more a result of him coming into his own as a writer, and finding his voice, and fearlessly challenging himself with each new work. Regardless of how it came about, we are lucky to have him. He's pushing both Splatterpunk and Extreme Horror ahead – expanding them, playing with them, taking them in new directions and pushing new boundaries. And look, as an author who has been heralded over and over again for the last two decades when it comes to pushing boundaries, trust me when I tell you, that is no easy trick. Hell, at age 54 with 60 plus books under my name, I didn't think there were any boundaries left. And then along comes Gretchen Felker-Martin, Aron Beauregard, Daniel J. Volpe, Samantha Kolesnik, Wesley Southard, Kristopher Triana, Wile E. Young, Candace Nola, Christine Morgan, Rowland Bercy Jr., C.V. Hunt, and the rest of this new fourth generation, with Carver Pike at their head like some clean-cut, country boy reincarnation of Lemmy, and the boundaries I didn't even think existed anymore? They just blow them right the hell up, leaving a fine red mist in their chaotic wake.

Suddenly, Wrath James White, Bryan Smith, Ryan Harding, Monica O'Rourke and myself are stuck having to play catch up. And I shudder to think what the *really* old guys like Edward Lee, David J. Schow, and John Skipp are having to do to keep pace. (Love you, guys!)

I love it. As a reader and fan of all forms of horror fiction, it delights me to see this melding taking place. And as a writer of all forms of horror fiction, it pleases me to see that there are still new places to go and new ground to tread.

I suspect Carver will begin treading into some of Horror's other sub-genres very soon, as well. You can see the beginnings of it, here in this book. It's right there in how he approaches mental illness. As I said above, he's got heart. And he has things to say. Could we see a Carver Pike quiet horror novel? Or a Carver Pike cosmic horror novel? I bet we will. He has many faces left to show us, and I'm here for it. I discovered his work during the pandemic, and I've quickly become a fan.

Anyway, I'll shut up now, and let Carver take over. He has some things to say to you, here in the dark. You may think you're ready, but you have no idea...

(You might want to turn some Motorhead on in the background).

– Brian Keene
Somewhere along the Susquehanna River
April 2022

1

Family is family. Remember that. No matter how crazy things get. Family is family.

It was a promise he'd made his wife. Andrew would be as patient as possible. He would try to understand each of her family members' quirks, and boy, did they have their quirks.

Gore was due home any minute, and like a concerned father, Andrew sat in his windowsill with his hands cupped around a mug of hot chocolate and his current mystery read face down beside him.

It's nearly one. He knows how worried I get. We've talked about this. He agreed to get home at a decent hour.

Andrew had issued an ultimatum: if the guy wanted to have a roof over his head, if he wanted to be welcome at the dinner table, if he wanted to be accepted as part of the family, he'd have to abide by a few rules.

One o'clock in the morning is not a decent hour.

Then again, *he* wasn't a child. He'd be home soon. He was probably rushing home right now.

As if on cue, the doorknob rattled a few feet away. Andrew hadn't seen the approach, but Gore was great at sticking to the shadows. He was one sneaky son of a bitch.

Andrew stood, unlocked the door, and backed away. He snatched up his book and dashed to the living room where he sat on the couch as if he'd been there all evening.

When Gore entered, he kept his head down and his hood pulled over it. He was always like this. Solemn and silent.

"So," Andrew said, clearing his throat. "How did it go?"

The man turned his shadow-hidden face toward him. The dim hallway light refused to penetrate the darkness of his hood. Even the bulbs seemed afraid of him.

Andrew's overactive imagination kicked in and, for a moment, he imagined the light sending thin, frail fingers toward the young man and those fingertips hesitating at the fabric of the hood, flinching a few times as they considered pulling back that veil but then deciding against it and retreating.

"Gore," Andrew said. "I'm speaking to you. How did it go?"

The man lifted his clenched fists, turned them toward the ceiling, and opened them. Even in the room's faint light, Andrew could see they were slathered in blood.

Andrew took a deep breath and sighed. This meant the doorknob would also be covered in it.

"I see," Andrew said. "So, it went—"

"Well," the man growled.

His voice always came out low and gravelly. Each time he spoke, and it was rare that he did, Andrew imagined a pit from hell opening up in the man's gut. He could see the twisted, agonizing faces of those trapped souls trying to reach out. Then the man would slam his gullet shut with a clack of his teeth, and those souls would once again be trapped.

It took Andrew a second to come to his senses and realize Gore was still standing there with his red palms held out in front of him. "I suppose I shouldn't ask for more details."

The shake of Gore's head was barely noticeable, but Andrew saw it and decided not to push for more information. The less he knew the better.

"I'm glad you had a productive evening," Andrew said, and then nodded and tilted his head to the right, letting him know he was free to go to his room.

Gore huffed, shoved his hands into his pockets, and walked away.

Great. Blood in the laundry, too.

Andrew waited until he heard the creaking of the stairs before going out to the garage to retrieve the cleaning supplies. It didn't take long to wipe down and bleach the doorknob. It never did. This had become a bit of a ritual lately. It seemed Gore was great at sticking to his rules during the job, but once he found the comfort of home, he got lazy. This left Andrew with the duty of cleaning up after him.

Oh, how I wish he'd get lost.

Gore was family though. Andrew's wife, Beth, had lots of strange family members. She was too good for Andrew. How he'd landed an angel like her was beyond his own comprehension. He could look past her guests' peculiarities if need be. As long as it made her happy. As long as it kept her *his*.

Dammit, I'll need to clean the bathroom and bedroom doorknobs, too.

Everything Gore touched on his way to bed would need to be wiped down.

By the time Andrew finished and made it upstairs, his wife was sound asleep. He cursed under his breath at Gore, the asshole who'd caused him to miss some alone time with his woman. Whenever possible, he liked being by her side as she read her favorite book, he read his, and they had a nice cuddle as the night wound down.

Every once in a while he'd get lucky. Tonight, as it was nearing half-past one, there would be none of that. He held her anyway and enjoyed the scent of her freshly showered hair.

She hadn't gone to bed long ago, and that frustrated him even more. The things he put up with for her. Way too many damn family members. Her bleeding heart had bled onto him and he suffered for it.

"Goodnight, gorgeous," he whispered as he kissed her forehead and allowed himself to drift off to sleep.

2

"We don't have any Fruity Pebbles."

Through the gummy eyelids that accompanied not getting enough sleep, Andrew looked past the pig-tailed little girl standing at the side of his bed and saw that it was only seven o'clock. His alarm for work wasn't set to go off for another hour. He hated when Beth got such an early start. If she was around, he could get more sleep, but she wasn't so he'd have to tend to the cereal situation.

"Eat the chocolate stuff," he murmured, knowing damn well she wouldn't. She was a sweetheart when she wanted to be, but other times she was a downright brat. He supposed most six-year-olds were.

"Eww, that's gross," Alexandra, or Alex as he'd gotten used to calling her, replied with a whine he'd learned to adore. It was definitely an acquired taste.

He'd married into this family. It had taken a long time to get used to everyone's likes and dislikes. At first, he'd raised his voice a lot. He'd been a video game playing bachelor for all his thirty years. Then, he was madly in love. Now, he was a thirty-two year old with no time to play his games and much more patience than he'd ever had in his life.

"Please eat the chocolate stuff. I need more sleep." His voice came out muffled through lips mashed against his pillow. He refused to commit to becoming fully alert. There was still a chance she might retreat and leave his room. It was doubtful, but it was possible.

"Stayed up late again?"

"What would you know about it? You're just a kid."

"I know when I stay up late, I'm *really* really tired in the morning."

"Good. You know how I feel. Can you let me sleep another hour?"

"But we don't have Fruity Pebbles."

"I know. You said that already."

"Can I have some pancakes?"

"Is Paloma awake yet?"

"No, not yet."

Paloma was a live-in helper – housekeeper/nanny – with strict working hours so Andrew only had to pay her minimum wage, with room and board included of course. As much as he wanted to tell the little girl to wake her, he knew he couldn't without it resulting in overtime and since he'd forget to scribble it down in his notepad, he'd have to take Paloma's word on how many hours over she worked. He found it much easier to deny any overtime. If he only allowed her to work forty hours per week, he only had to pay her forty hours per week.

He wasn't a cheapskate, he was just trying to get by on a meager salary and help an illegal immigrant with no place else to go by paying her a fair wage but not a cent more since he couldn't really afford what he was paying her now. He needed the help, and she did too, so they were scratching each other's backs. Alex, not understanding the concepts of money or time, would bother Paloma 24-hours a day if she were allowed to.

"She'll be up soon," he said, "then you can bug her."

Alex stomped out of the room with all the huffs, puffs, and groans she could manage on her way down the stairs. She wouldn't wait for Paloma. She'd throw her temper tantrum now, but she'd forget about it in five minutes once she was sitting in front of the TV with whatever cereal she found in the kitchen.

Andrew didn't give a shit. She could bring on all the drama of Broadway. He still had... fifty-three minutes left to sleep.

As usual, his desires didn't quite line up with reality. He'd always been a counter, a clock watcher, and as soon as he looked at those red digital numbers, he knew these fifty-three minutes would be spent lying in bed with his thoughts. Alex, his stepdaughter, had seen to it that he would not be getting any more rest this morning.

Instead, his mind went over the facts. He was tired. Bone tired. He might even say exhausted. He'd known when he met Beth that she came with a lot of baggage. Yet, he'd inherited this great big house in the rich part of town, so he'd accepted it all with open arms. He definitely had the space to take care of her family, but it turned out, space wasn't the only criteria. Patience was needed, as well as endurance, and even the ability to turn a blind eye from time to time like he had last night.

Her kids, fifteen-year-old Peter and six-year-old Alex, weren't so bad. Peter pretty much took care of himself. Like most kids his age, he was glued to his video game system. Alex needed a lot of attention, but Andrew could handle her. She was his daughter now, after all.

It was the other family members mooching off him that really pushed his buttons. Both of Beth's siblings were living with them. Gore was a twenty-something punk. Of course, that wasn't his real name but to call him anything else was practically blasphemy. Ruby, Beth's sister, was a bit of a whore. Most disturbing had to be her grandfather, Dennis, who liked to be called Father Dennis. He was an ex-priest who must have been knocking at death's door. The dude was ancient and barely left his room.

If Andrew didn't love Beth as much as he did, and if he didn't have Paloma around to help do the cooking and cleaning, Andrew knew he wouldn't be able to handle things the way they were. It felt like he was running a loony bin half the time, and that was where he worked, so he literally spent 24 hours per day in an insane asylum.

Forty-five minutes left to sleep.

Andrew's head throbbed and he knew it was from a lack of rest. He got migraines easily and felt one coming on last night while reading his book and waiting on Gore to arrive. If he could rest his mind, he might be able to sleep it off, but of course, he couldn't. His thoughts continued.

At least he didn't have to pay a mortgage. That was a blessing. His father, the founder of Mason Bank, which had closed long before his death, lost his life along with Andrew's mother in a car accident. Andrew was eighteen at the time. All he'd inherited was the house, its furnishings, a few pieces of jewelry, and a little cash. The money was gone. It dried up quickly, but still, if it weren't for the house, Andrew wouldn't be able to handle the new life he had with Beth and her family.

With Paloma being an illegal immigrant, she was happy with the skimpy earnings she received, as long as she was allowed to live in the house without paying any bills and was able to eat with the rest of the family. It really wasn't a bad gig, and she helped Andrew immensely.

Thirty minutes left to sleep.

A sigh of frustration escaped him as he threw his blanket off and forced himself up to a seated position, his legs hanging over the edge of the bed.

Why even bother?

Through the window in front of him, he saw his nearest neighbor on his riding lawnmower, and he knew he'd gotten up at the right time because if his sleep had been disturbed by the roar of that motor, he would have been pissed.

It was nearly eight o'clock, and nobody else in the neighborhood seemed to mind the asshole across the street running his mower first thing in the morning. Most of them were already up and starting their day by now. Andrew, who usually worked the later shift, was only up this early because he'd agreed to some overtime to help a coworker and because he needed the extra cash – and because Alex couldn't simply eat the chocolate shit.

Inside the shower, Andrew welcomed the hot water on his face and body. He looked down at himself and slapped his belly, thinking he probably needed to lose some weight. He'd been eating more freely lately. It was part of married life. He knew he wasn't a bad looking guy. He'd always been somewhat physically fit, and women seemed to like his brown hair and matching beard.

As he washed, he let his hand linger on his balls and grazed them a few times with his fingertips. It felt good and he started to harden as the streams of hot water pounded his head. He closed his eyes and imagined Beth on her knees in front of him. It had been a while since she'd welcomed him home from work with a blowjob. Those perks seemed to be pre-marriage mostly. She'd never been exactly wild in bed, but he'd been pleased.

They'd made love often enough. She was fondest of the missionary position and that was okay with him. He'd always secretly wished she were a little more willing to try new things, but he had to accept her how she was, and she'd always been kind of shy about sex.

When she did go down on him, the lights had to be out, and he was never allowed to return the favor. Now, sex hardly happened at all. She was always tired, they were worried about the kids interrupting, or they couldn't make too much noise because her siblings and her grandfather were always near.

Andrew stroked himself as he remembered what it was like to feel her legs fall open for him. How she'd look into his eyes and smile. He'd never been able to see her face clearly because the lights were always out, but he knew she was happy. He could feel it in her kiss. She wasn't able to have more kids, so she allowed him to finish inside her, and that was the best feeling in the world.

Today, he'd finish in the shower. Beth would be upset if she knew he was masturbating. She seemed offended by it, like it was proof she wasn't enough for him. In all honesty, lately, she wasn't. He needed this so his mind wouldn't run astray. It kept him sane. Maybe he would try with her again tonight if he got to bed at a decent hour.

By the time he was dressed for work, Alex was sitting cross-legged in front of the TV with a syrupy plate in front of her on the floor. Water ran in the kitchen, and he knew she'd woken Paloma. She knew better. She'd already gotten grounded for this twice.

"Did you wake up Paloma?" he asked as he stepped into the living room and stared down at her empty plate.

Alex looked up at him, her hair in pigtails, and smiled. He had to admit, she was the cutest damned thing, but she knew better.

"Nope," she replied. "Nope. Nope."

"Are you lying to me?"

She shook her head. "Nope."

"Alexandra?"

"She is not lying." Paloma's voice carried a thick Nicaraguan accent.

Andrew turned to see the older Latina standing in the kitchen doorway still wearing her long nightgown. Her bun was unraveling. Sometimes Paloma covered for Alex, so he still didn't buy it.

"Paloma," he said.

"I promise, Mr. Mason. She didn't. I came out to get coffee started before showering and she told me she wanted pancakes."

He nodded and looked down at Alex whose smile beamed back at him.

"I need to get to work," he said. "You behave for Paloma, okay? I might bring some ice cream back tonight if you're good."

The little girl cheered. "Okay, Daddy."

His heart melted. Yes, she could be an absolute brat sometimes, but she'd recently taken to calling him Daddy. He'd never demanded that of her, had never even asked her to call him that, so he found the gesture sweet.

Turning to Paloma, he asked, "Did Beth leave any instructions for dinner?"

"Umm," Paloma replied, thinking about it, "yes, she did. She told me to make *ropa vieja*."

"Mmm. Perfect."

Ropa vieja was their favorite of Paloma's meals. The name of it was funny as it basically translated to "old clothes," but it was delicious. Flank steak slow cooked in her special sauce with onions, green peppers, and whatever else she threw in there.

"Do me a favor and make sure Peter doesn't spend the whole day on the Playstation," he called out over his shoulder as he headed for the door. "He's been getting headaches lately from staring at that screen all day. And that doesn't mean switch to his phone!"

He closed the front door and heard Paloma's response on the other side. "Okay, Mr. Mason."

Peter wouldn't listen to her. Teenagers never did. He tried not to be too hard on the boy, but it was true he was getting headaches. Andrew wanted to buy some of those special blue-tint glasses meant for gamers for the boy's birthday. Maybe he should buy them sooner.

"Ka-ching," he said to himself as he walked to his car.

Sometimes he felt like a walking cash register. Everything cost money and it wasn't lost on him that it would take approximately an hour or two of his workday to earn what it would take to buy those glasses. Again, he wasn't a cheapskate, and of course, he was happy to do what was needed for his family, but nothing made him feel more like a loser than comparing work time to dollars spent.

Nothing makes me feel more like a loser than reminding myself I'm not a cheapskate. Maybe I am a fucking cheapskate.

He wished he could be more like his father, before the bank went under, and truly provide for his family. If he could only be the founder of *something*.

He blinked once and it felt like it took way too long to open his eyes, so he closed them again for a minute, giving himself a moment of silence, knowing it might be the only solitude he'd experience all day. He pressed a thumb against each eyelid and watched the odd blend of colors ignite there, bursting in time with the thumping of his head. A migraine was definitely coming, heading his way, like a storm forming on the horizon. Headaches he could handle. Even migraines he could manage. As long as this one didn't bring nausea with it.

Yeah, I'm bone tired. I'm so damn tired.

If Gore went out again tonight, he wasn't going to wait up.

Andrew started his car and pulled out of the driveway.

3

Myles-Bend State Psychiatric Hospital was located high on a hill that overlooked a small town called Lawson. The entire town revolved around the hospital, so you were more likely to find the place in a pamphlet given to your not-quite-there grandmother than on any U.S. map.

The hospital looked exactly as expected. Dull brown with peaked towers that seemed to only exist to make the place look more menacing. Each exterior brick was a different shade than the one next to it, like a smoker's mustache that was mostly grey from old age but was also streaked with rusty nicotine stains. The flowerbeds to both sides of the main entrance hadn't been tended to in quite some time.

Andrew figured the facility wasn't properly funded, but how much money could it possibly take to throw a coat of paint over the walls and send in a gardener to at least put in fake flowers that would last longer?

The yard behind the building was much prettier, as that was the area some patients were allowed to roam, but out front, it was quite intimidating. Andrew laughed to himself as he thought of the building being a lot like a mullet haircut. Business in front, party in back.

Nothing much would change here. At Myles-Bend, you could always depend on things remaining the same. The patients would continue to be crazy, and he would go on receiving a paycheck. That was all that mattered anyway. Nobody starved and nobody died prematurely, so nobody gave a shit. In all his years working here, hardly anyone ever truly got fixed, but if they were locked up inside, they were unable to harm anyone on the outside.

It was a sad truth, Andrew thought, knowing he wasn't making much of a difference. At one point in his life, he'd considered being a high school teacher where maybe he would have been able to reach a few kids and change their lives for the better. He'd even considered law enforcement where he could have saved lives and cleaned up the streets. But he'd ended up here, at Myles-Bend, where he felt more like a babysitter for people who half the time didn't even know where the fuck they were, let alone who he was.

The criminally insane took up the top three floors of the building. Only security and staff assigned there could ride the elevator that high or exit the stairs on those floors. The bottom levels housed the non-dangerous guests, or as Andrew often referred to them, the less-dangerous guests. Some of them were far from being innocent and safe to be around unrestrained, but since they hadn't killed anyone – on record – they were treated differently from the deranged patients upstairs.

Myles and Bend, the doctors who'd founded the place, had been fans of the lobotomy. Everyone in town knew about it and had heard the screams emanating from the building. This was back in the day, but the long stretch of years between then and now didn't stop scary stories from spreading. Kids would dare each other to step up to the door on Halloween. Sometimes, just for shits and giggles, staff members would spend the holiday standing in random windows with sheets over their heads to give the kids something to tell their school friends.

Andrew was one of those staff members. Only a few of them had a sense of humor. Olivia, his best friend, was one of the others. They were psychiatric technicians but referred to themselves as orderlies because it rolled off the tongue a lot easier. They both only had access to the bottom four floors, which was fine by them.

Even the doctors, nurses, and orderlies who worked at the higher elevations seemed a little bit strange. One doctor never smiled at all. Another smiled too much.

It was the smiling one who passed Olivia a wave on the way to the elevator as Andrew walked in and approached the orderly station. She returned the smile but didn't wave. When the elevator doors closed and the creepy doctor was out of sight, she said, "You have to be of a certain mindset to work up there. Did I ever tell you about Stan?"

Of course, she had. They'd shared every story possible over their years working together. Stan was the douchebag who stole her earmuffs. Andrew liked her stories though, so he only shrugged when she asked. Her green eyes lit up and she tightened her blonde ponytail as she got into her best story-mode stance.

"It was a dark, stormy night," she began, waving her fingers in front of her face and bringing them down as if to symbolize rain. Andrew thought they looked a little too much like jazz hands and chuckled.

"What?" she asked.

He put up his own jazz hands and she laughed before rolling her eyes and snapping back with, "Fuck off."

"Go on with your story."

"Okay, I will." She bit her bottom lip, a gesture that used to drive him nuts. Nuts as in he found it absolutely adorable.

The truth was Olivia was beautiful. She was way too pretty for him, and he was proud to say they dated for a few weeks. The sex had been amazing, but she didn't take anything seriously and it bothered him that she was able to turn things off and on whenever the mood suited her.

One day she would be hot with him. Totally flirtatious. Couldn't keep her hands off him. The next day she'd be totally cold. It would be more like they were friends. She would even talk about other guys. The switch would flip again and suddenly they'd be back at her place fucking.

It should have been amazing. Most guys would love a relationship like that, but Andrew had always wanted more, and when it became clear she wasn't the one to give him that, he cut ties with her. The interesting thing was, neither of them really ended the relationship. It kind of dwindled on its own. She asked if he wanted to come over one night, he said he wasn't really in the mood, and the subject was never brought up again.

Sure, she'd flirted from time to time. He had too, but once he got married, she seemed to respect his new situation and kept the flirting to a minimum. Cutting it out entirely wasn't in her nature, but she understood it would be completely one-sided. Andrew was enamored with Beth and wasn't interested in a fling or anything even close to it. He was devoted to his wife.

"It was a dark and stormy night," she repeated, "and that motherfucker, Stan, stole my earmuffs."

The rest of the story didn't matter. She'd started it with the most important part. Stan was a motherfucker, and he stole her earmuffs one cold and rainy night, a night before it snowed, and she was left scraping ice off her own windshield with freezing ears. Add to that, the jerk never called her again.

He was lucky it was only her earmuffs. Once, a guy stole a book of CDs out of her car when she broke up with him. It had all her Weezer albums in it. She threw a garden gnome through his window when he refused to return it. Then she drove home blasting 'Beverly Hills' and singing at the top of her lungs.

"You look like shit," Olivia informed him as she handed him the clipboard containing the notes of the orderly on shift before him.

Andrew grabbed it, glanced at it, and said, "Thanks. I haven't slept so great. Have a headache coming on. Migraine I think."

"Want one of my pills?" she asked.

He hated accepting them from her because he knew her migraines came on often and she only got so many pills per month due to insurance restrictions.

"Let me try to fight it first," he said. "If coffee doesn't help, I might take you up on it."

"So, how are things with Beth?" Olivia asked as he checked the clipboard again.

"Beth," he said, letting her name linger for a moment as he tapped a finger against one of the names on the board. "Beth's fine. Did you see this? Scarborough's daughter came to visit again and said something to set him off. He's been pissing in the corner of his room all day."

"Thank God we don't do janitorial work," Olivia said.

"Yeah, but Phil does and he's not gonna be happy about it."

"Phil's never happy."

She was right. Phil never was. He wore the same stern expression whether he was wiping off a dusty countertop or scrubbing shit off the cafeteria floor. Yes, someone had actually taken a shit on the cafeteria floor once, twice, or a few times.

Glancing up from the clipboard, Andrew looked around the place. Posters adorned the walls, all positive motivation and advertisements except for the corkboard with special announcements for the guests. That was where one would find all the schedules, like the meals, orderlies' shifts, and the movies that would play each Friday evening in the rec room.

Everything seemed bathed in blue, outlined in darkness, and it was noon. Andrew had worked every shift the hospital had to offer, and he'd realized it looked the same at midnight as it did at noontime. Three in the morning could have been ten in the morning.

At one of the staff meetings, he brought up the fact that it was always dark in the hospital. Not nighttime blackness, but if he had to explain it, he would say it always felt like twilight. It could be as sunny as possible outside, but inside it felt like there were storm clouds looming overhead. There were very few windows at Myles-Bend, other than the barred-up ones inside the patients' rooms, but even if there were more, Andrew knew it would always feel like there was a hurricane brewing outside the glass.

"Depressing," he muttered, but Olivia heard.

Her ears perked up. "Depressing?"

"This place," he said. "How can anyone hope to get better when it's so fucking dull, dreary, and depressing."

"Dead, despairing, and decrepit?" she replied.

"Huh?"

"I thought we were playing *Words that begin with the letter D.*"

"Fuck off," he replied.

They had great banter between them and lately, with so many people clogging up his household, Andrew had to admit he kind of liked being at work. At least here, he knew what his responsibilities were. At home, he felt a bit lost. Almost like he was needed by everyone except the one person he wanted to need him. He couldn't help thinking about a time when he and Beth would sneak off to be alone. It didn't matter who was around. They would find special moments together.

Now, time for everyone else at home seemed to matter more, and being here at work seemed less like work.

And you're not committing a crime by covering up whatever Gore is up to tonight.

Gore. What a piece of shit. And he was family.

"So, how's the married life treating you?" Olivia asked.

Hadn't she already asked him that? She seemed to be digging, and he wasn't sure he liked it.

"It's going good," he said. "I guess."

"You guess? Beth's a hottie and she's definitely interesting."

"Interesting? What's that supposed to mean?"

"Nothing."

Andrew set the clipboard down on the counter and noticed Olivia was biting her lip, as if holding back her words.

"What?" he asked again.

"She's dull, Andrew. I'm so sorry. But she is. And…" She squinted her eyes and pursed her lips, like it was causing her great pain to finish. It wasn't, but she wanted to be dramatic about it. "Well, you were more fun before you met her. That's all I'm saying. You deserve better." She threw up both hands, guarding her face as if warding off an attack. Like Andrew was known for throwing fireballs when he got angry.

"Seriously?" he asked. "She's great. Come on."

"Is she though?"

"Olivia—"

Faces of Beth

"I'm just saying. I think she's taking advantage of you, and you can do better."

"Like who? You?"

Olivia laughed. "Me?"

He lifted an eyebrow in her direction.

"Okay," she said with a laugh, "you can't say we weren't pretty good together."

"We weren't even together! So, no, we weren't pretty good together."

"No?" she asked, looking genuinely surprised.

"You know what I mean."

She rolled her eyes. "I still say you deserve better."

"I love Beth," Andrew said as he picked up the clipboard and walked away from the orderly station. "I love Beth."

"Keep telling yourself that," she teased.

"Bitch."

"Asshole."

They both laughed.

Olivia's shift started two hours before his and would therefore end two hours before his. All orderlies were on a similar schedule. Overlapping them made sure there was always someone on duty and if someone didn't show up on time, there was still someone there to fill in until the tardy employee arrived. There was a station at the other side of the building too, near the back doors, with orderlies maintaining the same schedule. There were never fewer than two orderlies on each floor at the same time.

Upstairs, they kept more on duty because the patients were often younger, stronger, and a lot more dangerous. Down here, they were mostly over the age of seventy and didn't have the energy to cause much trouble.

Charlie Dap was polishing his shoes when Andrew walked past his room.

"Hi Charlie," he called out to the old man who always wore pajamas but spit-shined his business shoes every single day as if he needed to prepare for a long day of walking Wall Street tomorrow.

Charlie responded to the greeting by lifting a shoe in Andrew's direction.

Lady Anne Clemson was next up on the right. She didn't bother anyone but claimed she was royalty who'd been locked away for telling family secrets. She'd often call orderlies to her room with complaints that tabloid reporters were watching her from within the woods outside. Nobody was out there. Nobody lived on the hill, and nobody would march up there to snap photos of her. Yet, it did keep the orderlies entertained.

"Lady Anne," Andrew called out with a wave as he passed her.

"Good afternoon, Andrew," she replied. "May the day take you where it may."

He scrunched up a corner of his mouth as he passed, trying to make sense of her ramblings. He figured the day absolutely would take him where it may. He hoped it would take him someplace great.

The next room was occupied by Agatha Halstead. Agatha was very quiet and loved to read, which wasn't a problem in itself. In fact, she was much more peaceful than most of the other patients – if she was engrossed in her book. Once the story was done, she would completely lose her shit. Either she'd kick up a fuss if she didn't like the ending or she'd bawl her eyes out if it was a tearjerker. As Andrew passed her door, he peeked in to see how far she was into her paperback.

She appeared to be about halfway through. The cover showed a handsome man with a chiseled chest carrying a damsel in distress in his arms.

Romance. Could go either way.

There was enough left of that book to give them a little more time before she reached its finale and exploded on everyone around her. At the speed she read, he figured they still had another day or two.

"Agatha," he said as he passed her room and waved.

"Andrew," she called out to him, "come here."

He turned and leaned into her doorway. He wasn't going to fully commit to entering.

"Do you believe what this son of a bitch did?" she asked.

He waited for her to elaborate because he had no idea who she was talking about or what the person did.

"Liam O'Rourke," she added.

Andrew knew no Liam and wondered if they'd gotten a new patient since yesterday. Sometimes they moved one of the patients from upstairs down to a lower floor if they'd exhibited no violent tendencies. Surely Olivia would have mentioned it if that were the case.

"Heather Swan left the man to whom she was betrothed so she could ride out into the Irish countryside with Liam. And that son of a bitch told her she was too good for him, and he would not take her with him."

So, Liam was a character in her novel.

"What an asshole," Andrew agreed.

"I'm telling you right now," Agatha continued, "if he doesn't throw her onto this horse and make love to her like a real man, so help me God…" She shook her head and squinted her eyes.

Andrew said a silent prayer that Liam would do exactly that because if he didn't, Agatha was going to throw a fit in approximately two days' time.

"I'm sure he will," Andrew said.

"I sure hope so."

"You have a great day, Agatha."

"You too, Andrew."

He passed the rooms of Toad Phillips, real name Pierce, who liked to make the ribbit sound of a frog for no apparent reason, Leona Barret who believed Nazis were out to get her, Adrian Lockheed who ate with his toes – held his fork between his big toe and the one next to it, and Carmine Piazza who thought the FBI, CIA, and even the KGB wanted to pick his brain for all the secret Mafia intel he'd collected over the years.

The worst was Old Lynne. Dog Lady as some of the orderlies called her. To Andrew, she was simply Old Lynne. As long as she was sitting still, she seemed completely normal except for her dark, dull, dead looking eyes. Her stare reminded Andrew of the demons on the show *Supernatural* because he swore they were as black as night. Her hair was long, frizzy, and ashy grey. It was usually wild, unkempt, and looked downright animalistic. She didn't talk much. It was the way she moved around that earned her the nickname "Dog Lady." She always moved on all fours. What freaked Andrew out the most was her uncanny ability to get out of her room, even when the door was locked.

"Lynne," he said with a wave, knowing she wouldn't respond.

She always sat, staring out her window, as she did now. Only her crazy grey mane was visible.

"Hope your day's going great," he added and was about to walk away when her head turned.

Her body remained stoic, but her head turned to the left where he could see one of her lifeless eyes and her long, pointed nose. Sometimes he thought he saw an Adam's apple at her throat. Of course, he knew she was a woman, but her throat seemed too bony for a lady.

Old Lynne acknowledged him with a smile that crept too far up her cheek. It didn't seem natural, and she stayed like that for what had to be a full minute or two. It was enough time to cause chills to run up and down Andrew's spine, arms, and legs.

He should have walked away. Most people would. This was entirely too much time spent watching someone who was only watching back.

All was silent.

Until a hand touched Andrew's shoulder and he gasped, jumped in place, and spun around to see Olivia standing behind him. She had a hand cupped over her mouth and her eyes squinted in hysterical laughter.

"Oh, my God," her muffled voice said through her hand. "I got you so bad!"

Andrew closed his eyes and leaned back against the wall. "I hate you."

"You love me," she replied as she looked into Old Lynne's room.

He glanced that way too and saw that the old lady had turned back to the window. Leaving Olivia behind, Andrew scurried away.

"What's wrong?" she called out from behind him.

"Piss off."

She continued to laugh, following him all the way back to the orderly station where he plopped down in a chair and glared at her.

"You're truly an asshole," he said.

"Oh, stop. You'll get me back."

"I'm so gonna get you back."

"The old lady really spooks you, huh?"

"Yeah, she does."

Sometimes he thought there was a chance some of the patients could be possessed rather than insane. He knew the science of it all suggested that was impossible. They were simply delusional. Some had past drug abuse issues, some had lost it as they'd grown older, but still, Andrew wondered if something more sinister was at work.

Like the old man they called The Quiet Man. The other patients gave him the nickname because he hardly said a word. He was tall, at least 6'5", and was extremely frail. His skin was pale, sickly looking, and he had dark bags under his eyes. He stared at the corners of the rooms as if watching something there. Sometimes his lips would move as if talking to the shadows. Andrew found him to be a bit unsettling, but not necessarily frightening.

If there was anyone in the hospital that scared him, it was Old Lynne. She'd never done anything to him. He just didn't like being around her. That creepy grin she seemed to turn on specifically for him. The way she'd turn her head so he could see it and then freeze and remain perfectly still until he chickened out and looked away. She knew he didn't like her. It had become a game to Old Lynne, a game Andrew didn't care to play. He stayed the hell away from her as much as he could.

When he glanced back at Olivia, she was fiddling with her phone. He watched as she swiped left. Then she swiped right. She was at work and looking for her next booty call. That was all he'd been to her – a three-week stand.

"I think Old Lynne's possessed," he said.

"Old Lynne is crazy," she whispered.

Andrew shook his head. "Possessed."

"Did you hear her speaking in tongues again?"

He whipped his head to the right and stared at her with his mouth agape. "She spoke in tongues?"

"Yesterday," Olivia replied. "I didn't tell you about that? Holy shit. How did I not tell you?"

"I don't know. Seems like something you should have told me, don't you think?"

She paused for a second and then laughed. "Look at you. I didn't tell you because it's bullshit. I made it up. Of course, she didn't speak in tongues. She's not possessed. She's just old. And needs to brush her hair more."

"Have you ever known her to have a visitor?" Andrew asked.

Olivia's gaze shifted to the ceiling as she thought about it. "I don't think so."

"Because she's fucking possessed."

The rest of their shift went much like so many of their other shifts. George Anderson and Bonnie Grey got into an argument at the dinner table because Bonnie claimed that George kept picking his nose and wiping his boogers on the table. Andrew investigated and he had to admit, the green smears on the white table did look a lot like they might have come from the old man's nose. Bonnie, who argued with everyone, refused to stop shouting until George was moved to the next table and seated beside Lady Anne.

Someone took a shit in the hallway and, of course, Phil wasn't happy about having to clean it up. It didn't help that the janitor's shift was over at five and the pile of steaming poo was discovered at fifteen 'til. Andrew thanked God it happened right then and there because if it had occurred after Phil's shift was over, it probably would have fallen on him to clean it up.

Olivia wouldn't have volunteered to clean it which meant it would have come down to a good old-fashioned game of Rock, Paper, Scissors. Andrew sucked at that game and always lost.

As it turned out, they were engaged in the game over an entirely different matter when the lights went out. They were battling over who would bring snacks to this Friday's movie night. The patients ate popcorn and drank fruit punch, but Olivia and Andrew always brought snacks of their own.

She'd just thrown her paper over his rock when the lights stuttered, gasped, and blinked out.

Total darkness.

The patients were already locked in their rooms for the evening.

It happened often with the building's old wiring. Electricians had checked it out a number of times and none could give a good explanation. The power simply went out sometimes, the generator would turn on eventually, and usually, within an hour or two, the lights would pop back on, and all would be normal again.

Olivia and Andrew had their own suspicions on why the building had random issues with electricity. They'd spent many boring shifts going back and forth with things they believed might be happening on the upper floors at Myles-Bend. Everything from shock treatment to the electric chair for getting rid of problematic patients.

"Electric eels," Olivia called out as soon as the lights went out this time.

This wasn't how he wanted to spend the rest of his shift.

Andrew sighed. "For fuck's sake."

"That's my guess," she continued. "They've got this vat of electric eels, right? And they're using the power to regenerate their... well, power. So, when they're fully charged, they stick them in the bath with prisoners—"

"Patients," Andrew reminded her.

"Whatever. They stick them in the bath with 'em and zap! Whammo! You've got a drooling, zombie-like, well-behaved pris... patient."

"Sounds reasonable," Andrew agreed.

"I'm out of here in fifteen," Olivia reminded him, "with or without lights."

If the situation were reversed, he would never leave her in the dark, but he was the man of this friendship, and she didn't seem all too concerned about his safety nor was she worried about his mental state.

He was clearly more afraid of some of the patients than she was. In fact, she'd never really mentioned having a fear of any of them.

He was about to give her a hard time for wanting to leave him alone when a door slammed down the one hallway he hated traversing in the dark.

"What was that?" Olivia asked.

Andrew stepped away from the orderly station and walked slowly toward the hallway, trying his best to keep his sneakers from squeaking against the floor. He failed with one of his steps and his rubber sole squealed beneath him.

"Shh," Olivia warned him, "you might wake up Old Lynne."

It wasn't funny. At least to him it wasn't. Behind him, he could hear Olivia stifling her laughter. She hadn't been around the last two times the old lady had snuck out of her room. He wasn't sure how she did it. Once the doors were locked, like they were right now, they could only be opened from the outside. If a patient had an emergency, they could press the buzzer on their wall, and it would alert the orderly on duty.

Yet, Old Lynne had managed to get out of her room twice. Nobody could ever explain it. Both times, the security cameras showed her door closed. They never showed it open. But they did show her galloping wildly down the halls on all fours looking like some pale bony creature with wild hair in the green glow.

Andrew only took a couple more steps toward the hall when he stopped in his tracks. The slapping of bare feet and heavy palms against the tile floor was loud and slow. Something was moving in the dark hallway, deliberately stalking toward them but trying to move slowly enough to hide its approach.

"Andrew?" It was clear from Olivia's shaky voice that she heard it too.

Olivia was no longer laughing. She crept closer to his side, slinked an arm through his, and snuggled up close.

In any other situation, he would have pushed her away. He had no desire to be close to her. This time, his need for safety and security overpowered his fear of overstepping flirtatious boundaries.

Even Olivia wouldn't be thinking along those lines at a time like this.

"What is that?" she whispered. "It can't be…"

Andrew didn't need to answer her. She knew it was Old Lynne. He'd told her the stories, but it seemed like she didn't believe him, and nothing was scarier than knowing a lunatic was outside her room and you were alone with her for the most part.

The orderly on the other side of the building would respond if called, but they had their own duties to worry about, and he would never call them unless absolutely necessary. Of course, last time he'd needed the help once he realized she was out of her room.

This time though, Olivia was still here. She hadn't ended her shift, and he finally had proof that the old lady was out of her fucking mind.

"Do you think it's her?" Olivia asked.

The smack of what sounded like damp skin echoed down the hall. Andrew could imagine her sweaty palms hitting the tiles. She was old and it wouldn't take much exercise to cause sweat to drip down her neck, arms, ass, and saggy tits.

"It's her," he said. He didn't need to see it to know it. The sound of her gallop was unmistakable.

The generator kicked on, causing the lights to flicker as it worked to power the enormous building, but it too was old, and it would cough and sputter for a while before it would do its job to the fullest. It would be the job of the emergency lights keeping them from being plunged into total darkness. These dull bulbs placed every ten feet or so at the bottom of the walls gave the corridors an eerie orange glow that lit the path but didn't quite penetrate the darkness in the middle of the hall. Most of the building remained quite dark.

"What do we do?" Olivia asked.

"What do you mean? We find her and put her back in her room."

"Oh, hell no."

"Who's the chicken shit now?"

He was still. He knew that, but at least for a moment, he could pretend she was the scared one.

Laughter flowed from within the dark hallway where the old lady was racing around like a dog. It wasn't all-out hysterics, but it was a creepy snicker that had a menacing quality about it, like she'd done something evil and couldn't wait for everyone to figure out what it was.

Andrew closed his eyes for a moment and was greeted with horrible visions. He saw Old Lynne with her wild grey hair and her black, oily eyes. He could imagine that sickening grin of hers in the darkness, her dentures moving in her mouth as she quietly cackled and crept through the halls in search of him. Maybe she could climb the walls or would come spider-crawling across the ceiling.

No, she's only human. She's not actually a demon, no matter how fucking creepy she is.

His eyes sprang open as Olivia squeezed his arm tighter.

The sound of Old Lynne's galloping was coming closer. It was faster now, almost at a frantic pace, and the eerie giggle grew louder.

Andrew and Olivia backed away from the hallway as the old lady, as naked as Andrew had imagined her, charged out of the dark corridor, passed the orderly station, and hurried around the atrium area. Her tits shook, her hands thwacked against the tiles, and her wild mane blew back in what should have been nonexistent wind. To Andrew, the air felt still, yet her hair flowed around her as if she'd stumbled upon a breeze.

As she bolted by, she turned her head and looked in their direction. Even in the darkness, her grin was obvious. She was smiling at them, and the corners of her mouth seemed to stretch wider than normal. Andrew swore they reached halfway up her cheeks. Her head was cocked at an odd angle, and she kept moving forward even with her eyes on them. Then, she tilted her head back and let out a painful moan that sounded like it might have damaged her vocal cords.

"My God," Olivia said.

Old Lynne ran into the opposite hallway and disappeared in the darkness. She was headed toward the elevators but without a keycard, she wouldn't be able to access them.

"We have to get her," Andrew said, hearing his own voice tremble.

"I don't want to."

"Me neither, but it's our job."

"What the hell is wrong with her?" Olivia asked. "Is she possessed?"

Andrew would have laughed if he wasn't scared shitless. As it was, he couldn't even manage an "I told you so."

As they contemplated chasing after her, the old woman came rushing out of the hallway, back across the atrium, past the orderly station, and right back into the hallway that led to her room. Andrew and Olivia moved quickly into the hall, but she was already gone. The darkness hid her room, but they heard the door slam.

Neither of them moved. They stood at the entrance to the hallway peering into the faint light provided by the emergency lighting.

When the lights suddenly popped on, it caused both of them to jump.

They both laughed. Olivia put her head against his shoulder and a hand on her own chest.

"My heart is about to rip out and leave without me," she said.

Andrew had forgotten that her shift was about to end.

"Yeah," he said, "mine too. And my fuckin' headache's gone."

They both laughed.

"Believe me now?" he asked.

"I believe you, and I don't want to be here tomorrow at all without you."

"I don't want to be here tonight without you."

"If it weren't for the situation, I'd think you were flirting with me."

"Fuck off."

She giggled. "So... uh... are we gonna go check her door or what?"

"Yeah, please. I don't want to do it after you leave."

Olivia accompanied him to Old Lynne's door where he pulled on it and found it locked firmly in place. Andrew hesitated before glancing through the slot in her door, afraid he might find her black, cold, lifeless eyes staring back at him, but he didn't. She was in bed with the blanket pulled up to her neck, and she appeared to be fast asleep.

This made no sense. Unless they'd failed to lock her door in the first place, there was no way she could have gotten out.

But she's gotten out twice before.

Andrew was going to have to order an investigation into this under the guise he was worried about her safety. The truth was, he wanted it done for his own sanity – and *his* safety – because he couldn't take much more of this shit.

Olivia left for the evening and Andrew spent the next two hours alone. Nothing significant happened. Old Lynne remained in her room, and at a few minutes to eight, Patrick showed up to relieve him.

As Andrew walked out to his car, he glanced back at the building only once and stared at the dark windows. He found the one that belonged to Old Lynne. Nothing seemed out of the ordinary, but he couldn't help thinking about how she'd been staring out of it earlier, and he wondered if she were there now, watching him.

4

"Did you bring pizza?"

Andrew closed the front door to his house and leaned against it for a second. He didn't feel ready to step through the hallway and face the others. He wasn't in the mood to entertain. He wondered if he tiptoed past the living room and quietly made his way upstairs, would he be able to climb into his armchair and read for a few minutes without any interruptions?

If Peter was playing one of his games and Alex was in her bedroom, then—

"Did you bring pizza?" Peter repeated.

The boy wasn't going to stop until he got an answer. At least Beth would be home soon. She always got home at about nine. Andrew kicked off his shoes and lined them up with the others along the wall, next to the door.

As with most teenagers, Peter didn't bother saying hello or asking how Andrew's day was. He only wanted to know what might benefit him about the moment of his stepdad's return. Right now, that meant food.

Peter was sitting where he usually was at about this time, in front of the TV with his Playstation controller between both hands.

"Tell me you brought pizza, bruh," Peter said as Andrew dropped his work bag down on the floor.

As an orderly at a psych ward, Andrew didn't carry a briefcase full of important papers or a satchel with expensive tools. No, his bag carried a box of Cheez-It crackers, a canister of instant coffee (because he wasn't fond of the stuff the hospital offered), wet wipes in case of a bathroom emergency, and other odd stuff that could possibly come in handy during his shift. None of it was necessarily important.

"I'm sorry, man," Andrew said, "but I didn't bring pizza. There's some pizza rolls in the freezer though."

"Not the same," Peter replied as he leaned his body to the right as if that might make the car on the screen handle the corner a little better.

"What are you playing?"

"GTA."

Grand Theft Auto. Perfect game for a fifteen-year-old.

Andrew moseyed over to the couch where he sat down next to his teenage son. He watched as the boy controlled his onscreen avatar who was dressed in a nice suit but wore a baseball cap. The guy was running down a busy city street. As he passed a woman in a pink dress, he suddenly lashed out and punched her in the face. The woman screamed and threw up her hands to shield herself, but Peter's character kept swinging at her, hitting her with a barrage of punches until she bled and fell to the ground.

Peter laughed.

"Damn," Andrew said, "why'd you do that?"

"I don't know."

"What's the object of the game?"

"I'm playing online right now."

He said it as if that was supposed to explain everything.

"But what are you supposed to do?" Andrew asked.

"Whatever."

Andrew watched as the onscreen character opened a car door, pulled the driver out of the vehicle, and threw him onto the street.

"Watch this," Peter said as he made his character pull out his gun and shoot the man several times.

Faces of Beth

Almost immediately the Playstation controller started flashing red and blue. The chase was on. Peter's character got into the victim's car and took off as police cruisers came at him from all angles.

"Are you winning?" Andrew asked.

Peter shrugged. "I don't know."

Andrew was only fucking with Peter. Of course, he knew what the game was about. There were missions to complete, there was money to be made, and there was a lot of fake shit to spend that virtual money on. Peter seemed interested in none of it. He only wanted to randomly hurt people in a simulated world.

"Do anything exciting today?" Andrew asked.

"Nah."

"Where's Alex?"

"In her room."

"And Paloma?"

"Asleep."

"Is anybody else home?"

Peter shrugged.

"Has Gore gone out?" Andrew asked.

Peter paused the game and set the controller down on the couch between his legs. "So, like, I told you I wasn't gonna call you Dad, right?"

"You said that," Andrew acknowledged.

"Mmm kay. But I do think you're pretty cool. And I think I can talk to you."

"You can. What's up? Is there something you need to talk to me about?"

Peter stared into his lap. "It's Gore."

Andrew took a deep breath. He hoped Gore wasn't going out tonight. He really couldn't handle staying up half the night to clean up his mess again. He'd already decided he wouldn't. He was too tired. Plus, he missed having quality time with his wife. If they didn't have sex soon, he might explode.

"What about Gore?" Andrew asked.

"He's weird. Kind of crazy. I mean I know he's family, but I try to stay away from him. He kind of freaks me out. I have to pass his room to get to mine and sometimes his door's open and he's sitting there, doing nothing, only staring... at nothing."

Andrew knew what the kid was talking about. He'd seen it himself. Gore would sit and sulk. He'd listen to depressing music with lyrics he seemed to be deeply into. At one point he'd taken to cutting himself. That phase seemed to be over, but Andrew still worried about the guy. He was the kind of person you expected to come home and find hanging from a noose.

"One time he wanted to talk to me," Peter said. "He called me into his room and when I went in there, he started rambling about how society had gone to – excuse my language – but how society had gone to shit. How people's faces were fake filtered selfies, and their lives were lies. Something like that. He said the only truth was evil. That evil was everywhere, and I should be careful. That I should watch out."

"Yeah, Gore... he uh—"

"Why do you help him?" Peter interrupted and it caught Andrew off guard. He hadn't realized the kid was so in-tune to his surroundings considering his eyes never left the TV screen or his phone.

"Help him with what?" Andrew asked, deciding to play dumb before he accidentally gave something away that he shouldn't.

"Cover up his kills," Peter replied, and Andrew's blood turned to ice.

Hearing it out loud brought with it a reality he wasn't prepared to accept. Of course, he knew what he was doing each time Gore came home and left bloody handprints all over the place. He'd wondered the same thing himself. Why did he help Gore? Was it because he didn't want Beth to be hurt if he got locked up?

But what if you get locked up, Andrew?

That would hurt Beth even more. Still, he couldn't help feeling somehow responsible for helping Gore clean up his mess. He felt like the Alfred to Gore's *Batman*.

Peter was still waiting for an answer, so Andrew went with, "Well, Beth loves him, and I love her, so I do what I can to keep her happy."

"I don't understand why she cares so much about him," Peter replied.

"Family is family. Blood is blood."

Peter chewed on the inside of his cheek and thought about Andrew's words.

"Be careful, okay?" he finally said.

Andrew ruffled Peter's hair. "I will, kiddo."

Peter slapped Andrew's hand away. "Cut it out, man." Then, he picked up his game controller and went back to slaughtering people on-screen.

5

Andrew was finally in his reclining chair in the bedroom, when he heard Beth softly singing her tune as she made her way up the stairs. She always sang or hummed 'Like a Prayer' by Madonna only much slower than the version of the song Andrew remembered. He asked her once what it was about that song she liked, and she responded much the way Peter did when asked why he was hurting people in his game. She shrugged her shoulders and said, "I don't know. I've just always liked it."

When she stepped into the bedroom, Andrew swore the light in the room brightened. Beth had that way about her. She brought with her a sense of peace he could never explain. She was *home.* All his frustrations fell to the floor and all the day's mayhem melted away.

It was silly, he knew, but he'd always imagined her a Disney cartoon princess stuck in this hellish human world. If anybody should be able to speak to animals, sing through conversations, and move to her own melody, it was Beth.

Andrew closed his book and admired her for a second, watching her make her grand entrance. To her, she was simply stepping into the room, but to him, she was enhancing the space, sprucing it up, working her magic over the spot that had seemed so drab only moments before when he'd been alone.

When Andrew stood from his chair to meet her at the door, Beth's lips parted in a smile. She was so innocent, all the time, and he knew it was his duty to protect her from the world outside their home, from everything under their roof, and even from herself.

They often spoke of moving out to the country and buying some land to farm. Neither of them had experience in this area, but both knew they'd have a much more wholesome life far removed from everyone else. If they could learn to live off the land and depend only on each other, they'd be much happier. It seemed like a dream Andrew could almost reach out and touch. He'd been YouTubing how-to-farm videos lately. It was a tiny step in the right direction, but at least it was a step.

"What are you looking at, mister?" Beth asked, going through one of her playful routines.

"The most beautiful woman in the world," he said as he clutched his heart and fell onto his ass at the foot of the bed trying to look like he'd suffered a heart attack but looking more like a gunshot victim from an episode of *Gunsmoke*.

"Well, I must apologize," she replied while giggling, "but I am a spoken for woman. Married before the eyes of God. I will not be tempted by a handsome devil."

"Let's see how good you are at warding off this devil," he said as he bounced once more on his ass and shot up to his feet, taking hold of both her hands.

Her long brown hair was down, wavy over her shoulders, and her makeup had mostly faded. It had been a long day for her too, but she still found it in her to be frisky. He loved that about her. She smelled of the sweet perfume she always wore and when he stood to wrap her up in a hug, he inhaled it and smiled.

The hug didn't happen because she stepped away from him and smiled that gorgeous smile of hers with her big, pouty lips and her warm brown eyes. At first, she was only being a tease, but then she seemed to come to a realization and her face screwed up in disgust. "Eww. Wait. You're still in your scrubs."

He'd been so tired when he got home that he'd put off taking a shower. Beth tried to escape him, but he still held her left hand and refused to let go. His fingers brushed her palm, and he felt the raised scar there from a cut she'd received long ago. He'd asked her about it before, but she couldn't remember how she got it.

"Drew!" she squealed. "Seriously, you stink!"

"Ah, damn," he said, stepping back. He knew how she hated the hospital smell on him.

"You smell like bedpans and old people," she said.

He laughed. "Beats smelling like the shit someone took on the floor tonight."

"That's gross."

"Well, when the mood's dead…"

"The mood is definitely dead."

Andrew backed away from her and plopped onto the foot of the bed again.

Thinking of work brought back a glimpse of Old Lynne on all fours, staring at him as she strode past. Chills ran down his spine and he had to fight the grimace threatening to break through on his face. Beth was quite intuitive, and he knew it wouldn't take much for her to ask him about it and if she did, he'd be forced to relive it as he explained. He really didn't want to think about the crazy old woman from work right now.

This was his safe haven.

"Did you eat anything?" Andrew asked.

Beth laughed. "Nothing makes my stomach growl with hunger like talk of people taking shits on hospital floors. But no, I didn't eat, and I'm starved. What did Paloma make?"

"What you told her to make. *Ropa vieja.*"

"My favorite."

Andrew was thrilled to have Beth to himself. She seemed to be in good spirits. Alex, Peter, Ruby, Gore, and Father Dennis were in their rooms. If everything worked out the way he hoped, he'd have a nice, relaxing dinner with his wife and then he'd shower and quite possibly fall into bed with her where they'd make sweet passionate love tonight.

Only he knew that wouldn't be the case when, as they ate dinner in the bedroom, Beth kept squeezing her shoulder and complaining about how dog-tired she was. They'd been married long enough that he knew all her signals. Anytime she mentioned a headache or being exhausted, there would be absolutely no sex. If she talked about feeling loose or being needy, he could be secure in ripping his own pants off and then going for hers.

Andrew did change out of his scrubs and into a pair of shorts and a T-shirt so his wife wouldn't be disgusted by him through their meal. Dinner was delicious, as it always was. Paloma was one hell of a cook.

They then watched TV together, him in his reclining chair with her lying down in the bed next to him. He was ready to shower but he knew if he disappeared for even a few minutes, she would fall asleep, and even if they weren't going to have sex tonight, he missed her and didn't want to lose even a second of the time he could be spending with her. He could shower once she fell asleep.

"So, how was your day, baby?" Beth turned off the TV and asked. "Talk to me a little bit before my eyes slam shut."

He reached out to her, and she took his hand in hers, rubbing at his knuckles.

"It was okay," he said.

And it was, but the truth was it felt like any other day. They all felt so routine. She hated his complaining though, and he didn't want to give her any reason to roll over and turn her back to him tonight. She was trying her best, like he was, and he needed for them to be on the same side tonight. Too many evenings ended with them in disagreement and feeling like they were on different teams.

Tonight, he needed to feel they were partners.

"Tell me about it," she insisted.

"Alex woke me up because she was hungry," he said.

"Ugh, she knows better," Beth said. "I'm sorry."

"It's no big deal. She's a kid. Work was okay. Same ol' same ol'. Came home and talked to Peter a little bit."

"He loves you, you know?"

"Meh. He deals with me. Not sure I'd quite call that love just yet."

"What did you guys talk about?"

It was one of those moments when he had to decide whether to tell the truth or lie. As much as he hated lying to her, any talk of Gore seemed to turn things sour.

When he didn't answer, she gave him a stern look and said, "Tell me."

"He's concerned about Gore," he admitted.

Beth rolled onto her stomach, sideways on the bed so she could face him, and rested her face in her hands, elbows against the bed. It was the cutest damn look he'd ever seen from her, and he wished he could strip off his clothes, slide into bed with her, and take her from behind just like that.

"Gore?" she replied.

"Yeah, he thinks Gore's weird. Freaky. Scary maybe. I don't know. You know how Gore is. He's always saying off-the-wall shit."

"And he spoke to Peter about it?"

"Apparently so."

She rolled her eyes and sighed.

"You know Gore went out again last night, right?" he asked.

"I didn't know that. No."

"Yeah, he came back pretty late. Blood on his hands again."

"He's got issues, Drew. You know that."

"I know."

"Ever since we were kids, he'd go out and kill animals and stuff. I mean, of course I feel bad for the little critters, but it's Gore and—"

"I know, baby," he said.

He didn't have the heart to tell her he was pretty sure it wasn't animals he was out there killing. If she thought he was slaughtering the occasional raccoon or putting down a possum every now and then, so be it. She didn't need to know the truth, whatever the truth actually was. He'd never witnessed Gore's wrongdoings, so he was still able to play ignorant, but he knew the truth.

It was the reason he caught himself watching the news more often now. Every missing person or dead body discovered somewhere made him wonder if Gore had anything to do with it.

"I'm sure it's no big deal," he said, "I'm tired. That's all. I stayed up late to make sure he got in okay and I'm tired."

"You don't have to wait up for him, honey," Beth said. "He's not a kid."

"I know, baby. But he tracks blood all over the house, so I like to clean it up."

"Do you think I'm too much of a burden?" she asked. "Me and all my baggage?"

The baggage, at least the adult part of that, was really wearing on him, but he couldn't tell her that. She was too sensitive. She'd start talking about how she should probably leave and let him get on with his life. That got them nowhere. He was never going to let her go, not unless it was because she wasn't in love with him anymore, and he really believed that would never be the case.

"Of course not," he said as he leaned over and kissed her on the forehead. She kept her eyes closed even as he backed away, as if she were savoring the feel of his lips on her.

"I know this isn't easy. It's a lot to handle. I'm a lot to handle—"

"You're not."

"But I am. We are. My family is a lot to—"

"Let's not talk about it tonight," he interrupted her, "we're both tired."

She yawned. "You're right."

"I'll take our plates down," he said.

And by the time he returned from the kitchen, Beth was out cold. As he did often, Andrew sat in his chair and watched her sleep. He adored her so much. He couldn't help thinking about what Olivia said. That Beth didn't deserve him. She absolutely did and he was pretty sure he deserved her too. They'd found each other after so many bad years on their own. Her ex had been a verbally abusive, narcissistic prick who didn't understand her, and after that, she'd gone at it solo for five years.

"God bless you, Beth," he said as he stood to go into the bathroom, opting to use the one out in the hallway because he preferred the harder spray of the showerhead.

At least that was what he told himself. The real reason, he hoped, would make an appearance tonight.

6

He'd hoped she'd pay him a visit earlier in the day when he'd ended up masturbating in the shower. Ruby wasn't one to get up early though. She never did. He wasn't sure she'd show up this time either, but he purposely left the bathroom door unlocked just in case. The first time it happened, he'd accidentally left it open.

It was shortly after he'd been introduced to her. This was even before he'd married Beth. They were only dating, getting serious, and he'd allowed them all to move into his house.

At the time, he didn't yet understand what that meant as far as a lack of privacy. He'd never had to hide his favorite foods or lock any of his doors. This had always been his domain. He'd been able to walk around the place naked if he felt compelled to do so. Then *they* all moved in, and everything changed. He'd always preferred the shower in the hallway bathroom even though there was a larger tub in the master bedroom, and it didn't occur to him that someone might walk in if he didn't lock the door.

He'd been in the shower when he heard the bathroom door open and close. Andrew always enjoyed his water steamy hot so there was a natural mist, and the smoky glass door was fogged up to the point he couldn't see through it.

"Beth?" he'd asked.

He'd heard only a giggle in return, but he knew it was her. Or at least he thought it was.

Even when she stepped into the shower with him, completely naked, he didn't recognize the difference. The water spray hit her fast and hard, soaking her quickly. Her back was to him, her hair was drenched, and she simply reached back to grab him.

That was the first time they fucked.

Since then, they'd performed the same act a number of times.

It was wrong. He knew that. He loved his wife, and this was her twin sister. They were identical, but where Beth was the quiet, sensitive, vanilla kind of woman who always wanted to have sex in the missionary position, Ruby was the complete opposite.

Ruby loved to give blowjobs. She'd greedily shove Andrew's face into her pussy, she was willing to fuck in every position possible – notice Andrew thought of it as fucking with her and making love with Beth – and Ruby would even let him do butt stuff. She loved anal.

Still, if he had to choose, he would always choose Beth. Unfortunately, his wife took the choice out of his hands by denying him the sex he so desperately needed. There was no love between Andrew and Ruby. It was only fucking for the sake of their sanity.

Andrew refused to let Ruby bring other men into the home, so he was fulfilling her needs as much as she was meeting his. They satisfied each other's sexual cravings.

Tonight, when Ruby snuck into the shower with him, she immediately dropped to her knees and looked up at him with those slightly squinted, animalistic eyes of hers as she opened her mouth, put out her tongue, and scooped up the head of his cock. He liked seeing it rest there against her bottom lip as her teeth touched the top of his shaft.

"May I?" she asked him, mumbling the two syllables, but he understood perfectly.

He nodded and that was her cue to go to work sucking him so feverishly his toes curled, his ass clenched, and he eventually came so hard he thought he saw stars. Ruby swallowed every drop. Beth, when she did go down on him, always made him tell her when he was going

Faces of Beth

to come so she could pull away in time and finish with her hand. He hated that.

Andrew wasn't a pig. At least he tried not to be. Somehow, as sick as it must sound to others, he felt that it was better keeping it in the family like this. The first time they had sex, he broke down and cried after. He hated feeling like he'd let his wife down, but Ruby had held him tightly and promised him that her sister wouldn't be as upset as he thought.

She said they shared a past unlike most people and some of that past included a situation with a man or two. Plus, Beth hated confrontation. Even if she found out, Ruby assured him there was a strong chance she'd never say anything. She was the type who'd rather pretend she didn't know than rattle the world around her by exposing the truth.

Andrew doubted that, but the thought helped him feel better about it.

Tonight, as usual with Ruby, he was able to get hard again almost immediately after. All it took was Ruby playing with his balls. Once he was hard, Ruby put one foot up on the tub and opened her pussy wide for him. Andrew glided right in, dropping his forehead to her shoulder when he felt her warmth. She had a silky smoothness about her, a wet warmth that always grabbed hold of him and made him feel as if he'd entered a heated, forbidden chamber. His Shangri-La.

Her orgasms always came faster than any woman he'd ever been with in the past. She was the horniest of all the women he'd experienced too, which might have been the reason she was able to finish so easily. She didn't fake it. He knew that by the way her pussy trembled and clenched him. He could feel her insides convulse, and it always brought him to climax with her. She whimpered and moaned into his ear until he quickened his pace, gripped her ass with all his strength, and rammed his cock into her until he spurted his seed deep inside.

Then, when he was done, she'd quickly clean herself, kiss his cheek, and leave the shower. She always left the bathroom first.

For a long time, he felt guilty going back to bed with Beth, but like everything else in Andrew's life, fucking Ruby had become routine.

Only this was a part of the routine he actually enjoyed. No complaints there.

As he toweled himself off, he once again thought of what Olivia said about Beth not being good enough for him, and he chuckled. If she only knew what was really going on. *Beth* was too good for *him*. He was a lousy asshole who took advantage of not only his wife but her sister as well.

Later, in bed, he lay in the darkness and watched his spouse sleeping peacefully and he felt his cock stir as he thought about Ruby and how great tonight had been. He wished he could do it again, right now, but he couldn't risk it. Ruby had to come to him, and that usually happened in the shower. That was the way it had always been done. It was the only place and time Beth was sure to never interrupt.

7

Andrew wasn't proud of what transpired in the shower. He might have liked it as it was happening, but guilt always followed. Ruby wasn't his wife, no matter how similar they looked, and deep down he knew Beth didn't deserve to be treated the way she was, even if she never found out about it.

But he was a man with needs, and already in their short marriage, Beth had stopped performing her spousal duties. Duties was a horrible way to put it, he knew that, but they were married, and he enjoyed making love to his wife. Missing out on that one special part of their relationship hurt. They hardly had sex at all anymore and they were a young couple.

Was he an asshole for what he was doing? He figured he was. Every other person on earth would think so.

As he lay down in the dark bedroom, in his spot beside Beth, he scooted closer to her under the blanket and watched her sleep. She was so tired. Each breath went in through her nose and softly rumbled past her lips on the exhale.

Ruby was gone and he was alone with Beth. He wondered if Ruby felt any guilt after. Did she even care? Did she realize the damage they were doing to his wife and how much it could hurt her if she found out?

You could have waited. Beth would have made love to you eventually.

It was time for his conscience to deliver its verdict. For it to drop the gavel on him and remind him how lucky he was in life and how close he was to messing all that up. If Beth found out, she would take everyone and go. Or, according to Ruby, she would hold it all inside and not say a single word. He wasn't sure which would be worse. Knowing she was silently suffering or feeling her wrath?

Andrew turned over because he couldn't stand to look at her anymore. His heart hurt when he did, and as he glanced over at the moon seeping through the slots in the blinds and casting a faint light over his reclining chair in the corner of the room, he thought for a moment, and only the briefest of moments, that he might prefer it if Beth left and took everyone with her.

No more early mornings with Alex, no more arguing with Peter over online video game purchases "accidentally" made with Andrew's credit card, no more cleaning up the bloody messes of Gore, no more visits from the creepy grandpa, and no more post-sex guilt because of the time he spent with Ruby.

You don't mean that. You love Beth and deep down, you love all the others too. They're family.

"What a fucked-up family," he whispered to himself.

"Huh?" Beth asked in an adorable, sleepy voice.

He rolled over once more so he could hug her. Her body was always so warm against his. Andrew faced her, slid one knee between her legs, and lay an arm over her shoulders. It was the best face-to-face cuddling he could create. She wasn't exactly in *spooning* position.

With his eyes closed, he thought about his and Beth's first date. It was a picnic, on a hill that overlooked a sleepy town. He'd placed a lunch of KFC's fried chicken and side dishes in Styrofoam cups inside a brown, wicker basket. He'd even found one of those old-fashioned picnic blankets with the red and white squares, the checkered kind that was a must in any movie where a picnic took place.

The sun shone down overhead, and he remembered Beth wouldn't eat. It wasn't that she didn't like him or that she wasn't hungry. She simply didn't like eating in front of people. He knew that beforehand though and—

Andrew's memory of the picnic blurred and became a dream as his exhausted mind finally took over and whisked him off to sleep.

They were still at the picnic. His mind had kept them there, but the town below wasn't filled with people completing their daily errands.

Instead, they were ants.

The insects didn't seem all that peculiar to him though as he munched on his fried chicken and wiped his greasy hands on the checkered blanket.

"It's funny how ants are so free to move about," Beth said.

"But we're free to move about."

"Are we?"

Beth's fist was up to her mouth and the knuckle of her thumb rested against her bottom lip. She made this gesture quite often when she was deep in thought. As with every mannerism of hers, Andrew found it cute. Everything about her amused him.

Andrew had to turn his back to Beth to follow her gaze. They watched as an ant exited the post office. Another entered the bank. Two of the insects sat on a bus stop bench conversing. An ant got into a car and drove away.

All the things people usually did in real life, in this real town, were being done by these ants, and none of it seemed odd at all. These ants absolutely seemed to belong down there. Andrew did kind of wonder where the ant now exiting the bank kept his money when he wasn't wearing pants.

"It's interesting how they keep going and going," Beth said. "Living life without any real expectations, only hoping to make it through the end of the day so they can get up and do it all over again."

Andrew wondered if she was talking about the ants or people.

"Caught up in routine," he said.

"Very much so. The difference between people and ants is... ants are loyal."

As she said the word loyal, Andrew felt a pinch on his index finger and looked down at the grass where a red ant had crawled onto his knuckle and bit him.

"Ants follow a queen, kind of the way humans should follow God. Did you know that when a woman is being raped, she is supposed to yell the word fire instead of rape?"

"I've heard that, yes," he replied as he flicked away the ant.

"Do you know why that is?"

"Because people respond faster to help put out a fire. When someone is getting personally harmed or raped, they tend to look the other way."

"Yes," Beth said. "Like Kitty Genovese. Do you know that story?"

"No," Andrew admitted.

"She was a bartender in the 60s in New York. She got raped and stabbed to death in an alley behind her apartment building. People saw her and heard her screaming for help and did nothing. They say over thirty people were around and could have stopped it or at least called for help. She died with all those people right there. She was alone on a street full of people. Or so they say."

It occurred to him he was dreaming this conversation, so he wondered where he'd heard this story before. Was it real? Were these facts? Or was this a made-up dream story?

"See? No loyalty," Beth added.

Andrew's eyes were still on the town below where the ant that had entered the bank was now exiting and crossing the street. Two black beetles, larger than any of the ants, approached the single ant and climbed atop it.

The sky above Andrew and Beth darkened with storm clouds and a wind suddenly kicked up.

"Unlike humans," Beth continued, "ants are all on the same wavelength. They help one another. They have many friends ready to attack."

In the street below, every ant in the area stopped what it was doing and rushed toward the beetles. Even the ant that had been driving the car earlier arrived on the scene, slamming on the car's brakes, and stepping out to help its brethren.

"They protect each other," Beth added. "They are all ready to fight to the death for one another."

The ants converged on the two beetles. The larger black bugs squealed in pain as the smaller, vicious ants chewed into their legs and ripped them from their bodies.

"To stop evil," Beth said.

There was a finality to her statement like the story was over, so Andrew turned back to look at her.

And found her holding a white, plastic knife from the fast-food restaurant.

"Ants are loyal," she said.

Her face transformed to that of Old Lynne. Droopy cheeks, that wild grey mane of dry, frizzy hair, and eyes as black as coal.

Then she brought the plastic knife down in a stabbing motion, right at his face.

Andrew's eyes burst open.

He'd rolled over again and was facing his reclining chair.

Only this time it wasn't empty.

Seated there was the shadow of a man he knew all too well. One who always frightened him in the middle of the night. The old man's shoulders were square, and he sat perfectly upright, staring back at Andrew with his face lost in the shadows.

With his eyes adjusted well enough to the darkness, Andrew could make out the appearance of the priest's large, round, wide-brimmed hat, and he was suddenly paralyzed with fear. Unable to get up and hardly able to breathe, Andrew stared back at the man.

The figure rocked slowly in the chair, its face focused on Andrew.

"You shouldn't be in my room," Andrew forced out through clenched teeth.

He wanted to say so much more, but every time he was in the priest's presence, he shut down like this. He couldn't get up and he could barely speak. He'd heard of this phenomenon before and that it happened often with people experiencing night terrors. Only they usually couldn't move or speak at all.

"Keep it down," the old man said in a hushed, hoarse tone.

Andrew hated the priest's voice. It scared the shit out of him. He couldn't move his body, but out of the corner of his eye, he saw that the bathroom light was on. He could see the glow around the edges. The old priest only visited him when he was alone, never when Beth was around.

"Father Dennis," Andrew said.

"Yessssssss," the priest replied, holding onto that "s" so he sounded like a demonic snake.

He's only human. He sleepwalks. That's all. He's only human.

"And you are the sinner," Father Dennis added.

"We are all sinners, are we not?" Andrew forced out, his voice trembling as he spoke. "You taught me that."

The old man laughed, and Andrew flinched. He hated the old man's chuckle.

"Indeed," Father Dennis replied. "Indeed."

"Leave me alone," Andrew insisted. "I'm tired. I have to work tomorrow."

"Work, yes, with O-liv-i-a. What a beauty she is."

This wasn't the first time the old man had mentioned her. He wasn't sure how he knew about her unless Beth had talked about her in front of the others. She'd made comments in the past that told Andrew she was a bit jealous.

"And how about Old Lynne?" Father Dennis added.

Andrew's shoulders tensed and his breath quickened.

"She is an old friend," he said, "and she tells me she likes you. Likes your scent. Would like to eat the meat from your bones."

"That's enough," Andrew said. "Go to bed."

Father Dennis slowly rose from his chair and stepped closer to Andrew. He stared down at him from the darkness that shrouded his features. Andrew wished to God he could move. That he could stand up and face the old bastard, but he couldn't budge. It was like sleep paralysis, but it only happened in the old priest's presence.

"Beth," Andrew whispered, trying to alert his wife, and hoping maybe she could make the evil bastard go away.

"Call to her," Father Dennis said. "Please, call to her. Then we can talk about your sexual extravaganzas with Ruby."

Andrew couldn't respond. He felt like he was choking on his own tongue, and he wasn't sure whether it was caused by the priest or by his own fear of getting caught.

"Yes," Father Dennis continued, "I heard Ruby gagging on your cock earlier."

Andrew finally breathed and found his voice. "That's enough."

"You should tell her to keep it down next time. Everyone can hear you."

"Get out of my room."

"You give it to her good, don't you? Cramming your cock into every orifice."

"Get out."

"Finishing down her throat sometimes while she drinks you dry."

He wanted so badly to scream out for Beth, but he was terrified she'd hear what Father Dennis was saying.

Andrew looked up at the shadowy figure in the wide-brimmed hat and begged. "Please."

"Sinner," Father Dennis declared.

"Yes, I am."

"Like the nun."

"The nun?" Andrew squeaked out.

Father Dennis laughed as he walked to the foot of the bed. "Ask Gore about the nun."

This was the first he'd ever heard about a nun and before Andrew could get more information, he heard the priest's heavy footsteps head for the door. Then the door opened and shut with a click.

Andrew's body remained frozen for at least another few minutes. Until he heard the bathroom door open, saw the light glow for a moment and then shut off as Beth hit the switch, and then felt her body slide into bed next to him and cuddle him.

He gasped as his body came unfrozen.

"Baby?" Beth asked as she spooned him from behind. "You awake?"

Andrew fought to control his breath. He was worried she'd sense his fear.

For a second, he considered telling her about the old man's visit, but he didn't know what to say about it. He couldn't tell her about Ruby, and he was afraid if he told her about the visit at all, she'd ask her grandfather questions that would lead to info she didn't need to know. He wasn't really sure about their relationship or how well they communicated. So, he lied.

"No, I mean, yes," he stumbled over his words. "I just… I had a nightmare."

"Oh, I thought I heard you talking to someone when I was in the bathroom."

"No. I was asleep."

8

The old man was definitely off his rocker. Who would still prance around in the middle of the night in their old priestly get-up and big round hat for no other reason than to pass judgment on someone?

Father Dennis. That's who.

Andrew woke, exhausted again, to find that Beth had already left. They rarely woke up next to each other unless it was the weekend. On those days, she'd turn her back to him and drag one of his arms over, yanking him into the spooning position where he'd hold her as they drifted back to sleep. He loved those mornings. The rest felt too routine.

And routine it was. Andrew eventually got out of bed, shuffled to the shower, poured his clothes over his body, brushed his teeth, and went downstairs to talk to Alex for a little while. She was as chipper as could be. This morning's topic of conversation was whether or not she could have a rainbow cake when her birthday rolled around. He was okay with that but ultimately it would be up to Beth.

At work, Olivia didn't seem herself. She was unusually solemn. When she wasn't making her rounds and didn't have anything specific to do, she had her nose buried in a sudoku book. She worked on puzzles other days too, but today he sensed she was a bit *off*.

First, he tried to ignore it and focus on his job. He figured she had a bad date or maybe some guy who'd promised to call her, after a rowdy night in the sack, hadn't kept his word. For as freewheeling as Olivia was, she also had a sensitive side. She needed to be the one in control. If a relationship was casual because she wanted it to be, she was fine, but if it were the guy calling the shots and leaving her hanging, she couldn't stand it.

When Andrew returned from walking the halls and checking the patients, he found Olivia sitting at the orderly desk, staring into the open, empty atrium. He followed her gaze and saw nothing fascinating. Only an empty, dark, dreary space.

"Okay, what gives?" he asked, plopping down in the seat next to her.

She jerked slightly as if his words had flown over and shocked her.

"Huh?" she asked.

"What's wrong with you, Liv?"

"Nothing," she said. "I didn't sleep well last night."

Andrew remembered the shadowy silhouette of Father Dennis sitting in his reclining chair when he opened his eyes in the middle of the night. He shrugged his shoulders to loosen them up.

"I hear ya," he replied. "I had a bit of a rough night myself."

"At least you didn't have a priest visit you," she said.

He sat up straight. Goosebumps rose on his arms. He doubted he heard her correctly. Surely she hadn't said—

"The scariest thing I've ever seen," she added.

"A priest?" he asked.

"It was a nightmare, but it seemed so real. It was crazy. This guy, Dan, that I'm kind of seeing, well, he was asleep next to me. I was facing him, drifting in and out of sleep myself, when I heard a man clear his throat behind me."

Andrew leaned closer in his seat, *needing* to hear the rest of her story.

"I couldn't turn around," she continued. "I was so scared. Then he laughed, but like a deep laugh, kind of under his breath."

Andrew knew that laugh, but it couldn't be the same one he was familiar with. His came from Beth's grandfather. Olivia's had to be a nightmare.

"I finally turned around," she went on, "and I saw him standing near the window. A tall man, with priest's clothes, and a big, round hat. But I could feel that he wasn't a priest. At least not of any religion that was good. He was evil. This is stupid." She scoffed. "I mean, come on. Stupid, right? I'm sure it was only a dream."

"What did he say?" Andrew asked.

"He mentioned you."

"Me?"

"It's embarrassing."

"Tell me."

"It's not true, okay? He said he knew I wanted to fuck you again. He said it just like that. I mean what kind of priest talks like that?"

Andrew knew what kind of priest spoke like that. The same one who'd visited him last night, but that would be impossible. Father Dennis had visited him, and he was too old to travel across town to Olivia's house.

"Is that all?" Andrew asked.

Olivia shook her head. "He said I should fuck you and then I should kill you."

Andrew waited for a second. He knew Olivia well and this would usually be the moment she'd smirk and then slap his shoulder and say something like, "Gotcha. You're so gullible."

But she didn't, and he could tell from the look on her face she wasn't joking.

"Anyway," she said as she picked up her puzzle book, "it was only a dream, I'm sure. It bothered me though, and when he disappeared, it took me a little while to go back to sleep. In the morning, I knew it had all been a dream, but I'm telling you, Andrew, it felt so real."

Andrew sat in stunned silence until Olivia finally tossed her puzzle book onto the desk, stood, and walked away calling out over her shoulder, "Well, I promise I won't try to fuck and kill you."

Olivia laughed, but Andrew didn't. He was worried about Father Dennis and thought it might be time to talk to Beth about him. It was a risk. She might find out about his fling with Ruby, but the old man scared the hell out of him, and he thought maybe he could convince Beth to make him go away.

Beth wasn't home when Andrew arrived at the house, so he hung out with Peter for a little while. The boy, as usual, was wrapped up in a video game. In this one, he was a shotgun-wielding soldier from the future. He battled demons and cackled with laughter as their heads exploded with each blast from his weapon.

"Killing demons this time, huh?" he asked as he plopped onto the couch.

"Yep. Watch this." Peter made his on-screen character spin, roll across the ground, and then come up behind a demon where he pulled a giant machete from his back and wrenched the evil bastard's head back while simultaneously slicing the blade across its throat. The monster's head came off in his hands. The body fell to its knees before collapsing to the ground in a puddle of blood. "Yesssssss!" Peter announced. "Take that, demon!"

"This game is pretty graphic," Andrew said.

"It was my favorite for a long time, but I beat it a bunch of times. It's still fun though. Demons deserve to die."

Andrew watched as the boy worked the buttons on the controller. His face was so intense. Mouth drawn taught, eyebrows furrowed, and a cold, icy stare. He only smiled when he was about to kill another demon. *Demons deserve to die.* The boy had made the statement as if he'd been personally harmed by one in the past.

Peter's concentrating look reminded him of Beth. Back when she had more time to spend around the house, she would do some needlepoint and she used to stick her tongue out like Peter was right now. She'd pinch it between her lips as she focused on the task at hand. He missed those days. Now, it seemed she was hardly ever home and when she was, they were usually in the bedroom getting ready for bed.

They'd been married a short time and already it was all feeling so... *blah.*

You're falling back into depression, man. Snap out of it.

He'd suffered through depressed episodes in the past and had even

Faces of Beth

contemplated suicide at one point. It was actually Beth who'd pulled him out of that stupor. It was when they'd first met. She was going through so much in life and the way she managed to smile back at him, even when he knew she was feeling down, inspired him. It made him realize that he could push through this. He wouldn't be a victim of his own mind or that depression demon that threatened to snuff out his life.

"You want to try?" Peter asked, holding the game controller out to him.

He shook his head. He loved playing games, but he feared if he picked up that controller, he might never want to put it down. He had too much on his plate these days to allow himself to sink back into that fantasy world. His PC was in the basement, and his past life of after-work online gaming into the late-night hours was down there with it.

Andrew stood from the couch. "Looks like you've got this under control. I think I'm gonna head to the bedroom and wash up."

"Beth should be home soon," Peter replied as he got back into his game.

You mean Mom. Andrew hated that the kids sometimes called her by her name. It was disrespectful, but he didn't feel like bringing it up right now.

Not wanting to greet her in his hospital scrubs again, Andrew showered and changed into a pair of slacks and a sweater. He sprayed a few spritzes of cologne on his neck and chest in case the hospital smell still lingered on him. He wanted to be a good husband and it was the small things like this Beth seemed to appreciate.

Later, when his wife finally arrived home and met him in the bedroom, she once again seemed too tired to talk. She had dark rings under her eyes and her hair was a mess. She closed the bedroom door behind her and rushed to him. He caught her in his embrace, squeezed her tight in a hug, and whispered, "Man, I've fucking missed you."

"Have you?" she teased. "I bet you didn't think about me at all."

Andrew scoffed. "You're all I've thought about."

You and your creepy-ass grandfather.

She inhaled his scent. "I've missed you too."

He relaxed and she stepped toward the closet, removing her blouse on the way. Andrew admired her pale skin, following the curve of her spine until it swelled into her full, beautiful ass. He wanted to hike up her skirt further and take her from behind, but he couldn't handle being pushed away. His ego had been damaged enough.

When Beth moved all of her hair over to one shoulder, Andrew knew what she wanted. She didn't actually need help with her bra clasp, but she knew that he liked assisting her, so she waited for him. He smiled as he moved close to her and unclasped her bra. She sighed in relief and pulled it from her shoulders, covering her breasts with her arm.

She glanced over her shoulder at him, and for a moment, he thought she might want to make love, but then she blinked her eyes, giving him the signal to close his.

"You drive me crazy," he said as he threw himself onto the bed, rolled onto his back, and closed his eyes.

"You know I'm shy," she replied.

"I know."

He kept his eyes closed until he felt her crawl onto the bed and lie down with her head on his chest.

"Long day?" he asked.

"How did you guess? I look an absolute fright, don't I?"

"A fright? No. Overworked, maybe a bit."

"They're going to drive me mad," she admitted.

"You can't let them."

"All day it's bickering and arguing and slamming doors and—"

"Remember, you have to think of it as just a job. Yes, you spend more time there than here, but go in, do your time, and come home to me."

"I know. I'm just tired, Drew."

"Then stay home with me."

"You know I can't."

"You can. You have to learn to push everything that's not *us* aside. We have this big house, and I make enough to take care of us. You need to relax more and be present here, with me."

"Alex is needy, Peter's always asking for money for this or that—"

"Sometimes you have to stop worrying about everyone else's needs and focus on ours. On yours and mine. Ours."

Andrew felt wetness seep through his T-shirt and realized she was crying. He leaned down to wipe away her tears and kissed her long and lovingly.

"I love you, Beth," he said.

She smiled back at him. "I know you do. And you know I love you."

"I do."

That was the extent of their conversation. Tonight wasn't the night to discuss Father Dennis with her. It would only cause an argument. Anytime he mentioned anything stressful in the house, Beth crumbled.

As exhausted as he was, Andrew wasn't ready to sleep. It was still relatively early, so he kissed Beth on her forehead and left her resting in their bed. By now, Peter would be in his room, so he'd have the living room TV to himself.

He crept downstairs and made some microwave popcorn before settling down to the next episode of his favorite TV series. Dumb reality shows were his guilty pleasure. He dealt with so much drama in his real life that he liked seeing real people stress out about ridiculous shit like not finding love the first night they met someone.

Love Buggers was only about thirty minutes through episode five when Gore came shuffling down the stairs. From his perch on the couch, Andrew saw him reach the bottom of the stairs and look toward the living room. As always, he wore a hooded sweater with his face covered in its shadows. Of course, Andrew had seen his face often enough, but it said a lot about the man's character that he chose to remain hidden most of the time.

"What's up, Gore?" Andrew asked.

"Going out," the young man replied.

"On a Thursday?"

"It's ladies' night."

"Of course."

Gore turned away from him and pulled his jacket off the coat rack near the door. He put it on over his sweater.

"Try not to stay out too late, huh?" Andrew suggested.

Gore turned to him, face down, and breathed heavily the way he always did. Andrew could see his chest heaving up and down.

"At least don't make a mess when you come in," Andrew added.

A sound came from the young man that sounded a bit like a scoff. Then Gore was gone, out the front door.

Andrew got to his feet and rushed to put on his own jacket and shoes. It wasn't the first time he'd considered following Gore when he went out for one of his nightly escapades. In fact, he'd actually gone all the way out to his car once before, put the key in the ignition, and even backed out of the driveway. Then a million thoughts hit him.

What if I see something I can't unsee?

What if I witness Gore killing someone?

What if Gore does a great job of covering his tracks, but I leave my own fingerprint lying around and end up getting fingered for the murder?

In the end, Andrew had re-parked his car and gone to bed.

Not this time. This was his chance to finally find out exactly what went on out there. For so long he'd cleaned up Gore's bloody messes, and deep down he knew something was not right about the young man. He figured he was killing someone, but since he'd never actually seen him do the deed, he was able to pretend he was overreacting. He could rationalize it because he didn't actually *know* what Gore was doing out there.

He was done wiping up bloody doorknobs without a damn good explanation behind it.

Perhaps Gore would have his reasons.

Even the name Gore sounded – gory.

Where did he come up with that name?

He'd asked Beth about it once and she'd mentioned something about an old rock band he'd been in and how they'd all had nicknames. He was Gore. There was another guy called Bone and even one labeled Flesh.

Gore took Beth's car like he always did. Tonight, as Andrew followed him, he noticed the license plate had been covered with duct tape. The guy was definitely up to something, and he didn't want the car to be traced back to him or to Beth. Andrew could appreciate that.

If Gore knew he was being followed, he showed no sign of it. He drove calmly through town. Andrew followed a few car lengths behind, appreciating the darkness. During the day, he would have never done something like this. His car was too easy to spot. In the darkness, all Gore would see was headlights and since he wasn't zigzagging here and there, racing through red lights, or doing anything else that would give Andrew away if he copied him, following him was relatively easy.

Before long, they arrived downtown, and Gore pulled into a daytime pay lot that was fairly empty and free at night. It was one of those *at your own risk* kind of lots meaning no security was on-hand to watch the cars. With his license plate duct-taped the way it was, it made sense he'd want to stay away from street parking and the potential for cops to drive by.

Andrew, however, could park along the street, so he drove a half a block farther and pulled alongside the curb. He exited the car and walked toward the lot, sure that Gore wouldn't exit and walk toward him since all the bars and restaurants were in the opposite direction.

Pulling his own hood over his head, Andrew was careful not to follow too closely when Gore came into view. The young man walked with his head down and didn't stop at the main downtown thoroughfare. He wasn't interested in the ritzier joints. It became clear to Andrew that they were headed toward Bly. Everyone in the area knew Bly Street was where you went to get drugs or hookers.

Andrew once got a black eye near Bly. He and his buddies overstayed their welcome at a shady bar where the locals didn't like yuppy college kids. After a short brawl outside, it was clear the yuppies should have partied elsewhere. It turned out if you looked tough enough, you could even lose a fight and still get laid. Andrew's friend Griffin got the girl, but he also got crabs. It was Bly Street after all.

Since then, Andrew stayed far away from Bly.

Tonight, he didn't have much of a choice because that was where Gore was headed, and even though it seemed clear the young man could take care of himself, Andrew found himself fearing for the guy's safety.

Maybe you should turn around and head home. Just wait, sip some coffee, read a book, and clean the bloody doorknobs again.

It was too late for that. He'd already come too far.

Bly was dark, dingy, and it seemed even most of the streetlights stayed far from here. The only illumination was the flickering of neon signs. Andrew read them as he followed Gore.

Dax's Pawn Shop.

Hammer Down Guns & Ammo.

Cash Fast Check Cashing.

Ruby Slippers and Strippers.

Hook's Pub.

Sleazy Dog Adult Store. XXX.

Andrew kept following Gore until the hooded young man turned left into a place called Wicked Waltz. On the sign, a woman outlined in pink neon lights was bent over with her dress hiked up. Behind her, a man wearing an old-fashioned gangster suit gripped her hips and drove into her. The woman's mouth opened in pleasure each time he thrust forward. Her mouth would close as he backed up.

Nice.

At first, Andrew thought it was a strip club. It seemed like the kind of place Neanderthals would go to get their dicks sucked. Bass boomed from the other side of the door and before Andrew could grab the handle, the door burst open, and out stumbled a sweaty man with glitter all over his face and a woman in a white tank top with no bra beneath. Her dark nipples were clearly visible under the shirt fabric.

"Sorry, buddy," the guy said, so drunk he could barely stand up straight. The woman helped him walk. She eyed Andrew like maybe she was making a mistake going home with this drunk guy when such good looking, fresh meat was stepping through the door.

Andrew smiled at her and entered the club.

The place was smokey despite the fact people weren't supposed to be smoking inside bars, clubs, and restaurants anymore. It didn't surprise him. This was Bly Street and people didn't follow rules here.

Faces of Beth

The cops wouldn't be doing any surprise inspections. They only showed up here when it was too late, if they showed up at all.

Andrew appreciated the club's darkness. Purple strobe lights flickered from corners, but that was the only light other than a pink neon bulb that ran along the length of the bar which took up the entire left wall. To the right was a crowd of people grinding up against one another to the music.

One guy bounced up and down with his hand down his pants, clearly jerking himself off as he danced.

Two women kissed erotically, groping each other as their tongues collided in a slobbery waltz.

The Wicked Waltz.

It was the perfect name for a place like this.

"Want a drink?" came a voice to Andrew's left.

He glanced over and saw an older woman who looked rough like she'd been the spouse to several abusive partners. Black rings were painted around her eyes, giving her a raccoon-like appearance. It dawned on Andrew that he was being judgmental. She could have been the nicest woman in the world. This might have been the end to the shitty path she'd been led down and now here she was, alone and miserable, serving drinks to assholes on Bly Street.

"So, you fuckin' twat? Want something to drink or what? I ain't got all night."

Nope, he'd been absolutely right to judge her.

"A Bud, in the bottle," he replied.

He wasn't going to drink anything out of a glass, and he wouldn't touch anything he couldn't watch the bartender open. She quickly returned with a bottle, twisted the top, and handed it to him.

"That'll be ten bucks," she said.

"Ten bucks?" Andrew replied. "For fuck's sake. It's a beer."

"It ain't beer we specialize in, stud," she said, nodding toward a red door in the back corner. "You want a simple fuckin' beer, you go to the grocery store. You come here because you want dick, pussy, ass, or blow. Or all of it for all I care. Entry is free but drinks aren't."

Andrew was careful with his wallet as he tugged out a ten and slammed it on the counter. The bartender waited a second, like she was expecting a tip, and Andrew laughed. When she didn't budge, he rolled his eyes, pulled two dollars more out of his wallet, and put them on the bar.

Twelve dollars for a fucking beer.

Andrew felt like a sucker for leaving her a tip but figured she probably didn't get paid much tending bar here. He definitely wasn't going to order another drink from this place.

Now, where the fuck is Gore?

It took a few minutes to realize he was nowhere in the crowd. That red door in the corner kept pulling his attention to it so he finally decided to have a peek. He deserved to at this point, after paying so much for a damn beer.

To get to the door, he had to move through the crowd of dancers. They didn't make it easy. A tall woman's sweaty shoulder rubbed against his cheek and Andrew winced, instantly wiping a damp smudge off the side of his face with the back of his hand. Someone grabbed his ass and squeezed. Then someone grabbed his cock and did the same. He was violated left and right. A big tattoo-covered guy blew cigarette smoke in his face. A woman with hot pink hair blew cherry smelling vapor at him. Someone spilled a drink on his leg.

When you get home, you are immediately getting into the shower.

Finally, he made it to the red door and stepped through.

As soon as he did, he heard moans, sighs, and cries coming from all over the place. The room was bathed in red, and it took a moment for his eyes to adjust. His nose caught on much more quickly and the musky scent of sweaty bodies assaulted his senses. It reminded him of the time he stumbled into his apartment complex's sauna as a kid.

He was only twelve years old and had been in the pool but wanted to try the sauna. His mom took him in there just as three couples were leaving. He didn't know what had gone on in there, but he'd always remember that smell, the condom filled with semen on the floor, and the way his mom ripped him out of the room as soon as she caught on.

That sauna smell came back to him now only it carried with it some new scents. This aroma consisted of armpits, sweaty balls, soaked and

Faces of Beth

unshaved body parts, bodily fluids dripping on random surfaces, leather from sofas and floggers, blood, a little bit of accidental feces, and mixed sweet scents from fruity lotions and lubes.

As his eyes adjusted, Andrew noticed he'd entered onto a ramp with a metal railing that led him to the far side of the room where spectators stood watching a hodgepodge of sexual scenes taking place. To stand at the entrance would keep him highlighted and too easy for Gore to spot, so Andrew hurried into the crowd so he could hide among the others.

There, in his hiding spot amongst the crowd, he saw things he'd only glanced at on the Internet, back before he'd met Beth. When he was single and he watched porn sometimes, he would click randomly on videos and would end up down rabbit holes where he'd stumble upon sex videos he never meant to find. Nothing bad, but of course he saw sex parties and things like that. He'd never experienced anything live and in the flesh like this.

In front of the crowd was a lit-up, checkered dance floor. On it, he noticed a couple was going at it. The woman was bent over some kind of fuck-cushion, giving the naked man behind her easy access as he drilled into her from behind. Other naked people were around the couple, on their knees, touching her with their hands. They weren't doing anything sexual but just touching her, running their fingers across her back as the man continued to fuck her from behind. They told her things like "You're beautiful," and "You're so sexy," and "You're a queen."

In the corner, another couple gyrated in a sex swing. The woman cried out, "Yes!" as she rode the man's cock. Others helped her by lifting her up and slamming her down on the man. Each time they did it, she cried out in pleasure.

From there, things got a little crazier. It seemed the tamer scenes were closer to the door but as Andrew moved toward the back of the room, he found things got darker and bloodier.

Another woman gripped a long-haired man's ponytail, snapping his head back, while she fucked him from behind with a strap-on dildo. She was completely naked other than the harness around her waist. The man's face was bloody, like she'd broken his nose. He hissed through gritted, bloody teeth, "Please keep going." "Shut the fuck up," she replied as she slammed his face against the wall in front of him. The guy reacted with a smile and more blood running down his neck.

Andrew was in awe. He'd had his nose broken before and it didn't feel good. Having it mashed like that, even during sex, had to hurt like hell.

Next, two men sat side by side on a cushion. Each had a hand around the other's cock while the other hand sliced the other's chest with a razor blade. Both men looked to be in pure ecstasy. Was it from the pain of the cutting, the masturbation, or both? The people watching were all touching somebody near, stroking them over their clothes, reaching into zippers, hiking up dresses or skirts.

Up ahead, Andrew could see there were more violent scenes taking place, but his eyes were drawn to the side where, near what looked like the back door, a man leaned close to Gore, whispering to him. Andrew's immediate thought was drug deal. The two conversed and Andrew hung back in the crowd to watch. Nobody else seemed to be acknowledging them. Why would they with all the fucking going on in every corner?

As Andrew watched, it seemed the guy talking to Gore was getting aggressive. He put a hand into the hood where it looked like he might be gripping Gore by his hair. Then the man leaned in and the two kissed. The man's face pressed against Gore's.

Andrew couldn't fucking believe it. Was that what he'd been up to all this time? Visiting sex clubs so he could get *his?*

Here I was thinking he was in trouble, and he was only—

Gore lifted a hand to stop the man and pushed him away, but the man wasn't ready to stop. His hand came up to Gore's chest where he groped him and went in for another kiss.

It was clear Gore wasn't into this.

Nobody else was watching.

Nobody cared.

Gore was on his own against this aggressive son of a bitch.

Beth's young, hooded brother tried to back away when the other guy pulled a knife and opened it, holding it up close to Gore's neck in the darkness. Andrew watched in awe as the guy led him toward the back door then reached once more into the hood, grabbed Gore by his hair, and threw him through the door.

Only then did a couple of people glance over, but all they saw was the door open and slam shut. Then their attention was back on all the couples fucking.

That was all Andrew needed to see. It didn't matter what Gore was up to, he was family, and Andrew needed to help him.

Andrew burst through the back door and out into a dark, damp alleyway.

It was too late.

The man, the aggressor, lay on his back. One dull lamp post shined down on him. Blood gurgled from his lips. His throat had been slit. As he lay dying, he reached out to Andrew for help with a look of confusion on his face. His knife was on the ground next to his outstretched hand.

Gore stood staring down at the dying man, his hands at his side, one holding a straight razor, the other balled into a fist. His chest heaved up and down angrily like a ferocious animal ready to pounce for a second time but waiting to see if its prey was fatally wounded.

Andrew had tried to play along with all this. He'd tried not to interrupt things, but he'd never expected it to go this far.

"Beth!" Andrew yelled.

Gore looked back at him, his hood removed, and sneered. Then he lowered his head, and when he lifted his eyes the next time, the young killer was gone.

Standing over the bloody man, clutching that straight razor, was the woman Andrew had married. It was Beth standing there trembling under the lamp post, unaware of what had just happened. Her hair dangled half out of her sweater from where the man had tugged at it.

The guy had attacked, and Gore had done what he was created to do – protect.

Andrew ran to his innocent wife.

"Beth, please, give me the razor," he begged.

She didn't even hesitate. She handed him the bloody weapon.

"What happened?" she asked.

"This guy tried to hurt you," Andrew replied.

And he had, but Andrew knew that wasn't the whole truth. Gore had gone out looking for a fight. He'd come to the bar in search of this. He'd wanted to find someone who might be looking to force himself on a young woman like Beth. An innocent woman hiding a deadly secret.

The dying man on the ground shook his head and then went still. A pool of blood had formed around him.

"He tried to hurt me?" Beth asked.

"Yes," Andrew replied, "and Gore wouldn't let him."

"Oh my God," Beth whimpered.

"Come on," Andrew said, pulling Beth's sweater hood up over her head, "let's go home."

Andrew wasn't well-versed in getting rid of bodies, and he figured in a place like this, this kind of thing happened often. He couldn't imagine there was much evidence or probably much give-a-damn on the cops' part. There were no cameras around and nobody here would say a word. So, he led Beth back to her car and insisted she follow him home.

9

What a fucking night.

Beth was visibly shaken when they finally made it home. While she went into the house and got into the shower, Andrew cleaned her car. He scrubbed the steering wheel, the gear shifter, and every other place she may have touched with bloody hands. Gore would have been much more careful, but he'd fled and left Beth a nervous wreck. It seemed she'd touched damn near everything.

When Andrew finally made it to the bedroom, the shower was still running. Beth was always the get-in-and-get-out type, so he knew she was having a hard time in there. Luckily for him, the bathroom door was unlocked.

The bathroom was filled with steam and through the frosty shower door, he could make out Beth's form sitting on the floor. He expected to find her sobbing or praying or making any kind of noise really. Yet she was totally silent.

"Baby?" he called out.

No response. Inside the shower, the water poured down with such strength it was possible she hadn't heard him, so he tried again. What he didn't want to do was yank open the door and scare the shit out of her. She'd already been startled enough tonight.

"Baby, you okay?" he asked.

"Daddy?" she replied from the other side, and he already knew his wife was gone.

Beth had shrunk into herself and opened one of the other doors inside her mind. Six-year-old Alexandra had answered the call and was now sitting inside the shower. For a moment, he was concerned about opening the door. He didn't want to see a little girl naked.

It's your wife. It's only your wife. Alex is in her head.

His personal pep talk was enough to convince him to pull open the shower door. There she sat, cross-legged, like she often did in front of the television. Her hands were clasped together at her lap, and she was rocking back and forth. Water drilled at her face and body with so much heat her skin was red.

Andrew reached out, and as his arm fell beneath the shower spray, he yelped and yanked his arm back. "Jesus!"

"It's hot," Alex agreed, continuing to rock back and forth. "It's really hot, Daddy."

"It's way too hot, baby," Andrew yelled as he turned the cold water on to mellow out the temperature.

Looking down at the innocent face staring back up at him, it was so hard to imagine that was the same person he'd seen murder someone in an alley only an hour earlier. It was hard to believe it was his wife at all. She smiled at him and even though she didn't have her hair in pigtails the way Alex usually did, he could tell by her childish grin that it wasn't his wife looking back at him.

When one of the others left their room, which is what they called it when one of her alters, or personalities, took over her mind, Beth slunk back into her room – her special hiding place inside her mind, and it was only a matter of time that decided when she'd come back. Only when the others had outstayed their welcome or something shocking jolted her back to reality would she come back to him.

With all the tenderness of a father helping his daughter out of the tub, Andrew wrapped a towel around Alex and led her to the bedroom. She trembled in the cool air-conditioned room as he dried her off and pulled a loose-fitting gown over her head. He found her least sexy underwear in her drawer and asked the six-year-old to step into them carefully before pulling them up to her waist.

Then he led her to the bed, tucked her in with a kiss on her forehead, and blessed her goodnight.

"Will you read me a story?" Alex asked with eyelids that could barely stay open long enough to finish her question.

Instead of denying her, he said, "Sure. Let me look for the perfect story."

He knew she would fall asleep while she waited for him, so he pretended to go look for a book while he secretly returned to the bathroom where he quietly locked the door, sat down on the toilet, and sobbed into his shirt.

When morning came, Andrew was afraid to open his eyes. For the first time in a long time, nothing in particular woke him, and he was in no rush to get to work. Tonight was the Friday night movie and his shift started later. He'd forgotten about his loss in the Rock, Paper, Scissors game the other day. It was his turn to bring snacks.

Your wife is a murderer with multiple personalities, and you're worried about forgetting snacks?

Andrew realized he was totally fucked-up. His priorities were a mess, but in all honesty, nothing had changed last night.

He'd suspected all along that Gore was out there killing people. When his wife donned that hoodie sweater, she was definitely up to something, and he'd decided a long time ago, back when he first met Beth, that he would protect her at all costs.

From the first time he saw her at Myles-Bend State Hospital, Andrew knew loving her wasn't a choice. As the daughter of a high-powered lawyer, she had enough money to check herself into a place that might be able to help but not quite the funds to allow her to disappear altogether. She once told Andrew if she could afford it and knew how to take care of herself well enough, she would have moved to a cabin high on a mountain and lived all by herself, perhaps with a little dog, like *The Grinch*. "At least that way I'd only be bothering myself, and I'd sure be good at keeping myself company." She'd laughed at the end, and Andrew was smitten.

Beth's father visited her shortly after her arrival at Myles-Bend, and it had been Andrew who stepped in and demanded he take his hands off her when he tried to forcefully drag her out of the building with one hand wrapped around her hair and the other locked on her arm.

Andrew remembered it like it was yesterday.

"You're fucking coming with me," Steven R. Stamp demanded as he pulled her out of her room and into the hall that led to the front atrium and main door.

How the man had gotten into the building was a bit of a mystery. Then again, the security officer on duty worked for a contract company and Andrew was pretty sure all it would have taken was a hundred dollar bill to gain access.

All Andrew knew was there was a strange, well-groomed man in a suit and tie dragging a patient out into the hallway.

"Hey!" Andrew had yelled upon seeing the forceful tactic Mr. Stamp employed. "Take your hands off her."

With the shocked look of a man knowing he'd gone too far, her father let go of her and glanced into her eyes before looking back at Andrew and raising his hands as if to say, "I haven't done anything wrong."

Andrew rushed toward this gorgeous young woman he'd never seen before. Having only started his shift a few minutes before all this kicked off, he'd had no idea they'd received a new patient earlier that day.

"Are you okay?" Andrew asked as he gently took the new patient by the arm and pulled her away from the aggressive older man.

She smiled back at him, and he instantly felt his heart melt. "I am now."

"I was only trying to—" Mr. Stamp started.

"How did you get in here?" Andrew asked.

"I... the uh... that's not important. I need her to come with me."

"She'll be going nowhere with you," Andrew declared. "It seems to me she's a lot safer in our care, Mr.—"

"Stamp," her father informed him. "As in Stamp, Silver, & Boston."

He'd said it as if that was supposed to frighten Andrew or at least inform him he was making some kind of big mistake.

"I'm Andrew of Myles-Bend State Hospital, and I'm going to call security if you don't find your way back out to the entrance where visitors are supposed to remain until escorted into unsecure areas of the building. You see, this is a secure area. That means you NEVER get to come back here. Not even with an escort, Mr. Stamp."

"I see," Mr. Stamp said, using his thumb and index finger to smooth down his salt and pepper goatee.

He did see and for a few months, he made Andrew's life a living hell. Phone calls and written complaints led to disciplinary action. For a little while, Andrew thought he might get fired over the situation. If it didn't mean he'd have to stop spending time with Beth, he wouldn't have cared. He could have gotten a job someplace else, but once he looked into her big brown eyes, he was lost to her. She owned him. And she learned to love him the same.

Of course, Mr. Stamp disowned her the moment he found out who she was marrying. Even though he'd shown on day one how willing he was to protect the man's baby girl, a man like Mr. Stamp didn't like to lose. It was clear he'd lost the day Beth said, "I do."

As Andrew lay in bed and thought about the past, a smile formed on his lips.

He was happy because thoughts of his time spent courting Beth reminded him no matter how strange his day-to-day life was right now, he was with the woman he loved, and nothing could get in the way of that.

Not Alex, not Peter, not Gore, not Ruby, and not even Father Dennis.

They were all Beth in some weird way. They were all parts of her he had to learn to appreciate differently. He'd chosen to think of them as family members because it was a way to make his mind adjust to something beyond his control. If he could rationalize it, he could accept it.

At first, he'd had a difficult time believing she couldn't change personalities on a whim. It frustrated him when it happened. Sometimes he felt she was doing it on purpose to avoid an argument or to get out of a difficult situation even though everything he learned in the hospital told him otherwise.

It took some time to understand and, yes, they had their arguments and misunderstandings, but Andrew found ways to come to terms with it all. He loved Beth beyond society's regular rules and standards. While her mind created personalities as coping mechanisms, his mind created family members to add some normalcy to their lifestyle so he wouldn't lose his fucking mind.

When Andrew finally made his way downstairs, he found Alex seated in her usual place. This time she wore blue jean overalls, a pink T-shirt with cherries all over it, and she had her hair in pigtails. The interesting thing about Alex was she seemed to have a dusting of freckles even though Beth didn't have any. It was like they floated on the breeze and landed on her face whenever she was in Alex-mode.

He was sure they were a part of his imagination, or perhaps they really were there, and Beth simply covered them in makeup when she was *herself* or *out of her room* as they called it.

"Good morning, little one," Andrew said as he walked into the living room and sat on the couch.

She was watching some animated show that seemed strangely computerized. He couldn't help thinking back to his own childhood when most of the stuff he watched on TV had a mixture of puppets and humans. They always seemed to be working together, like this odd alien race of puppets was forced to blend in and work side by side with mankind. Like they couldn't possibly count to ten, tie shoes, or practice good manners without this good old-fashioned interplanetary teamwork.

"Good morning," Alex replied in her usual high-pitched, sing-song child voice.

Each of Beth's personalities had a different pattern of speech and a different pitch. If one were to close their eyes and speak to each one, they'd never guess those voices came from the same vocal cords. It hurt Andrew's throat to even think about trying to mimic the little girl's tone.

Andrew remembered the first time he'd encountered Alex at Myles-Bend. He'd read about Beth's dissociative identity disorder, or what many people still referred to as multiple personality disorder, but he hadn't yet experienced it. Or, he actually had, but he'd confused Ruby's sexual flirtation as Beth simply coming on to him while high on one of her meds.

So, when he walked into her room one afternoon and found her sitting cross-legged on the floor putting tinker toys together, he was at a loss for words. She'd invited him to sit with her and play. He accepted the invitation because he didn't want to be away from her any more than was necessary.

Now, watching her rock back and forth in front of the TV, he was grateful she'd never morphed into Alex while they were making love. That would have made him feel horrible. Luckily, even though she consciously didn't seem to be in control of the switch, her body – or at least the other personalities – seemed to subconsciously be able to handle it. Not in control as in Beth could show up whenever she wanted, but in control as in each had a role to play and they didn't seem to step on each other's toes.

For example, Beth knew how to drive a car. It was understood by Andrew and Beth that it probably wasn't the safest thing for her to be cruising around town, but she had driven before and had never switched to little Alex while behind the wheel. She'd remained Beth or one of the other adult personalities that could handle *that* task like Ruby or Gore.

Most of the knowledge he had about Beth, he'd gathered himself. The doctors at Myles-Bend had tried their hardest to get information from her or from any of her personalities really, but she'd been stubborn. She'd checked herself into the hospital to get help, but she refused it at every turn. She knew she had a problem but at the same time seemed convinced she didn't have one. At one point, Andrew was able to get out of her that she'd checked herself in for safety and security purposes only. Not to get rid of the problem, but to control it.

Obviously, with the loose cannon known as Gore, she hadn't learned to keep her violent side in check. In fact, nobody at the hospital knew she had a *violent* side. She'd always been pleasant. Even when she was Gore, she only had a bit of an attitude. If Andrew had been asked to explain Gore back then, he might have used the words *goth, dark, unfriendly,* and maybe *secretive.*

Murderer would have never crossed his mind.

With all that was going on with Gore, Andrew felt the need to take Alex out of the house. Nothing got her to put her shoes on and get ready faster than the promise of her favorite breakfast.

"I was thinking," he said, "maybe we could go for some blueberry pancakes."

Alex whipped her head around and beamed with delight. "Blueberry pancakes? Now?"

"If you're up for it."

"Yay!"

Alex leapt to her feet and ran to Andrew, wrapping her arms around him in a big hug. Of course, physically she didn't change when she was in this childlike form, but the way she seemed to sink into herself and bend her knees slightly, keeping her shoulders lower, did give her a shorter appearance. Everything about Beth, when she was Alex, was – smaller.

"Get your shoes on," he told her.

"Oh, I will!"

Beth wasn't pretending to be a six-year-old racing off to get her shoes so she could get her favorite breakfast. She *was* that elated child.

Alex disappeared and came back in less than a minute with her shoes in her hands. She dropped to the floor, put them on, and pulled the Velcro tight over them. The shoes were black, a color all her personalities seemed to agree with. If he'd gone with any other color, he would have had to buy a different pair of shoes for each of them. Peter wouldn't have been caught dead wearing pink sandals.

Andrew would never make his adult wife sit in a car seat, but he did feel more comfortable with her sitting in the backseat, as her childlike self wouldn't know how to react in the case of an accident.

On the way to the diner, he played some of Alex's favorite songs and hoped she wouldn't suddenly switch to being Peter. The teenage boy wasn't a big fan of pancakes, nor did he like being dragged out of the house when he could be home playing his video games. If the switch did occur, Andrew would need to make a U-turn and hit McDonald's before heading home.

Nothing changed, everything ran smoothly, and a half hour later, Andrew was seated across from Alex watching her stab her fork into her pancake happy face's blueberry eyes. Next would be the strawberry nose and then the banana smile. This was her routine. Eventually, she'd make her way to the actual pancakes.

Andrew sopped his biscuits up with gravy and sipped coffee while he watched her.

"You can't see so well with one eye, can you?" she asked her pancake face. When it didn't answer, she stabbed the other eye and added, "How about now, blind man?"

A snicker escaped Andrew and Alex glanced up at him with a furrowed brow.

"Hey, what are you laughing at?" she asked.

"You, goofball."

She laughed. "This is sooooooo good."

Across from them, an older couple stole glances at them, obviously curious about the grown woman acting like a child. Andrew glared at them with a look that told them to mind their fucking business. They seemed to get the message as the woman lifted her coffee mug to her mouth and the man nodded once at Andrew before starting a new conversation with his wife.

Now that they had some sort of privacy, Andrew decided it was time to bring up a serious subject to Alex. He leaned forward and at a low volume said, "I need to talk to you about something."

This was the real reason he'd decided to bring her out for breakfast. He knew if he got her all excited like this, she'd tell him nearly anything.

"Okay," she said, her eyes growing wide as she dug into her pancake and ripped off a piece of the syrupy substance.

"How do you feel about the others?" he asked.

"The others?"

"The rest of your family."

"Oh," she said, chewing her food and swallowing it with an exaggerated gulp. She washed it down with a swig of orange juice.

"Like Gore," he pressed her. "What do you think of him?"

"He's kind of scary," she said as she avoided making eye contact with him. This was how she always behaved when he tried to pry information out of her.

"Scary how?"

"I don't know. He stays in his room most of the time but when he comes out, I stay in my room. He's scary. He's kind of mean."

"I can see that. Has he done anything to make you feel this way?"

She shook her head. "No, I think he's a good guy but he's still scary. Sometimes I think you might be in danger. And I don't want anything to happen to you, Andrew. You're my daddy now. I feel safe with you."

"You didn't always feel safe, right?" he asked. "Did something happen at the hospital that I don't know about?"

She had to stop and think about that for a second, but then she shook her head.

"What about before that?" he asked. Remembering what Father Dennis said, he decided now was the time to ask. "Was there ever a nun?"

Alex dropped her fork. It bounced off her plate with a clang. The older couple looked over once more but as soon as Andrew turned his attention on them, they went back to their conversation.

"I'm sorry," Alex said as she reached for her fork.

Andrew caught her hand and rubbed the back of it with his thumb. His eyes fell on the scar at her palm, and she jerked her hand away.

"It's okay," he promised her. "You're safe now."

She shook her head. "I don't think so. Gore said we can't talk about that."

"Tell me about her," he insisted.

Leaning forward so she was closer to Andrew, she whispered, "A long time ago. He..." Alex shook her head, confused. "She... she took us to her room. We didn't like her. She was scary."

"What was so scary about her?"

"She had black eyes. And a long tongue. Like a snake. She wanted to touch me."

Andrew wasn't sure he wanted to hear anymore.

"She always wanted to touch me. To touch... us," Alex added.

"I'm so sorry, Alex," Andrew said. "I'm so sorry you went through that. I'm going to protect you now. You don't have to worry."

Then, she suddenly sat back in her chair and ripped off another piece of pancake. She shoveled it into her mouth and shrugged. "I'm not worried. Gore protects us."

10

I'm not worried. Gore protects us.

Andrew considered not going to work tonight, but he couldn't afford the hit to his paycheck. He had bills, like everyone else, and paying Paloma wasn't easy. Plus, there wasn't much he could do around the house besides play video games with Peter and allow himself to be seduced by Ruby.

Alex was still out of her room when Andrew left for work, and if things went in their usual order, Peter would be up next. There was a chance Andrew could make it home before Gore pulled another one of his nights on the town. He'd have to stop him this time. This wasn't a game, and if he got caught, Beth would spend the rest of her life in prison. Andrew might too if they found out he was aware of the murders.

Murder. There's only one you're sure of and did you see the guy die?

The man in the alley was dead. He probably wouldn't show up on the news, but Andrew was sure Beth had killed him.

No, Gore had killed him. It wasn't Beth. It was Gore. Remember that.

Andrew was running late as he drove to the hospital, so he stopped by a gas station and picked up whatever overpriced snacks he could find. A bag of Cheetos, a couple of Hostess apple pies, a pack of Sour Bite Crawlers, two Snickers candy bars, and a couple of Cherry Cokes. Maybe he'd keel over in a diabetic coma and all the madness in his life would fade away.

It was only a joke. He might goof around about wanting out of his life, but the truth was he could never leave Beth alone. What would happen to her if he wasn't there? Would she check herself back into a hospital or would she simply keep rotating through her personalities until one of them did something that would get her in enough trouble to end up in prison instead of a hospital?

When he finally made it to work and set the bag of goodies down on the desk, Olivia opened it and rolled her eyes. "Really? I whoop your ass in Rock, Paper, Scissors and you only go as far out of your way as to stop by Go-Mart for snacks?"

"Go-Mart is more expensive than any other place, I'll have you know. I should have stopped by the damn dollar store. I probably would have found all this there for a hell of a lot less money."

"True."

"Besides, I've had a rough couple of days. I almost didn't come in at all."

"I would have killed you."

"I know you would have, but—"

"It's Beth, isn't it?" she asked.

"I really don't want to hear the I told you so speech tonight. I know you warned me about dating her and marrying her, but I love her, Liv."

He fell into the chair and rubbed his eyes with the palms of his hands like a sleepy toddler.

"You really do love her," Olivia said.

"I always have."

"I can't even imagine living with her and, well, all her others."

"It's not easy. I do my best to go with the motions, but it's exhausting sometimes."

"Still fucking Ruby?" she asked.

He removed his hands from his eyes and stared up at her. "You were supposed to forget I told you about that."

"I can't," she replied. "Remember, I've been there. Literally. With you I mean. I definitely have not been with Ruby." Olivia laughed. "So, of course, there was some slight bit of jealousy when you told me about the freaky sex the two of you get up to. I mean, you guys even tried the wheelbarrow move. *I* haven't even tried that."

Olivia stood and pretended to be holding someone's legs like wheelbarrow handles as she shook her head in disgust. "So, you had her like this and..." Her voice trailed off when she realized he wasn't really in the mood for her joke.

Andrew shook his head. "It feels wrong."

"What's feels wrong about what?"

"It feels wrong having sex with Ruby. It's not Beth."

"But it *is* Beth," Olivia argued. "It's totally Beth. Please stop sulking about this. And please don't complain to any of your guy friends. They'll laugh at you. I mean what guy doesn't want to have a sweet, charming wife who flips a switch and becomes some wild, super sex-charged nympho with a bad mouth?"

Andrew laughed. "I don't have any guy friends."

"Even better," Olivia replied. "Seriously though. What's to complain about?"

He obviously couldn't tell her about his wife's desire to sneak out in the middle of the night and murder men in dark alleys. So, he went with something a little less dramatic.

"Ruby says things Beth never would," Andrew said. "Her voice is sultrier and she's kinky as hell."

"Again," Olivia said, "what's to complain about? Hell, keep talking about her that way and I'll want to go over there and do her."

"Do her? What are you, a college frat boy?"

Olivia plopped into her seat. "I feel like it sometimes. Dan isn't going to work out."

As much as he didn't want to hear about Olivia's sex life, he thought it might get his mind off his own problems.

"Tell me more," he said.

Faces of Beth

"You sure you want to have this conversation?" she asked. "It's not really work appropriate."

"Is anything you say work appropriate? A second ago you were demonstrating the wheelbarrow move."

She laughed and shrugged her shoulders. "Dan won't go down on me." When Andrew didn't reply, she added, "I mean he won't eat my—"

"Whoa, I know what you mean," he replied with a chuckle. "Ruby goes down on me."

"Rub it in. I can't be with a selfish man. I mean he lets me go down on him, but he won't return the favor."

"Did you ask him about it?"

"I did, and he said it's something he's *just not into*. I told him romantic comedies are something you're *just not into*. Dungeons & Dragons is something you're *just not into*. Microwaveable mac & cheese is something you're *just not into*. Eating pussy is *not something you're just not into*. So, I told him to get the fuck out of my house and don't bother calling."

"Yeah, sounds like it's not going to work out."

Once again demonstrating her amazing ability to go from hot to cold in no time at all, like she had back when they'd dated, she changed the subject with no easing into it at all and said, "We should round everyone up for the movie."

With all the patients finally gathered in the recreation room, seated on foldable chairs, Andrew thought the place seemed rather pleasant. Nobody complained or accused anyone else of pissing, shitting, or wiping his or her nose on any of the furniture.

So far, so good.

When he pressed the play button on the DVD player and the large, rolldown white screen came to life with the movie *Hook* starring Robin Williams, the crowd of people seated in front of them cheered.

Andrew couldn't help letting his mind drift off to a time when Beth would have been seated in that crowd. She'd made friends with a woman named Nelly who was no longer here at the hospital. She'd been released to her family shortly after Beth left. Andrew wondered what happened to her.

Was she living a good life now? Was she locked up in some other hospital? Was she even alive?

The girl had suffered from psychotic tendencies and would go from pleasant and somewhat cheerful one minute to trying to stab an orderly with a ballpoint pen the next. Medication seemed to help her, as it did with many of the other patients, but that depended largely on what one would consider help. Being so drugged up they're unable to think let alone attack someone was hardly a solution.

She's probably in another institution.

While an adult Peter Pan got his ass kicked by Tinkerbell, the audience roared with laughter. Andrew was busy counting the patients while Olivia sat next to him, stuffing her face with sour worms and laughing along with everyone else.

Andrew had always liked this movie, but tonight he couldn't seem to concentrate on the film. Something didn't seem right. An uneasy feeling settled in his gut. As his gaze touched each patient's head, he took inventory of the Q-tip cotton look of the white hair at the top of most of the ladies' heads and the sometimes shiny, sometimes liver-spotted domes of the men's.

When he finished his count, he realized what that troubled feeling had been. Two of the patients were missing, and he knew instinctively which two they'd be. Sure enough, he went over the room again, and he was right. They'd been in the room at one point. He was sure of it. He'd counted everyone himself.

First, was the woman he feared. Old Lynne. The bony, decrepit old bitch who always found a way to torment him was doing it again.

And, of course, the other had to be the one they called The Quiet Man.

Andrew stood and walked around the room, making sure they hadn't slid to the floor. Sometimes patients would curl up on the floor to watch the movie or they'd find extra chairs and lie down across several seats.

"What are you doing?" Olivia asked.

"We're missing two," he whispered to her.

"No, we're not."

"I counted."

"Who?"

"Do you see Old Lynne? Or Jimmy Grainger?"

"The Quiet Man?" Olivia asked. "And Old Lynne? You've got to be kidding me. I swear I saw them both earlier. I personally went to her room and got her. His too."

"Well, they're not here now."

"I'll stay here then. Someone has to. You go find them."

"Fuck that," he replied. "You're mighty quick to volunteer to stay here."

"I love this movie."

"Bullshit."

"I do. Seriously."

He wasn't going to win this argument anyway. When Olivia put her foot down, she quite literally put it down. As if her canvas sneakers were filled with hardening cement, she was not going to budge.

"Fine," he said, "but I hope all the patients in here start throwing up on one another and you're forced to clean it up."

She laughed. "You would wish something like that on me."

"I would. *And* I hope your next three boyfriends just aren't into going down on you."

"Now that's evil," she snapped back as he stood to leave. "Take it back."

He wouldn't. He walked away, hearing her call out, "You've gone too far this time. Take it back."

"Fuck you," he called back, "I wish you a life full of giving head and never receiving it!"

She wouldn't hear that last part, but he still felt satisfaction in saying it, and the lighthearted banter broke up what could've been an ominous departure from the rec room. Leaving a room full of people to walk empty corridors to find the two creepiest patients in his care wasn't his idea of a fun Friday evening.

I'm quitting this job tomorrow.

It was a phrase he'd repeated often, but the pay was decent, and the benefits were good. He couldn't afford to search for a new job. Not with everything that was going on with Beth right now, so he'd suffer the torment of Old Lynne, find her scary ass, and throw her back in there with the others to finish the fucking movie.

The lights were as dim as always at this hour, and when he stepped out of the recreation room and let the door close behind him, all was silent except the muffled sound of Peter Pan waking up on a pirate ship. He liked the movie too, probably even more than Olivia did. He would have preferred something scary, but that had been strictly banned after the last time they played a horror flick, and one of the patients spent every night of the following week convinced her floor was the ocean and *Jaws* was trying to attack her.

Some people just had tile-floor shark phobias.

From what Andrew could see as he looked left and glanced right, the hallway was empty. Old Lynne's hallway was one more over, so he made his way toward the atrium where he could move to the next hall.

His feet tapped against the tile floor and brought back the sound of Old Lynne's hands and feet slapping the ground as she galloped. If he heard that sound tonight, he was going to haul ass back to the recreation room. Or out the front door, whichever was closest.

This time, he felt entirely alone in the building. His feet clip-clopped across the floor and echoed so loudly off the walls he had to stop several times to focus on the other sounds around him. The feeling he was being watched was irrational considering everyone was in the recreation room except the two he was seeking.

Unless they were dangling from the roof at the dark end of the hallway, it would be impossible for them to be watching.

Even though he knew it wasn't the case, his mind went there, and suddenly he was imagining Old Lynne and The Quiet Man side by side somewhere in a dark corner, stifling their wicked giggles as they saw him searching for them. Like some sick and twisted game of hide and seek.

They were both probably asleep in their beds right now. That's where he'd find them. They'd be—

A giggle sounded off from somewhere in the atrium. He hadn't imagined it. This was real. Someone was out there laughing and suddenly the false imagery he'd conjured in his head didn't seem so ludicrous. What if the two of them had actually teamed up and were hiding somewhere?

Andrew reached the end of the hall and stood at the opening to the atrium, peering over at the orderly desk. Aside from that one central hub, there was nothing else in the large open area. Only a couple of seats for visitors that were bolted to the floor and wouldn't serve as a reasonable hiding spot. To his left, over near the bulletin board, were a couple of fake potted plants that were as tall as he was but too thin for someone to hide behind.

The giggle came again and this time the hair stood up at the back of Andrew's neck. The skin on his arms could have been braille and he read his right arm with his left fingers, fidgeting in the dull overhead lights. Lightning flashed outside, informing him that it wasn't only the lack of windows making it feel like there was a storm outside. One was indeed on its way.

"That's enough," Andrew called out. "Lynne. Jimmy. If you're out here, you need to go to the recreation room and watch the movie with everyone else. You know the rules."

The air conditioner turned off and the sudden silence could have been a loud bang for how it made him jump. Andrew scoffed at himself and pinched the bridge of his nose with two fingers.

"What's the movie?" a soft voice asked. It seemed to come from a small child.

Andrew jerked his head around in the direction of the voice. It seemed to come from the hallway where Old Lynne and The Quiet Man's rooms were located. He walked in that direction, quickly crossing the atrium. He paused before turning into that hallway. It seemed darker there than it had any right to be.

"Lynne? Is that you?"

Silence.

"This isn't funny," Andrew announced. "I need everyone in the rec room right now."

"Is the movie good?" the voice came again.

This time it sounded like it came from behind him. He spun around and stared into the empty atrium. It was impossible. Nobody was there.

"What's the movie?" the voice screamed from behind him.

Andrew turned just in time to see Old Lynne take her final charge, naked and on all fours, before she leapt at him. Her pure black eyes and wild grey hair came at him with such speed and ferocity he barely had time to get his hands up. Old Lynne's mouth was open, her jagged teeth barred, ready to take a bite out of him. She growled and screamed.

He yelled and tried to fight her off, but she'd come at him hard, and her momentum knocked him backward. Sliding across the slick floor on his back, Andrew held his hands up to protect himself from the wild woman swinging her fists at him and shrieking like a crazed animal.

"He's coming for you!" she yelled. "And he'll fuck each and every one of you! He'll shove his giant purple cock up your ass!"

One of the security guards, a guy named Tony, must have been near because suddenly Old Lynne was being pulled off him, her sagging tits flinging back and forth as Tony tried to pin her arms at her sides. She was going crazy.

"The Father is coming!" she screamed, wrenching herself free from Tony. "He's going to eat your soul like he ate my cunt!" She slammed a hand between her legs and slapped her naked, hairy vagina. "He was here, you know? He ate me, Andrew!" She fell to her knees and continued to finger herself. "He ate me with his long, purple tongue just like he'll eat all your souls!"

Tony grabbed her again, yanking her hand out of her and pinning both her arms to her sides. "Grab my radio and call for help!" he ordered.

Andrew climbed to his feet and reached for the radio at Tony's hip, coming dangerously close to Old Lynne. She sensed it too and shoved her face into his, wailing like a banshee as she bit his ear lobe and jerked her head back at the same time, tearing the bottom portion of the lobe clean off his ear. Andrew howled in pain and brought his hand up to find blood rushing down his neck.

Old Lynne cackled with laughter. "He'll eat your soul!"

"Call for backup!" Tony ordered.

Feeling woozy after seeing the blood running down, Andrew fought to bring the walkie-talkie up. He held down the button and announced, "Code Red at Atrium 1! Code Red at Atrium 1!"

The radio crackled and then a tinny voice replied, "10-4, responding."

Old Lynne seemed to sense the jig was up because her breathing calmed and she stopped struggling. It only took about a minute for two more security guards to arrive. Once she was constrained, Andrew jammed a syringe full of Ativan into her arm. Lorazepam wasn't a drug he had to use often. Most of the time, the patients on the bottom floor were reasonable enough to respond to verbal coaxing methods, but this bitch deserved it. She needed to be knocked the fuck out.

With a rag over his ear, he watched as the guards carried Old Lynne to her room. They held her down while he strapped her to the bed. All this went on while Olivia enjoyed the movie. His ear stung and Andrew had to admit he was glad it was him who'd gone looking for the two.

The two. Where's The Quiet Man?

"She's fine now," Andrew informed the guards. "Thank you for your help."

"You need to get that ear looked at," the first guard to respond, Tony, said.

"Trust me, I will."

With a nod at Andrew, Tony followed the other guards out of the room, leaving Andrew alone with Old Lynne.

Her eyes were closed now, her breathing was normal, and she was covered with a blanket. Later, he'd return with Olivia and try to dress her in one of her gowns, but he wouldn't dare try that on his own.

"You got me, Old Lynne," he whispered to her as he backed out of the room and closed her door.

He backed right into The Quiet Man.

Andrew spun around and looked up into the skeletal thin face of the towering figure staring down at him, flinching in the process, and barely squelching the shout that wanted so badly to call out to the guards who couldn't be far away.

"Mr. Grainger," Andrew said, "you surprised me there. You know you should be inside the rec room right now."

The Quiet Man put a finger to his lips as if to say, "Be quiet."

"Don't try to hush me," Andrew warned him. "I'm serious. I need you to—"

The Quiet Man's mouth opened only enough to let words spill out, and his lips didn't move with them. It was like looking into the face of a wooden ventriloquist dummy.

"Andrew, it is not what you think. Be careful. It will live with you until you die."

"What are you talking about?" Andrew asked.

"It's her he wants."

"Her? Her who?"

The Quiet Man put his finger to his lips again and then turned and walked away. Andrew followed him as he slowly shuffled his feet down the hall, into the atrium, over to the other hall, and into the rec room where he found his seat and continued watching the movie with the others.

Andrew still held the towel to his ear when he approached Olivia.

"My God," she said, "what happened to you."

"Old Lynne happened to me. I think I need to see a doctor."

"Andrew—"

"I hope *none* of your boyfriends *ever* want to go down on you *ever again*."

11

It was late when Andrew arrived home with his ear stitched and bandaged. For a moment, he leaned against the entry hall wall and rubbed at his temples. Tonight was already a doozy and he wondered what kind of excitement lay ahead.

Please let them all stay in their rooms tonight. Give me Beth. All of her for at least one night.

His hopes were shattered when he heard Peter call out from the living room, "You like that? Huh? You want some more of that?"

Some hard rock song played on the TV as Peter revved an engine on his video game. The boy must not have heard him enter. Andrew jingled his keys a little louder to get the nightly ritual out of the way.

"Did you bring pizza?" Peter called out.

And there it was. As much as he wished Beth would come greet him at the door, the familiarity of Peter's usual question wasn't too bad. It would have to do.

I can deal with Peter. But, please, can Beth come back to me next?

If the rotation went as usual, she would be next, but nothing was a definite around here and even if he did get to spend time with his wife, it was unlikely she'd last through the night.

Andrew slid down the wall until his ass hit the floor and buried his face in his hands. Peter wouldn't budge from the couch and Paloma would already be in bed, so he'd have a moment alone.

Why did he feel so defeated? Why was it hitting him so hard right now? This had been his reality since their marriage. Before that even. Yet this was the first time it seemed to kick his ass the way it was now.

Because, yes, this has been your reality, but it was never like this. It was never this extreme.

You'd never actually seen your wife standing over a bleeding body like some crazed serial killer.

Your coworkers never dreamed of Father Dennis.

Old ladies didn't bite your fucking ear off!

Andrew dug the palms of his hands into his eyes and rubbed. It wasn't until he pulled his hands away that he realized they were damp. He wasn't full-on crying, but tears had formed in his eyes. If his dad hadn't taught him at a young age that it wasn't manly to cry, he might sob right now. It wasn't like he never shed tears, but he wasn't able to ugly cry like he wanted to. Sometimes he thought if he could simply fucking bawl it all out, maybe he'd pour it out of his system and feel better.

Sitting by the door wasn't going to fix his problems, so Andrew left his work bag on the floor and shuffled into the living room. There was Beth in her backward baseball cap, chewing gum and letting it pop. Her clothes were typical Peter attire right down to the Killswitch Engage T-shirt and ripped jeans. Most of the young man's shopping had to be done online since he had his own unique taste.

In truth, there was nothing unique about it, but Andrew wouldn't dare start that argument again. At least he wasn't wearing Insane Clown Posse gear anymore. For two months straight, the kid would only drink Faygo brand root beer and referred to himself as a Juggalo.

Looking at the boy now, it was pretty easy to forget that was his wife sitting there.

"Whoa, did you get in a fight?" Peter asked as soon as he glanced up from his game and noticed the bandage covering his ear.

"Yes," Andrew said sarcastically. "Sucker punched me right in the earlobe."

"Hope you kicked his ass."

"I totally did."

Andrew looked over at the screen and watched the boy run over unarmed citizens in the game. It dawned on him that each of the personalities seemed to have his or her own violent side. Gore, of course, was the truly violent one, and Father Dennis was a meanspirited, self-righteous son of a bitch.

Thinking back to the look on Alex's face as she stabbed the fruit on top of her pancakes earlier and watching Peter violently attack people in his games, it dawned on Andrew that any of them could be as mean as Gore. Even Ruby and some of the stuff she said during sex was questionable. She had a bit of a dominant side.

They were all the things Beth wasn't. She was sweet, innocent, and absolutely glowing with an aurora of light and goodness. The others filtered out all her anger, judgment, and vengefulness.

How had he never thought about it before? She was a diamond, and they were all her blemished facets. They circled up around her and protected her. But protected her from what?

The nun. When he'd asked Alex about her at breakfast, she'd said, "She had black eyes. And a long tongue. Like a snake. She wanted to touch me."

"Peter, you have a second?" he asked as he sat down on the couch a full cushion away from the boy.

"Not really," he replied.

Typical asshole teenage boy.

"Gotcha," Andrew said, "I guess I *won't really* have any money to give you for whatever you need next time for your gaming. For one of your *skins* or whatever you call them. Or so you can level-up or whatever it is you need to do."

Peter rolled his eyes, mashed the pause button, and dropped his controller onto the carpet.

"I'm also not buying you another controller if you break that one," Andrew warned him.

Peter scoffed. "God, man. You don't have to be so mean."

"You have an attitude, kiddo. Don't have one with me and I won't give you one in return. Deal?"

"Yeah, whatever."

"Thanks for pausing your game."

"Wasn't like I had a choice."

"I really need to talk to you. I won't waste much of your time, but this isn't going to work if you have an attitude problem."

Peter took a deep breath and blew it out. "Okay, sorry. What do you want to talk about?"

"The nun," Andrew said, and the moment he said that word, Peter squinted a little and stared back at him suspiciously.

Sure, Andrew could have eased them into the conversation, but Peter wasn't one to give up much of his time, so he'd decided to go straight for the jugular.

"Nah," Peter said, shaking his head. "We don't talk about that."

"What don't you talk about?"

"That," Peter replied stone-faced.

"I won't pry… much, but give me something, Peter. You said yourself you try to stay away from Gore. I think whatever happened with that nun is what's driving Gore to do the things he's doing."

"What's he doing?" Peter asked.

Andrew wasn't sure how this worked. How much of what one personality did would the others be aware of? It couldn't be much, or Beth would know about his flings with Ruby. Perhaps she did and was fine with it or was too disturbed to mention it.

"You don't already know?" Andrew replied.

Peter laughed. "You're acting strange tonight."

I'm acting strange?

Andrew decided to come right out with it. "I think Gore is hurting people."

"Probably," Peter said. "Do you mind if I get back to my game?"

"Tell me about the nun first."

Peter shook his head. "I already told you we don't talk about that."

Andrew knew this probably wouldn't be the strategy recommended by doctors, and he hated to threaten the boy, but it was the only thing he could come up with that might work.

"Fine," Andrew said, "then you're grounded from your games. Hand me the controller."

"What?" Peter asked. It was the first time he looked concerned about anything other than the nun.

"You're grounded," Andrew replied, "and to be honest, it's been a long time coming. You've been really sarcastic lately."

"Andrew, come on."

"Peter, talk to me."

"Andrew."

"Peter. The nun."

Peter chewed on his bottom lip. "I'm afraid."

It might have been the boy's words. It might have been the long day at work. It might have been a malfunction with the house's electrical system.

Andrew could have sworn the lights in the house dulled a little and the temperature in the room dropped. A light wind seemed to float from the front door to where they both sat now.

"You see?" Peter asked, obviously reading the look of worry on Andrew's face. "That's why we don't talk about it. Besides, Gore took care of *that*."

"Took care of what?"

The lights flickered but stayed on.

"Andrew," Peter said. "Please, stop talking about it."

Andrew stood and walked to the front door, making sure it was closed and locked the way he'd left it. He jiggled the knob and found it was closed tightly. The breeze wasn't coming from there.

"Huh," someone did a half-chuckle behind him.

Andrew spun around and stared into the dark space ahead of him. Past the carpet-covered staircase and back toward the laundry closet and door to the basement, someone stood in the middle of the hall. It was a dark, shadowy presence wearing what looked like a large, round hat. Its hands appeared to be at its sides, dangling down.

"Peter?" Andrew asked.

No response.

"Peter?" he called again.

"Yeah, hurry up," the boy replied from the living room.

Impossible.

Peter was in there. And if Peter was in the living room, who was standing at the end of the hall, staring right back at him? It looked like Father Dennis, but if this was the priestly old man, how was he here in the house with Peter around? Beth could only be one personality at a time.

"What's wrong?" Peter asked, suddenly standing in the archway between the hall and the living room.

Andrew looked at the boy and then pointed at the figure in the hall. "Who's that?"

"Who's what?" Peter asked, looking in the direction Andrew was pointing.

The figure was gone.

Father Dennis wasn't there.

You're losing your shit.

He really was losing his mind. Only one personality could leave its room at a time and right now, Beth was Peter, so Beth couldn't be anyone else.

"Did you really see something?" Peter asked.

"It was nothing," Andrew replied. "Maybe it was Paloma."

"Paloma isn't here. She's on a date."

"A date?" Andrew asked.

"Yeah, remember? She's seeing some dude from Paraguay or Uruguay or, you know, one of those places. I think she's screwing him, bro."

"Peter."

"Nasty, huh? Thinking of someone wanting to have sex with Paloma?"

Andrew instantly calmed down with the thought of it. Then he vowed to never think about it again. She was an attractive older woman, he would give her that, but she was also an employee, and thinking about her like that was inappropriate.

"Would you hook up with Paloma?" Peter asked on his way back to the couch, crouching down to pick up his controller.

"No," Andrew said. "No, I wouldn't."

Peter held the controller in his hand and was about to press the pause button to get back into his game when he looked back up at Andrew like he'd just gotten busted and said, "Wait, were you serious about me being grounded?"

Andrew rolled his eyes and headed for the hallway. "No, you're not grounded."

"Thank God," he heard the boy say.

After a quick glance around the house, Andrew convinced himself he'd been seeing things. It had been a long day. He needed to rest.

12

Orphan X was one bad dude. Andrew was in the middle of reading one of Gregg Hurwitz's fight scenes when the bedroom door opened. In the fuzzy haze of his peripheral, he saw Peter's clothes rush by. Then he listened for the lock of the bathroom door. He found it was best not to interrupt the changeover. How it went down was always a mystery to him. Did she change to Beth downstairs and then come up to the bathroom to switch clothes?

Or was Peter aware that the change was about to happen, so he came upstairs and changed clothes so as not to startle Beth? If he investigated, he could discover the answer, but it seemed wrong to pry. Beth and the others had their system down pat. Who was he to get in the way of that?

After a short shower, Beth came out wearing only a long T-shirt. Andrew's imagination told him there would be sexy panties beneath, quite possibly a thong, but he doubted he'd get to see it. Her hair was still wet when she made her way to bed and lay down beside him. Reaching for her own book on her nightstand, she opened it and leaned over to kiss his cheek before settling in to read.

Andrew watched her, stunned that she was ready to sink into her book without talking to him first. It was a sure sign something was bothering her.

He reached over and put his hand between the pages of her book. "Wait a minute. I've missed you. Talk to me a little bit."

Beth closed her book and turned onto her side, facing him, and he slid down to look at her. They used to lay like this often, talking late into the night, giggling at jokes, and feeling each other up like horny teenagers.

Looking at her now, he wished they could go back to that easier time. Sure, they had the same issues back then, but marriage was new. Everything was fresh. Who knew what the future held? He finally had the woman he'd fallen madly in love with at the hospital, and he wasn't going to miss a second of this life with her.

Here he was all these years later, wishing he could avoid her when she let the others out of their rooms. Wishing he could show up only when it was Beth in his bed and then disappear before anyone else took her place.

God, I love this woman. How could I love a woman so much and be forced to miss her so much even when I'm face to face with her so often throughout the day?

"You've zoned out," Beth said, interrupting his thoughts.

She found his hand and interlaced her fingers through his.

Andrew squeezed her hand tightly. "I'm right here. I'm always right here. When you go, when you come back, I'm here."

"I know, baby," she said, and he could clearly see the pain in her eyes. They glossed over and he knew she was going to cry soon if he didn't change the mood. It's what he should have done but being with her in this moment was a reminder of why he asked her to marry him in the first place. He loved her immensely. When she was present, when *Beth* was really present, their life couldn't be any better.

Andrew wished like hell there was a way to trap Beth and keep her here.

"You've been gone a lot lately," he told her.

She closed her eyes and tears finally dripped onto her cheeks. "I don't mean to be."

He brought their hands up to his lips and kissed her knuckles. "I know." Then he touched his forehead to hers and said, "Can I ask you something I don't think we've ever talked about?"

She nodded. "Of course."

"I know what the doctors told me years ago, but I've never asked you myself. Are you aware of what happens when one of the others is let out of their room? Do you remember those things?"

"No."

"Where do you go?"

"I don't know."

"You must go somewhere."

"I don't know. I guess I just, I don't know, I kind of—" She pursed her lips and her eyes welled up with tears. She hid her face from him and finished with, "Lose time?" She formed it as a question because she really wasn't sure. Blacking out was how the doctors put it. It was like she lost consciousness when it happened. To her, it was losing time. She would be in the process of doing something and then suddenly she'd wink out and come back to herself hours later.

Why did you even ask her that? Were you hoping for a different answer?

Andrew hated pushing her like this. He remembered watching her in the hospital when the doctors would press her for information. She would shut down and they would be relentless. He wanted so badly to rescue her from Myles-Bend, to save her from all the doctors' prying, poking, and pestering. Now, here he was doing it himself when he'd once promised to protect her and never judge her.

Marriage to him was meant to be a release from all that tension. He was supposed to be the freedom from all that fear. Their home was the one place she could truly be herself no matter how many of herselves there were.

He lifted her hand and kissed her knuckles again. "It's okay. You don't have to answer."

If he pressed her too hard, it would trigger one of the others to step out and help her. He'd seen it happen often. It could be a loud noise that scared her or something unexpected happening. Any shock to her system could cause one of the others to leap forward, push her aside, and deal with the triggering event.

"Breathe," he reminded her. "Breathe."

She listened to him, closed her eyes, and she inhaled slowly and exhaled.

"You look beautiful," he told her.

She smiled and wiped at her tears. "Please. I look horrid."

"You could never—"

"Andrew, I'm a mess."

Sliding one arm out from under him and untangling his other hand from hers, he took her cheeks in both hands and brought her face closer. "You look unbelievably gorgeous at all times. And I mean that."

She forced a smile that melted into his as their lips met. Beth moaned against his mouth as his tongue slid out, pressed between her lips, and mingled with hers. She was soft and a blast of emotions hit him, like a sandstorm stripping away all the recent drama, ripping off his rough flesh, and exposing his tender heart. He was in his feels as she kissed him back with all the passion he craved.

This was his Beth.

This was the woman he was in love with.

The kiss ended naturally with lazy tongue lashes and a final peck on the lips. They remained close with their foreheads touching.

"You really love me, don't you?" she asked.

"You know I do."

"Nobody has ever loved me like you do."

"Nobody has."

"What did you say?" she asked.

"I said nobody has ever loved you like I do."

"That's not what you said."

She seemed scared as she pulled away from him.

"Beth, what's wrong?"

She sat up with her back against the headboard and tucked her knees up under her chin. "You said nobody will ever believe me."

"That's not what I said."

"I heard you."

"Beth, please."

They were both silent for a minute or two as Andrew thought about the situation and what he might be able to say to calm her down. He scooted closer to her and put a hand on her knee. She was close to changing again. In fact, he wouldn't know if she was still Beth until she spoke.

Andrew hated seeing her hurt or confused.

"Beth," he prodded. "Talk to me."

She wouldn't, and as much as he wanted to let it go, he couldn't. He had a feeling he knew what was going on here, and he needed to get to the bottom of it. He didn't want to take his wife back to the hospital – to any hospital for that matter – but Gore had gone too far. At Myles-Bend, the doctors had never gotten to the bottom of it. Andrew sensed he was close.

"It's the nun, isn't it?" he asked.

Her head shot up from her knees, her eyes opened wide in terror, and she put a finger to her lips. "Shh. Don't. Please. Andrew, please don't. Don't talk about that."

"Beth, this is important. I know about her. I know she hurt you and the others are protecting you."

Her head shook violently from side to side as she begged him to stop. "No, no, no, no, no."

"It's okay, baby," he said as he cradled her in his arms and stroked her hair. "It's okay. We don't have to talk about it."

Beth fell asleep in his arms.

For a full three minutes.

Then she got up to use the bathroom and it was pretty clear by the way she sashayed out of the room that they were going to have sex tonight.

Beth looked over her shoulder once before entering the bathroom, and the look she gave Andrew – that hungry-eyed glance while biting at only one corner of her bottom lip – turned him on instantly. His wife was a gorgeous woman and she never failed to get him aroused. She might have the attitude of Ruby, but this was Beth. It was her body, no matter who controlled her mind.

As she took her time in the bathroom, Andrew couldn't help thinking about the first time Ruby had shown her face to him. Of course, he hadn't noticed the difference at first. Beth had always had a kind of quiet, subtle flirtatiousness about her. She'd lower her face and lift her eyes at the same time, bat her lashes, and smile. She might tell him that he looked handsome today. Things like that.

She was sitting outside in the yard, a right reserved only for patients who'd either checked themselves into Myles-Bend or those who'd shown no violent traits. Beth fit into both categories. She was holding a daffodil she'd picked from the grounds and was sniffing it when Andrew approached from behind.

He'd already decided he liked her. She was the one thing he looked forward to each day. They hadn't quite formed a relationship, but there had been some mild flirtation.

"It's nice out today," he'd said, startling her.

She whipped her head around and put a hand to her chest. "You scared me."

"I didn't mean to. I'm sorry. Mind if I sit with you?"

"Here?" She looked down at the bench where there was barely room for another person.

Orderlies often visited with patients. They'd actually been instructed to converse with them more since many of them suffered from depression and struggled with having little contact with the outside world.

"Can you make room for me?" he asked.

She smiled up at him and scooted over. He sat next to her, and she held the flower up to his nose for him to smell. He inhaled.

"Doesn't have much of a scent," she said, "but it's definitely an enhancement over the stench in there." She threw a thumb in the direction of the hospital.

"I suppose you're right. It does kind of stink in there, but we try our best."

"I know you do."

"Why don't you leave?" he asked, instantly regretting the question since he hoped to God she wouldn't disappear. He imagined showing up for work someday and going to visit her only to find she'd checked out.

"I don't want to live with my dad," she said.

"So don't."

"You don't understand."

"Try me."

"I can't be trusted. I... I change."

"I know. I've seen it."

She lowered her gaze to her lap and tossed the flower onto the ground. "You have."

Reaching over, Andrew touched her chin and lifted her head gently. "Don't be ashamed. I change too."

She looked hopeful. "You do?"

"I do. I try to be a good person, but people sometimes say I'm an asshole." He smirked.

She laughed. "You could never be an asshole. You're a sweetheart."

Andrew's chest swelled and he found it hard to catch his breath. He wanted so badly to lean over, kiss her, and tell her he was falling for her, but he couldn't. Not only was it unprofessional in every way and would probably get him fired, but he was a chickenshit and was terrified she'd laugh.

"I think you're amazing," he said.

Her eyes seemed to well up a bit. Then she turned away from him and he noticed her breathing had picked up, too.

"You really think I'm amazing?" she asked, her face still pointed away from him, looking out over the yard.

"I really do. You're unbelievable. In a good way."

She shrugged and then reached with her left hand over to her right shoulder where she massaged it, like she'd suddenly gotten stiff.

"Are you okay?" he asked.

When she looked back at him, her eyes were slightly squinted. She bit at the corner of her bottom lip. Something had definitely changed

Faces of Beth

about her. She was no longer the sad, distraught girl she'd been moments before. Her eyes shifted into his lap and ran over his stomach, up his chest, and back to his face. She was checking him out, and she wanted him to notice.

"She likes you, you know," she said.

Up until this point, he'd only seen her Alex, Peter, and Gore personalities. He'd been told she had more, but the doctors were still trying to figure her out. She was a tough one to read.

"Who likes me?" Andrew asked.

She rolled her eyes. "Beth does, dummy."

"I'm sorry?"

"Beth? The chick you're sitting out here flirting with?"

It finally occurred to him that she'd changed personalities. One of the doctors called it letting one of the others out of their room.

"And who are you?" he asked.

"I'm Ruby, stud."

"Ruby."

"I'm the fun one."

He didn't want to laugh in her face. It would be rude, but this was wild. She'd changed right in front of him. He'd never seen it happen before.

"You're the fun one," he repeated.

She reached over, cupped her hand over his pants, and grabbed his cock. "The fun one."

In his right mind, he would have yanked her hand away and demanded she never pulled a stunt like that again. But he wasn't in his right mind. There was nothing right about his mind at all because he was tempted to escort her back to her room and toss her onto her bed. He had the feeling she, Ruby, would be completely fine with it.

As if reading his mind, Ruby leaned closer to him and said, "Beth's a bit of a prude, but I like to fuck."

Of course, Andrew did not fuck her. He did escort her back to her room where he bid her farewell for the day before heading home to masturbate three times before the next morning. If he didn't get rid of *all that pent up sexual frustration, he might have done something that would have gotten him in trouble.*

She'd tormented him so much when she was at the hospital. He'd basically courted her when she was Beth, but then she'd switch to Ruby and wreak havoc on his body. He spent a good portion of his day in an erect state. Olivia noticed it and used to call him out, teasing him, but she never knew the full truth. He and Ruby were sneaking off sometimes to have sex in a storage closet where Andrew knew there was no camera watching.

Finally, he was able to convince her to check herself out of Myles-Bend and come live with him.

Only Olivia knew the truth and she would have never told anyone.

The whole thing was unethical, sure, but he'd fallen in love with her and now they were married, so how and where they met really didn't matter. She was his responsibility now, and he would take care of her. She might have had a whole gang of internal protectors, but truly taking care of her fell on him, and he would never let anything bad happen to her.

Now, as he waited on Ruby to get out of the bathroom, he thought about how she was as much responsible for him falling in love with Beth as Beth was herself. All the sweetness and love had come from Beth but most of the stuff that had turned him on had come from Ruby. If sex was a healthy part of every relationship, then his health was in Ruby's hands.

The bathroom door popped open and there Ruby stood, still wearing that long T-shirt. Her hair was up in a ponytail. She liked having her ponytail pulled during sex.

Ruby leaned against the bathroom door frame and ran a finger over her shirt, around the spot where her nipple lay beneath the fabric, and it only took a second for the hardened nub to press against her shirt.

"Took you a while in there," Andrew said.

Ruby smirked and lifted the shirt to show she'd shaved her pussy bare. "Beth was a mess. I needed to clean up so it would be easier for you to eat."

Damn, she wastes no words.

She stepped close to the bed and tapped a finger against her clit before turning off the light. "Eat up, baby," she purred. "Mama needs to cum tonight."

Andrew slid off the bed, lay her on her back, and dropped to his knees so he could please his woman. Beth might not remember this, but he definitely would.

13

Ruby didn't take it easy on him tonight, and after they were done, they both collapsed onto the bed where they curled up in each other's arms. Andrew spooned her as she giggled with the post-sex lightheartedness he loved. She always did that when she wasn't rushing out of the room or the shower.

It wouldn't last long. He wouldn't allow himself to remain naked behind her like this. Not because he didn't like it but because she could switch to someone else with no notice at all. He could find himself naked behind little Alexandra or worse, spooning Peter.

Or Father Dennis.

Thinking of Father Dennis gave him chills. He would visit tonight. Showing up after their sexual romps seemed to be the old pervert's thing. To pop up and tell Andrew how much of a shithead he'd been. To pass judgment on him. Of all the personalities, it was Father Dennis Andrew loathed most.

As soon as he had the thought, Andrew muttered a quiet apology. If the old coot really was a man of God, it had to be wrong to think of him like this. Andrew had never really been the religious type, but wrong was wrong, and he couldn't deny that talking shit about the clergy felt sacrilegious.

Once Ruby was breathing deeply, the signal she was asleep, Andrew eased away from her and rolled to the opposite side of the bed where he found his pajamas and dressed before sitting in his chair with a book. He'd wait for the old priest instead of being jolted awake to find him hovering over him.

Andrew put his booklight on the dullest, faintest setting and settled in to read a fantasy novel. He wasn't in the mood for the action-packed world of *Orphan X* tonight. He wanted to be swept away to a world that wasn't so much like his own. He needed ogres, elves, and dragons. Mystical creatures that could help him suspend his belief for a little while.

Even with all the evil in those worlds, he often thought he would rather spend his time in a place with dark mages, goblins, and orcs than here in his hometown. He could carve out a nice home in the side of a mountain and spend the rest of his days with Beth. Without the real world to interfere with their dysfunctional family of sorts, life might be okay.

He could watch Alex dance with faeries, fish in a magical pond with Peter, fuck Ruby by campfire, use wooden swords to spar with Gore, and sip tea with Beth on the front porch of their cottage. If they were truly alone, none of it would matter. Not in a fantasy world.

If he could will them into another world, he would. Let Gore run around the hills and plains, attacking otherworldly beasts instead of strange men at nightclubs. Let him be a warrior assassin instead of a demented serial killer.

What it must be like to be the inventor of these kinds of stories. To be the writer of an epic fantasy.

It often dazzled him how authors were able to put fingers to a keyboard and build a dimension or a faraway land that never existed before their say-so. How could a man or a woman live in a regular world like this one and go to work, meet up with friends, drive around, shop at the mall, eat at restaurants, and perform all the other mundane functions of this boring world and then retire to their computer, flip a mental switch, and be in an entirely different headspace?

So many worlds.

So many characters.

All within one person's head.

Like Beth.

It occurred to Andrew that Beth wasn't so different from these world creators. She'd built her own characters. She'd built her own home inside her head where each of her characters lived inside his or her own room and only came out when it was their turn.

What if Beth could learn to harness that energy in a different way? What if she was meant to be an author but lost sight of how to control her characters?

Would the world's authors all have dissociative identity disorder if they couldn't write? If they had no gift of the written word, would all their multiple personalities be stuck inside their heads?

It was an interesting thought. Andrew wondered if Beth had ever tried writing. Maybe she would be an outstanding author. Alexandra and Peter would make a great coming-of-age novel. Ruby would probably fit an erotica storyline. Gore would definitely be suspense thriller and Father Dennis – horror.

As that thought came to mind, Andrew glanced over at the bed and saw that Beth, Ruby, was gone. All that remained was the crumpled up sheet and comforter. How could he have missed her getting up? He hadn't heard the bathroom door close. He hadn't heard the bedroom door open. She'd simply vanished.

Andrew dropped his book and booklight into his chair, climbed onto the bed on all fours, and patted her empty spot with his hands, like she might actually be there and his eyes were only playing tricks on him.

She wasn't there.

"Beth?" he called out.

"You were thinking of me," came a deep, hoarse voice.

Hands grabbed hold of his hips and suddenly Andrew felt himself being dragged from behind, lifted up into the air, and launched against the wall. He smacked the hard surface with his back and slid to his ass on the floor.

The dark, shadowy figure of Father Dennis reached down, grabbed hold of Andrew's shirt, and hoisted him up where he slammed him against the wall.

Andrew was lifted higher than Beth's body should have been able to handle. Not only because of the strength it would take but because she was too short for this. Yet, Father Dennis was tall, at least 6'5", and had driven Andrew so far up the wall his head was nearly touching the ceiling.

"You should be ashamed," Father Dennis barked.

"Beth," Andrew squeaked out as Father Dennis's hands wrapped around his throat and squeezed.

Andrew wanted to kick out, but he didn't want to hurt his wife's body. But the closer he looked through his watering eyes, the more he became convinced this wasn't his wife at all. He couldn't see the face of this *thing* clearly because of the wide hat the old man wore.

"Beth isn't here right now," Father Dennis said followed by a wheezing chuckle.

"What... are... you?" Andrew managed.

"All your concerns. All your worries. All your nightmares. I am all there is."

"I don't—" Andrew's words were cut short. He couldn't breathe. He was blacking out.

"Ask her about the nun," Father Dennis said. "She needs to remember. They won't let her. But she needs to remember. Ask Gore about it. Let's see how angry we can make him."

"I—"

"Or next time I will snap your neck."

Father Dennis spun him around and flung him against the far wall like a ragdoll, knocking him out cold.

14

When Andrew came to, he was alone on his bedroom floor. His eyes fluttered open slowly at first but then he remembered the assault from the old priest and jerked fully awake. He slid his ass against the carpet until his back was against the wall and threw his hands up to guard his face in case another attack came.

How long have I been out? Where's the old man?

"Beth!"

He kept his back against the wall where he could survey the entire room without a sneak assault from the wicked old bastard.

Light shined into the room from the bathroom but only through the wedged beam of the slightly ajar door. The bed was empty and so was the rest of the room, but in the doorway stood a shadowy figure.

Andrew knew that form and hoped this time it was Beth here with him. As the figure walked into the room, all hope left Andrew's body. He could tell from the way the person walked with his arms out at his sides, so full of strength and anger, that it was Gore.

Beth's darker version came closer to him, squatted, and with his face mostly hidden in the shadow of his hood, he reached out and touched Andrew's forehead.

"Gore," Andrew said.

Faces of Beth

The beam of the bathroom light shined off the side of his face and Andrew saw eyes he knew so well looking back at him, but they didn't contain the warmth he knew from his wife. This glare held a coldness in it. Gore respected him, he suspected, but there was no love there. Yet, the tender touch on his forehead was different. This wasn't like Gore at all, and for a second, he wondered if this dark personality of hers cared about him. He seemed... worried.

As if he realized himself that he'd shown too much emotion, Gore yanked his arm away, stood, and stuffed his hands into his pockets. Then he turned and started for the bedroom door.

"Wait," Andrew said.

Gore didn't slow down.

"Please," Andrew added. "Please, wait. Are you going out?"

Gore stopped and grunted his answer. He was going out, and Andrew knew that meant he might be going on the hunt. His head ached and he was still shaken up from his encounter with the priest, but he couldn't stand by and allow his wife to take any more lives, whether the men deserved it or not.

"I want to go with you," Andrew informed him.

Gore stopped, with his head down peering at his feet, and grunted once more. Then, with a wave of his hand, in his deep, throaty growl, he said, "Fine. Come on then."

Andrew drove this time, with Gore giving silent directions. Most of it was through finger pointing to the left and right with each necessary turn. Sometimes, when Andrew asked a question, the silent, brooding figure in the passenger seat answered with a shrug, nod, or one of his grunts. Occasionally, he would say in a low whisper, "Yes."

It was so strange to him how his wife could have such a sweet speaking voice and had the singing voice of an angel, but once she packed herself into this hooded sweatshirt and jeans, she barely made more than throaty growls. When she did speak, it seemed almost painful for her.

"Turn here," Gore commanded while shaking a finger wildly at the right.

The turn was coming up fast and the light was green, so Andrew changed lanes as quickly as he could, cutting off a car in the process. It honked at him, and he held a hand up to wave as if the driver would be able to see him through the darkness of the night and the tinted windows.

He slowed down the best he could and turned right at the light.

"If you don't want to call any attention to us," Andrew said, "you might want to give me more notice before a turn next time."

Gore didn't respond until two blocks down when he pointed at an all-glass structure wedged between taller condominium buildings. The sign out in front of the club was lit up bright white with purple neon trim. It read: Platinum. That was all. One word.

Andrew was unfamiliar with the place but thought it looked like it might be an overpriced strip club where the dancers would probably prostitute themselves out but would insist they were *escorts,* not *sex workers*.

"What are we doing here, Gore?" Andrew asked.

"You'll see," Gore replied.

Andrew wasn't dumb enough to park in the business lot. There, they would encounter bouncers, valet parkers, and anyone who'd exited the building to get a breath of fresh air and drown it in cigarette smoke. No, they needed to park somewhere they could easily escape, and nobody would remember seeing their car.

His goal tonight was to stop Gore from hurting anyone, but if he failed, he wanted them to be able to make a clean getaway.

Gore barely waited for the car to stop before he hopped out and walked toward the club, leaving Andrew to hurry and follow. The bouncer at the door barely paid them attention other than to hold out his hand and accept the twenty-dollar cover charges which, of course, Gore failed to mention beforehand leaving Andrew to fork out a fifty to which he was informed he would not be getting change. This message was delivered by way of the bouncer pointing at a sign that read: $20 cover per person. Exact change only.

Inside, the crowd separated as the entry corridor branched off into two hallways. A neon sign above the left showed a naked lady on a stripper pole, swinging around it, with the pole between two enormous

Faces of Beth

tits. Gore pulled Andrew in that direction, ignoring the other option which led to a hallway beneath an electric sign with a naked man swinging his hefty dick around like a helicopter propeller.

Andrew was glad they'd veered left. With Gore, they could have gone either way.

As they entered the club, Andrew noticed most of the men and women patrons were dressed as if they'd come over straight from a business meeting. In his polo and khakis and Gore's jeans and hoodie, they were way underdressed until a group of what appeared to be college kids showed up. Now, Andrew felt like one of their professors.

"You look like you could do bad things to a good girl," a blonde with her hair in a messy bun stepped in front of Gore and eyed him up and down. She seemed to notice she was addressing a woman in men's clothes and then changed her tune. "Or maybe we can join together and do bad things to your man."

Andrew's eyebrows shot up and he had to stifle his laugh. He'd never considered having a threesome. He had his hands full with Ruby and when his wife was playing the part of the seductress, he was perfectly content.

Gore looked over at him as if wondering what he thought of the woman's proposal and for a second, Andrew thought this might be a trick. He wondered if Beth was in there waiting on his answer, checking to see what he thought of bringing another woman into their bed.

"No," Andrew said, finally finding his voice. "No thank you."

"You look like you might change your mind," the blonde said. She turned her attention back to Gore and added, "Maybe you can talk him into it. If not, if one of you wants a lap dance, I'll be at the bar. And if you want to buy a girl a drink…"

She didn't finish but walked away.

"Seems she liked you," Andrew said, giving Gore a nudge to his ribs.

"We're not here for her," he said.

Andrew scanned the rest of the club and saw many other women like the blonde, all dressed in skimpy clothing. At the center of the club was a T-shaped stage, but it was empty. Instead, the dancers walked around the main bar area and tried to solicit customers. He wondered if Gore had gone to bed with any of these women during his nightly rendezvous. Surely, he couldn't be murdering someone every time he went out.

When he was younger, Andrew went to quite a few strip clubs. None were as nice as this one. Here, it seemed the women were classier. Not so much in the way they spoke, as evident by the blonde who'd approached them, but their style and overall look was more refined. This wasn't the kind of joint he'd visited in college.

"Come," Gore told him as he made his way toward the back of the club.

Andrew followed him until Gore sat down at a round table placed to the side of the stage. Once they were seated across from each other, Gore said, "Order us each a beer." His eyes, Gore's eyes, were faintly illuminated by an overhead purple light and Andrew found himself glued to his gaze.

Her gaze.

A glimmer of hope washed over him as he thought about the woman seated across from him. He knew it wasn't Beth, but for a second, he chose to believe he was on a date with her. His heart broke a little at the realization that he so rarely got the opportunity to take her out for a night on the town. They didn't often get the chance to sit across from each other at a restaurant or go out to the movies or rent a hotel for the night like most couples.

"Can I get you two something to drink?" a waitress asked, pulling him out of his thoughts.

"Umm, yeah," he said, his eyes still on Gore who was staring at a group of people sitting on a wall-length couch on the other side of the stage. "Two beers, please."

"Two beers, got it, sweetie," the waitress said and then disappeared.

Andrew hadn't even gotten a look at the woman. He'd been too lost in his thoughts. In the sadness his marriage had brought him. He'd been so in love with Beth. He still was. But this life was so fucking difficult.

You won't give up on her. You love her too much.

"Beth," Andrew said, thinking there might be a chance that she'd shove Gore out of the way and show up right now to share a drink with him.

Gore whipped his head to the right and glared at him. "Don't."

Andrew nodded.

The waitress returned with the beers, set them down, and as she was about to walk away, Gore grabbed her wrist, causing the woman to stop and glare down at him. The bouncer standing next to a door on the far wall noticed and stepped toward them.

Andrew's heart skipped a beat.

"Got any coins left?" Gore asked.

The waitress smiled and held a hand up to stop the advancing bouncer.

"You're in luck," she said. "We're down to only four. I've got one on me, but I can get another if you're interested."

"We are," Gore said.

"Twenty each," she said, "I'll be right back."

She walked away and Andrew leaned forward in his chair. "Are you fucking crazy? That bouncer was about to come over here and knock both our heads off."

Gore scoffed. "He could have tried."

"And what's this about twenty each? She better not mean dollars. I already lost fifty getting in this place. I don't have another forty. I work my ass off for the money I do have, and I don't have it to waste for these experiments of yours—"

"I've got it," Gore replied.

The waitress came back, and she gave Gore two black coins in exchange for his cash. Then she pointed them toward the door the bouncer was guarding. Gore stood and led the way. The bouncer, who'd watched the entire exchange, opened the door for them and ushered them in.

Once inside, he closed the door behind them, and Andrew found himself squinting through the sudden darkness until his eyes adjusted to the dim light provided by torches set in sconces every ten feet or so that descended along with a winding staircase.

Andrew recognized wet, earthy scents, and realized they might be under one of the area's rivers. It reminded him of the smells one might encounter when walking through a cavern to see rock formations.

"You've been down here before?" Andrew asked, hesitant to make his way down into the bowels of the club.

He was more worried about the ceiling caving in than anything else. Andrew looked up and couldn't see anything above him.

Gore nodded and started down the stairs. "Twice."

Andrew didn't immediately follow. He'd seen horror movies, and this was how many of them started. He couldn't help thinking this was where the dark things would lurk. Father Dennis was sure to bring this up later. He'd remember this through Gore's eyes and would blame Andrew as he held him up by his throat against the wall and cursed him for the sins they would surely encounter down here.

Realizing his only options were to follow or to turn around and go back into the club above, leaving his wife to descend alone into the darkness below, Andrew crept down the stairs. He knew what Gore was capable of, but it was only a matter of time before someone bigger and badder came along and left his wife in a pool of blood – like the man Andrew had found her standing over in that alleyway the last time she'd gone out on one of her crusades.

"Fuck," he whispered to himself as he hurried to catch up with her.

He reached Gore about halfway down the dark stairwell. At about that same time, the sounds of sexual pleasure greeted him, along with the clinking of glasses being brought together in toast and murmured voices, soft laughter, and the shuffling of feet moving about below. The stone walls seemed to amplify the sounds and the lower they went, the louder the ricochet. They were about to step right into a magnificent party or what sounded like a social gathering to rival one thrown by the *Great Gatsby* himself.

Andrew's senses ceased making sense as the damp, earthy soil that

Faces of Beth

had once filled his nostrils now mingled with cigar smoke, perfume, and the musky scents usually associated with sex.

"Gore," he said, but the young man he was following kept moving downward.

Light poured into the stairwell from the bottom and as they stepped lower, the party Andrew expected finally came into view. Only he'd stopped at an odd spot where the upper part of the wall's archway kept the upper portion of the crowd out of sight, only allowing him to see the bodies of people from about the waist down.

From Andrew's viewpoint, the bottom half of glamorous evening-wear was on display right along with the pubic regions of naked servers and flamboyant guests.

Witnessing black slacks, a small flaccid cock, a red mini skirt, a shaved pussy, a very bushy pussy, a long gold evening gown, camouflaged pants, black leather pants, a giant flaccid cock, a shimmering, sequined dress, a medium-sized hard cock, and a kilt all bustling about, nudging each other as they moved around, was an interesting introduction to the party.

Andrew laughed and stepped lower, allowing himself a view of the upper half of the crowd along with the rest of the party.

Gore was already stepping into the throng, like this was a group he mingled with every day. Andrew, however, paused. He couldn't believe what he was seeing. His jaw dropped in awe as he took in the sudden plethora of colorful dresses and fancy suits blended with naked bodies, some pale and some beautifully tanned.

He stood before an archway that made him think of old Wild West movies set in Mexico. The wall itself seemed like it was made of old adobe clay with a torch to each side. From where he stood, he could see the guests meandering about. People sipped wine from glasses, champagne from flutes, and whiskey from tumblers. Beer wouldn't be allowed in a gathering like this.

Gore had already disappeared into the fray and Andrew wondered how they'd been allowed in at all dressed the way they were. Then again, they could simply get naked and match half the crowd.

"Excuse me," a man in a grey pin-striped suit and a cowboy hat said as he stepped around Andrew from behind, meaning he'd just descended the stairs.

Andrew had heard of underground BDSM dungeons before, and he'd foolishly imagined them to look like an actual medieval dungeon. This was close, being underground and all, but this was an old horse stable. Andrew didn't know a lot about the area's history other than there had been a lot of Civil War stuff that happened here, so a horse stable wasn't too farfetched.

Once he moved into the sea of bodies, he saw that each stable was now an elaborate sex room with its own scene being played out for a viewing audience.

Well-dressed members of what Andrew supposed were the city's elite walked from scene to scene, viewing the sites while sipping their drinks and fondling one another. This was foreplay. Most would probably retire home to vanilla sex, the kind of stuff he himself would do with Beth. Some might even fuck like he and Ruby. But he doubted any would put their lover on a cross like the young man in the first stable.

One of the college guys who'd shown up after he and Gore had entered the club was strapped to what Andrew was pretty sure was called a St. Andrews Cross. His cock dangled for all to see while a woman in black latex dragged a crop up his balls and across his body. The young man seemed to be loving it.

"Would you like a drink, sir?" a naked woman with curly red hair asked, gripping Andrew's shoulder.

For a second, like any man, he caught himself staring at her nude body. Her nipples were pierced, and a chain dangled between the hoops. Another chain connected at its center and disappeared down below. Andrew followed it before catching himself and yanking his attention back to her face where he found her smiling at him.

She winked and repeated her question. "A drink, sir? Or, perhaps, something else to quench your thirst? I'm quite affordable," she assured him, "and well worth it."

"No," Andrew said, feeling his cheeks burn with embarrassment. "No, I'm... um... my wife is here and... no. I'm sorry."

"It's perfectly natural," the server said. "If you change your mind, I'll be around."

Andrew turned away from the woman and chuckled. He couldn't believe himself. How easily he'd gotten lost in his thoughts.

Why the hell did I let Gore bring me here?

Speaking of Gore, there he was. Andrew spotted him up ahead and followed him past the next stable where a very well-endowed man had three older women on their knees, blindfolded, with their mouths open.

As Andrew walked by, he couldn't help glancing left and peering in at the action. This was all so new to him. It reminded him of the crazy sex shit going on behind the red door at the Wicked Waltz before Gore killed the man in the alley. That place had seemed so sleazy where this, this seemed erotically elegant in an odd kind of way.

A choking, gagging sound brought Andrew's attention back to the reality of the situation, and he looked around the crowd blocking the stable to see the man inside had shoved his cock into one woman's mouth. She was brunette with grey streaks in her hair and had sagging tits. She gagged and pitched forward, nearly puking, until he removed his cock. She spit on the ground and nearly vomited.

The crowd yelled at her.

"Puke you fucking whore!"

"Filthy cunt!"

"Fucking throw up, why don'tcha!"

"That's all you're worth, you fat cow!"

As they hurled disgusting remarks at the poor woman, she smiled back at the crowd and licked her lips, seeming to love it. The man had already moved to the next woman, whose silver hair dangled in front of her face in strands. He shoved his cock into her mouth and kept it there while she gagged. When he tried to pull away, she leaned forward on it, not wanting him to stop. Until she did, in fact, vomit on him. The crowd went wild.

"Yes!"

"Puke!"

"You gross fucking pig!"

"Fucking nasty heifer. Puke it up, grandma!"

She smiled with vomit dripping down her chin and spit out her dentures.

Maybe this isn't any classier than the Wicked Waltz. Maybe kinks of all degrees live within all social classes and only the judgmental and self-righteous believe they see the difference. Inside, we're all the same animal.

Andrew watched in awe, wincing, and trying not to vomit himself until he felt a tug on his arm and looked over to see Gore pulling him away.

"Come," Gore said.

Andrew followed.

The crowd behind him continued shouting.

"That's degrading," Andrew said.

"That's the point," Gore replied. "They want to be degraded."

"Why would anyone want that?"

Gore shrugged. He seemed to have no interest in that display of public humiliation.

It was the next stall that caused Gore to stop and join the crowd gathered there.

In this stall, on her knees, was a beautiful young woman. She was tied up with her arms behind her back. The rope was thin but skillfully woven into an intricate design. The artist who'd put her in this position was an older, blonde woman with her hair pulled back and braided into an interesting design of its own. A purple scarf covered most of her face, up to her eyes, where she tried to hide her crow's feet with dark mascara and eyeliner.

She had to be in her sixties, but her body was magnificent. She wore skin-tight leggings and a bodice-like top. Andrew wasn't well-versed in ladies clothing, but it was a sexy outfit.

The woman in control pulled on the rope, forcing the tied woman to lift at the waist where we could see the rope wound around her tits and spider-webbed at her waist.

So this is Gore's kink.

Andrew wondered if all Beth's personalities were into this kind of thing. Did Ruby want to be tied up? Did Beth? Wait, did they want to be the one tying someone up?

No, I don't think I'd like that.

"Remember that blonde woman," Gore whispered in my ear.

"The one in control?"

He'd already walked back toward the stairs.

Later, as they sat in the car, Andrew couldn't help being a bit pissed that they'd spent so much money tonight and only got a beer and a fifteen-minute peep show that included a limp-dicked frat boy on a cross, some vomiting ladies being humiliated, and a girl getting tied up.

"This was a waste of money, Gore," Andrew complained. "I would rather be home with a good book. Or watching TV."

"We're not done," Gore replied.

"We've been sitting out here for three hours."

"I told you to rest."

They sat silent a little longer before Andrew decided to interrupt the quiet with a question he knew might cause a quarrel between them, but it was as good an opportunity as any to bring it up.

"Gore," Andrew said, "tell me about the nun."

Gore, who'd been lightly tapping on the steering wheel with his index finger, stopped.

"There was no nun," he replied between clenched teeth.

His answer didn't surprise Andrew. Denial was the best way to avoid a subject.

"There was—"

"There was no nun."

"The others say you took care of it," Andrew said.

Gore grunted and it sounded a little like a laugh. Like he was amused by that.

Andrew decided to change tactics. "Why do you hurt people?"

"I don't hurt people," Gore replied. "Never. Never innocent people. Only evil, demons in human form. Evil people who hurt others."

The clock on the dashboard changed to three o'clock in the morning. Gore opened the passenger door and said, "It is time."

"Time for what?"

"Come," he said.

Just like that, their conversation was over. Andrew still had no answers other than denial that a nun existed and denial that Gore ever hurt innocent people.

It was late, or early, and most of the cars parked at or near the club were gone. Gore walked to an alley that led between the nightclub and one of the tall condo buildings it was wedged between. Andrew stepped over a few puddles and followed Gore as he opened a door in the side of the condo building and led Andrew into a cold hallway.

This place was fancy, a nice, newly built condominium building.

Gore led Andrew to a set of elevators, pressed the up button, and waited.

"Gore, where are we going?" Andrew asked.

The elevator opened and they stepped in. Gore pushed the button for the top floor. The elevator didn't budge. After a few seconds, a voice came over the speaker. "Can I help you?"

"It's Rachel," Gore said in a female voice that was sexy but sounded nothing like Beth or Ruby. "I've been here before. I'm here to see Angel."

"*The Rachel?*" the voice on the other end asked. "It's rare anyone comes back."

"What can I say? I'm a glutton for punishment. I should have never left."

"Hold on." After a brief pause, the voice came back. "Angel remembers you. Come on up."

The elevator moved and as it started to ascend, Gore turned to Andrew and with his deep growl, he said, "Remember the night I came home, and you found Beth with all those cuts and welts on her body?"

Andrew did remember. It looked like she'd been beaten half to death. He'd considered taking her to the hospital but knew they'd blame him. He assumed the injuries came from one of Gore's nights out. That perhaps he'd bitten off more than he could chew and had gotten his ass kicked.

"They call her Angel," Gore told him. "The lady with the ropes. In the dungeon. The one in control."

"The blonde?" Andrew asked.

Gore nodded. "Out there she plays by one set of rules. But she brings young women here every night. From the club. In here, she hurts them. Like she hurt me. I've seen her do it five times. She takes women in there and they never come out."

"How did you get out?"

"I escaped."

"Gore."

He put a finger to his lips to shush Andrew. He pointed at the digital screen showing they were already about to reach the penthouse floor.

"The door will open on a dark hallway. They don't like the light here. You stay in the hallway and wait for me."

"Wait," Andrew said, his heart suddenly speeding up. He wasn't prepared for this.

Who was the guy on the speaker? A guard? She has guards?

What if they have guns?

What if they shoot us?

What the fuck?

"Gore, I don't like this, man," Andrew said.

"Andrew, shut up," Gore said.

The lights in the elevator went out.

Andrew panicked. "What the fuck?"

"Calm down. I told you they don't like the light up here. It's triggered that way. The light goes out on the penthouse floor."

"I really don't like this."

"Shh."

The elevator dinged as it came to a stop.

The doors slid open onto darkness.

Gore stepped through.

Andrew hesitated, and he knew the doors were about to close. At the last second, he followed Gore into the darkness.

The hall was painted black as if the owner wanted absolutely no light to seep through, but at the end of the hall there was no door, only an archway that led into the next room, and that was where all the cries for help were emanating.

In that open room, a purple strobe light flickered, and it was only enough light for Andrew to catch a glimpse of some of the grotesque horrors happening there.

With his back pressed against the wall, Andrew watched a naked young woman with her knees on the cement floor, one cheek pressed against a cinder block pillow, cry and beg for help with blood running from her mouth as the blonde woman he saw downstairs beat her across her back and ass with a bamboo cane.

"Please!" the woman cried. "Mistress, I want to go home! Please! I don't like this game!"

"This is your home now," the woman they called Angel replied, "and this is not a game. There are no safe words here. We stop when you pass out or when we feel fulfilled. You should have never offered yourself to me, Princess."

As Andrew stared at the scene in front of him, he saw Gore move toward the end of the hall. He stopped only ten feet in front of Andrew and pulled his hoodie sweater off. He dropped it on the floor before removing his T-shirt and then pulling off his jogging pants and underwear. Naked and looking as sexy as the Beth he'd always known and loved, Gore walked the rest of the way down the hall.

Angel stopped hitting the woman bent over the block and held the cane over one shoulder as she watched Andrew's wife enter the room.

"Ohhhh," Angel said, "I do remember you. I fucked you so royally the last time that you couldn't quite get enough. Isn't that right, Princess?"

"That's right, Mistress," Gore said.

Andrew wanted to scream, "No!" But he didn't. He remained silent.

"And you escaped."

Faces of Beth

"I did. I thought I wanted out, but you're all I could think about."

"Mistress," a man called out from somewhere inside, deep in the darkness of the room, "what if she's got cops downstairs waiting?"

"Boris is nervous," Angel said. "Does he have reason to be?"

"I signed a contract, remember?" Gore replied.

"You signed a contract," Angel let that thought simmer for a moment. "Yes, you did. And nothing here is illegal. But just in case, this time we will get you on video, to share your many talents on all the social media sites. We wouldn't want you sneaking away again. Not that you would. I trust you've come back for the right reasons. I can see it in your eyes. You *need* what only I can give you."

"Yes," Gore said, "just fuck me again, Mistress. I've missed you."

"You will have to earn that – in pain."

Angel, Mistress as they all called her, laughed, and the sound that came out of her didn't sound human. Andrew heard it and wondered if Gore had been speaking in metaphors when he'd talked about killing only demons. Or was the older woman's voice only ravaged by screaming and yelling at her sexual slaves?

The blonde Mistress led Gore to a pipe that ran across the wall and made him hold onto it. Naked and vulnerable, Gore put both fists up against the pipe.

The lights continued to blink, and Angel tapped Gore's thighs lightly with her cane.

"Spread your legs," she ordered.

Gore did as he was told.

Angel placed the cane between Gore's legs and lightly slapped it against his pussy. "Do you like that?"

"I do, Mistress," Gore replied.

Andrew watched Gore's hands and noticed one wasn't fully gripping the pipe. From where he stood, he couldn't quite see the entire room. It sounded like there were other moans and cries for help. Other grunts and complaints.

He wasn't sure how afraid he should be in the situation because he still didn't understand how dangerous these people were but standing in the shadows without anything to hide behind left him feeling vulnerable, and for a second, he thought this *mistress* might have seen him.

She froze amidst all she was doing and stared into the dark hallway. Her eyes seemed to fix on him.

"Mistress, please let me go," someone called out from the room behind her. "I won't tell anybody. I promise. I'll never come back to the club. I'll never say anything."

It seemed as if Angel was ignoring the shouting and had her attention on Andrew. He nearly pissed his pants when she slowly raised her right arm, lifted the cane, and stretched it out slowly so it was pointed right at him. In the darkness, he couldn't be sure, but he thought her eyes were squinted like she was trying to make out his form.

If she'd stayed like that even a few seconds longer, he might have stepped out with his hands up in surrender. That's how sure he was that he'd been spotted.

But she wheeled around with her cane and pointed it swiftly in the direction of the shouting woman and yelled, "Boris, shut her up, or I will shut her up. She's giving me a headache, and if I get a headache, I swear on everything unholy that everyone in this room will pay!"

Moans and groans went up all over the room as people complained and begged for the girl to stop shouting.

There came a loud *thwack* that Andrew assumed came from Boris, followed by a whine and a whimper.

"Should I fuck her some more, Mistress?" came a man's voice.

"Go ahead," Angel said nonchalantly, like she didn't care at all about the woman they were speaking of.

Then came the sounds of Boris's pumping and wheezing along with the woman's moaning and sighing. Andrew couldn't tell if this couple's sex was consensual or not. Every few thrusts or so, the woman would complain, "It hurts," but would go back to hissing through her teeth until her next sigh and grievance.

"Please," the woman on the cinder block near the door cried. "I want to go home."

Angel slammed the cane against her. The girl cried out.

"Do you want the razors again?" Angel threatened.

Faces of Beth

"No!" the girl screamed. "God! No, please. No! Please, no."

"Then shut up!" Angel yelled. "You were suicidal when you came to me. We're going to see how close to death we can bring you. And if you keep on, I'll release those pictures of you to your parents and friends. You want that?"

The girl only cried this time.

As Andrew's eyes adjusted, he finally started to make out more of the horrors in the room. Far in the background, a young man dangled from his wrists by a set of handcuffs. He was naked and had cuts all over his body. None of them looked life threatening, but blood ran from all of them. His head dangled down like he was no longer conscious.

To his right, a man was being fucked by another man, and in between thrusts, the man doing the fucking was striking the other across his back with what looked like a cat o' nine tails. As the leather flogger-like instrument with knotted ends tore into the man's back, he shrieked in pain, but his hands and feet were shackled to the floor, so he couldn't escape.

"Monty," Angel said as she looked over at the men, "I think he has had enough for now. Pull out of him and rub some of the sauce on his hole."

The man doing the fucking pulled out of him and laughed, slapping the injured man on his freshly wounded back. The guy shackled to the floor remained in position and cried, slobber dripping down his chin.

"Not the sauce," he begged. "Please, not the sauce."

Andrew didn't know what the sauce was, but the injured man's reaction told him enough. In his mind, he imagined it was ghost pepper sauce or something hellacious like that. This sadistic bitch seemed like the type to rub hot sauce on a man's torn and tattered asshole.

"Not the sauce," the man continued to beg.

"You came back knowing the pain you would receive," Angel said to Gore, bringing Andrew's attention back to what was happening closest to him.

Angel moved out of view but returned with a long dagger and brought the blade to Gore's back where she pressed the tip against his right shoulder blade and softly brought it toward his spine. Gore tensed, and Angel smiled.

While the evil bitch's attention was stuck on the kinky shit she was doing with Andrew's wife, Gore seemed to have a plan of his own. Andrew watched as the fist he'd kept loose at the pipe slowly unfolded a straight razor, the old-fashioned kind barbers used to shave faces. As Angel was about to cut into his back, Gore spun out of the way and swiped at her throat with the blade.

Angel dropped to her knees with her fingertips at her throat. At first, it looked like she was only choking. Then blood began to pour down her body, soaking her like a crimson chandelier.

Gore leapt out of view and glass shattered.

The strobe light stopped flickering and the room went completely black.

A woman screamed.

The sickening thwack of a blade on flesh and guts repeatedly.

A man cried out in pain.

"I'll fucking kill you!" someone yelled, it sounded like Boris.

The same someone screamed in agony.

Then he coughed and it sounded wet.

More yelling.

Crying.

Thwacks.

Thuds.

Thumps.

Argh!

Hugh!

Humph!

Hack!

Thwack!

Please!

The sounds of death are hard to explain, and all Andrew could think was they all sounded wet. All the cries were throaty and wet. All the slices and cuts were deep – and wet. All the dying was heavy thumps – all wet. And the blood splattering and flinging this way and that – so wet.

When Gore reemerged from the room and moved barefoot into the hallway, his feet padded against the cold tile floor, and even they sounded wet. In his hand, he still held his unfolded razor.

The way he walked out, his hair slicked back with blood, his body so naked, and the strobe light flickering behind him. It took Andrew a moment to realize the woman coming at him with the razor in her hand wasn't coming to kill him, too. It was Gore and they were on the same side of *this*. Whatever *this* was.

Gore bent to retrieve his clothes and used his T-shirt to clean the blood off him the best he could before pulling his hoodie down over his head and pulling on his underwear and pants.

Behind her, the girl with her face against the cinder block was still in the same position, begging to be set free.

"What about the girl?" Andrew asked.

"One of the others will help her," Gore said.

They were about to step onto the elevator when a big, naked man ran into the hall, wielding Angel's dagger. "You think you can walk in and out of here like that, bitch?"

"Hold on," Gore said as he turned toward the man and walked back to him. Andrew thought he might be Monty, the man with *the sauce*.

"Come on, you cunt," the big man said, his huge cock dangling between his legs.

Andrew felt like he should do something, but Gore was handling himself well, and he was liable to get himself killed if he intervened.

As Gore approached, he leapt left, then right, where he ran up the wall and bounced off it with a move that was so blindingly fast Andrew barely saw the razor's blade cross the big man's throat but before Gore's feet touched the ground, he'd also cut a giant 'X' across his chest.

The big man stared back at Gore, clutched his throat, took a few steps back while choking on his own blood, and then fell backward.

As he fell, the rest seemed to happen in slow motion.

Gore and Andrew both yelled, "No!"

But there was no way to stop his massive, tree trunk of a body from falling on the young woman, and when he did, his torso smashed her head in, snapping her neck between the cinder block and the floor.

Her constant cries were suddenly cut short with a sickening "ungh" sound.

Gore stood looking down at the naked man's body, which covered the girl. He pushed him over with his foot, but the giant barely budged. All that could be seen of the girl was her ass and feet, still in the fetal position where Angel had kept her crouched over that cinder block pillow.

"What the fuck?" Andrew said.

Gore didn't respond.

"He just came out of nowhere."

No response.

"We need to go." Andrew tried to grab Gore's arm, but Gore slapped his hand away.

Andrew tried again and got the same response. After several more attempts, Andrew walked toward the elevator, calling out over his shoulder, "Gore, we need to fucking go, man."

Finally, he came to his senses and turned to leave.

When the elevator doors opened, Andrew asked, "What happened in that room?"

It took Gore a long time to answer, and when he did, he said, "The same thing that happened to the nun you keep asking about."

In the elevator, Gore anxiously tapped his foot, and when they reached the ground floor, he rushed out of the building and toward the car. He seemed worried or afraid.

As they approached the car, Gore threw the keys to Andrew and said, "You drive."

In the car, Andrew finally asked him, "What's going on with you?"

Gore remained silent. His words from earlier came back to Andrew.

I don't hurt people. Never. Never innocent people. Only evil, demons in human form. Evil people who hurt others.

The young woman hadn't hurt anyone. This had become more than vigilante justice.

What did that make Gore? What did that make Beth?

Andrew decided the question needed to be asked. Gore had to be confronted.

"Gore, that's enough of the silent act," Andrew said. "You just killed your first innocent person, didn't you?"

15

Gore didn't kill everyone that night in the condo building. The innocents were left alive. All except that one poor girl who died in the end. That one had been a mistake and it seemed to tear him up. He'd only meant to hurt the evil ones. He made sure Andrew understood that.

When Andrew asked about killing his first innocent person, Gore lost it. He told Andrew he might have seriously fucked up. Beth was innocent and should have always remained that way. Gore might have stained her, might have made her body a receptacle of evil, a canister that could carry wickedness, he might have opened their home to something truly sinister.

He went on and on about how the killing of the evil ones made him stronger and stronger. That's why he did it. But now he'd made the bad one stronger. This time he'd fucked up.

Andrew had listened quietly until he couldn't take it anymore and finally yelled out, "What the fuck are you talking about?!"

He'd had enough of the psychobabble bullshit. He didn't understand all this insane rambling. Gore never said more than a few words and suddenly he was spouting out ridiculous gibberish.

After Andrew snapped at him, Gore shut up completely.

Now, he couldn't help wondering what the crazy son of a bitch had been talking about. What had Beth in her serial killer form been warning him about? One thing Gore said kept running through his mind.

"The same thing that happened to the nun you keep asking about."

What did it mean exactly? Had Gore killed the nun? Was that why Beth and all her personalities refused to speak about it? Were they afraid of Gore and what he might do? Was Father Dennis angry about it?

Things seemed to change last night after they left the condo. Gore seemed nervous in a way Andrew had never seen before. He'd always seemed so in control of himself. The only other time he'd seen him lose control was after he'd killed the guy outside the Wicked Waltz, when Andrew had yelled Beth's name and he'd changed back to her, but that was more out of shock or surprise.

After that girl's death, it was like Gore changed. It was like he saw or noticed something that scared the shit out of him.

When they arrived home, Gore was silent until he went to the bathroom to shower. Andrew knew he'd change to one of the others, probably Beth once he was under the water's stream and felt more relaxed. He wouldn't come to bed as Gore, but he was still him when he turned back to Andrew before closing the bathroom door and said, "I was doing it to get stronger, Andrew." His voice was still deep and growly, but there was a softer undertone to it. Then he added, "I'm afraid I failed. We're not safe anymore."

Andrew thought about those words as he lay in bed staring at the illuminated rectangular frame of the bathroom door.

What do you mean we're not safe anymore?

He drifted off to that thought. At some point, he heard the bathroom door open and felt the sheets get pulled back, but he'd been too exhausted to care who was getting into bed with him. He was tired enough to get a whiff of shampoo and find contentment in the thought that his wife was finished showering and Beth was by his side.

Later that morning, as he opened his eyes and glanced around the room, he saw through blurred, sleepy vision that she'd already gotten up and left the room. Her spot next to him in bed was empty. The bathroom light wasn't on. She must've gone downstairs.

It was still dark.

The sun didn't rise this time of year until around seven. Not wanting to be fully awake yet, Andrew squinted through the darkness and saw the red numbers on the nightstand alarm clock. It was only half-past five. He'd barely slept at all.

Was Alex awake already?

She was always the first one up. Paloma wouldn't be out of bed yet. This meant the little girl was downstairs somewhere either watching TV or trying to figure out what to eat for breakfast. No wonder his wife was always so tired. Between the different personalities always stepping out of their rooms, her physical body rarely got enough rest.

Andrew's thoughts returned to the room from the previous night and all the wet sounds.

Wet guts pouring from open stomach wounds.

Wet blood dripping onto the tile floor.

Wet feet stepping down the hallway as Gore made his way back to him.

Wet...

Wet...

Wet...

What is that? That wet sound?

Andrew sat up in bed. The room was nearly pitch black, but he could see well enough to make out the furniture in the room and he could see he was alone. He swore he could hear something wet.

Rain pelted the bedroom window and wind howled outside. It was storming.

Yet there was a different wet sound. Something even closer. Inside the house.

It was like the sound a dog makes when licking water out of its bowl, only they didn't own a dog.

Did Beth, or Alex, leave the faucet on in the bathroom?

Was the shower leaking, dripping?

It sounded closer than that, like it was inside the bedroom.

Then he heard whispering, and he froze.

They weren't normal words but something indiscernible, like someone was speaking in tongues but in a hushed tone. More like yelling, harsh words but at a low volume.

Then came the wet sounds again.

Andrew crawled toward the edge of the bed, thinking he might find one of Beth's personalities talking in their sleep. What he heard between the wet slurping sounds wasn't quite comprehensible. It didn't sound like any language he'd ever heard.

Slurp.

Me sincia copes resnic hala.

Slurp.

Tumasta berestemos vasta.

Slurp.

Vos me sincia copes resnic hala.

As he neared the edge, it was the round, black hat that came into view first. Then the veiny, thin skin of his cheek, like crepe paper, as Father Dennis lay with his right cheek nearly touching Beth's, who was curled up in a ball, sucking her thumb.

Alex. Alex is on the floor.

She was sleeping like Alex. Completely out of it.

Father Dennis was straddling her on all fours, lying on top of her, holding her in his embrace as his long, snake-like tongue slid out of his mouth and licked her cheek. The wet sound Andrew had heard accompanied the smearing of his tongue as it slathered saliva against her. And the whispered words flowed from his mouth without his lips moving at all.

"What the fuck?" Andrew said, frozen in place at the sight.

Father Dennis's head turned toward him, cracking as it twisted at an angle that should have been impossible. His head moved around until it was almost completely backwards, staring at him in the darkness.

The priest's mouth opened, and a scream emitted from him that brought with it a foul stench that reeked of vomit and fresh shit.

"Get off my wife!" Andrew yelled.

Father Dennis launched himself forward with both hands out, his fingers curled and his nails long with jagged claws. His face no longer looked like the old man who'd visited Andrew so many nights in the past. He wasn't Beth's grandfather, just some old personality locked in his room who came out from time to time to scold him. This was something different.

And how is he outside her body? How is he not a part of her?

Andrew threw his own hands out to shield himself from the creature, but Father Dennis sank his claws into his forearms, lifted him up, bounced off the bed, and let go of him, launching him through the air.

Once his body left the bed, all he could do was flail his arms and thrash his legs, but he knew where he was going, and he knew there was no stopping himself as his back crashed through the bedroom window. Glass shattered, pain registered all over his body, and he sailed through and down. It happened so fast, and his back and ass slammed onto the top of Beth's car.

Rain poured over him, slamming against his skin and washing away the splinters of glass. Even over the sounds of the storm, he was sure his neighbors had to hear the commotion.

Andrew wasn't friends with the people who lived beside him or across the street. Sure, he waved hello sometimes, but that was about all. They weren't aware, as far as he knew, of Beth's condition. He figured they might have their suspicions that all wasn't right in their household. If they didn't before, they would now. People aren't typically thrown out a second story window first thing in the morning.

As he rolled off Beth's car and wiped glass off himself, Andrew ignored the neighbors who'd already pulled out their cell phones to record him from their windows. He hated knowing he'd be all over social media later. News reporters didn't even have to do their fucking jobs any more thanks to everyday Americans doing it for them.

He was tempted to flip off the girl across the street who'd made her way across her lawn, with her phone held high under an umbrella, but he didn't. He needed to get inside and make sure Beth was okay.

His front door was locked, and his keys were inside the house, but Paloma was already at the door when he attempted to knock.

"Mr. Andrew," she said, opening the door for him. "What is going on? My God. You are soaking wet. And you are hurt."

She took his hand and held up his arm where he had minor cuts from the glass.

"I'm fine," he said. "The glass... it... I'm fine."

Beth was by her side. No, it was Alex. Andrew could tell by the way she was squatted down and hugging Paloma's waist. She was terrified and clinging to her the way she did when they watched scary movies together.

Paloma touched Alex on the shoulder to calm her and then pulled the little girl from her waist and handed her off to Andrew while grabbing an umbrella from the basket by the door so she could look outside at the damage done to the car.

From inside, Andrew could hear her yell at the neighbors, "Go inside your homes. There is nothing to see here. It was only an accident."

It almost made him laugh.

Yes, I was getting ready for work when I accidentally tripped, fell out the window, and landed on my wife's car.

"I'm scared, Daddy," Alex said.

Andrew squatted down slightly so he would be eye to eye with her. Beth was shorter than he was but somehow, she seemed even smaller when Alex was in control.

"I know," he said. "Who is he? What can you tell me about him?"

She shook her head and whispered. "The nun. The priest. They found us. I think it's Gore's fault. He did a bad thing. We have to run."

16

The storm seemed to grow stronger as the morning went on. Paloma made breakfast and Andrew changed into dry clothes. His work shift started soon and while he didn't want to take Beth to work with him, in any of her forms, he couldn't imagine leaving her at home either, knowing that demon priest might show up again.

At least if he brought her to work with him, he could keep an eye on her. He'd considered calling in sick. It seemed like the logical thing to do, but they'd be no safer at home than they would be at the hospital, and as much as he didn't want to take Beth back to Myles-Bend, he felt the need to speak with Mr. Grainger, The Quiet Man. He'd said something to him the other night, right after Old Lynne bit part of his ear off.

It hadn't made a lot of sense at the time, but now he wondered if the old man had been talking about Father Dennis, or the creature pretending to be a priest. Mr. Grainger had said, "It will live with you until you die. It's her he wants."

As they raced toward the hospital, with the storm raging overhead, Andrew wasn't sure which of Beth's personalities was in the passenger seat next to him. The attack at the house earlier seemed to throw his wife into complete disarray. Her usual systematic transformation was thrown all out of whack.

Usually, it went from Beth to Ruby to sometimes what Andrew thought was Father Dennis to Gore to Alex to Peter and back to Beth. With slight variations here and there. Gore was the one who kind of came and went as he pleased at night. Sometimes he appeared. Sometimes he didn't.

Now, it seemed Gore was the only one who didn't want to show his face.

"I want to play my game," Peter said as Andrew drove toward the hospital.

"When we get to my work, I'll try to find you something to do," Andrew promised.

"Like what, checkers?" the young man shot back.

"No, not like checkers. I'm sure there's something else to do."

"Uno?"

"We have *some* video games. Not *Grand Theft Auto* but we have games. Besides, I brought your Nintendo thing."

"That'll do for a little while."

"We'll find you something to do. Don't worry."

"I know what you can do." This time the voice coming out of Beth's body wasn't Peter. It was the sultry voice of Ruby. "You can fuck me. Like you used to in the janitor closet. Remember that? The way you'd bend me over and pound me from behind?"

Andrew remembered quite well and even under the crazy amount of stress he was feeling, the thought of it made his cock stir.

"How I'd suck your cock when nobody was around to see it," Ruby continued. "How I'd purposely rip a hole in my pants, right under the crotch, so I could sit on your lap and fuck you easily and quickly? Will you fuck me today, for old time's sake?"

"Maybe," Andrew said.

It was a lie. He knew there was no way they'd be able to pull that off today. This wasn't about sex. This was about getting some answers. In fact, he hoped to make a phone call to her father while they were there and get some information about when and where she might have met a nun or a priest. As far as Andrew knew, she wasn't adopted, so it wasn't like she'd come through one of those religious orphanages. She'd mentioned attending different boarding schools and private schools in her youth, but she hadn't told him anything specific about any of them.

"I don't want to go back there, Andrew." This time when she spoke, it was Beth. The real Beth, and it melted Andrew's heart knowing it was his wife there next to him. Of course, she wouldn't want to go back to the mental hospital. She'd want nothing to do with that place.

"I'd never take you back there to stay," he promised, "but I need you to stay with me. To be near me."

"Will Olivia be there?" she asked.

"You know she will be. I work with her."

"She judges me. I know she does."

"Baby, she doesn't judge you."

"She always has. And you two dated. I don't like how she looks at me."

"Beth—"

"Take me some place else."

"Beth—"

"Please."

"Where?"

Beth remained quiet for a moment. Then she clapped her hands together excitedly and yelled, "For pancakes, Daddy! Let's go get pancakes!"

"No, not this time, Alex," he said, sadness filling his heart. If only his wife could stick around a little longer, maybe he would have taken her someplace else. But the fact she couldn't was reason enough for him to go to Myles-Bend. He needed answers and she wasn't going to be of any help today.

A husband and wife were supposed to be a team but with Beth, he was simply alone.

"So where are we going?" Alex asked.

"To Daddy's work," Andrew said.

The rain was coming down something fierce but with the windshield wipers, he could see the tall building up ahead on the hill even through the thick downpour. He pointed at it.

"See there?" he asked.

"There?" she asked, excitedly. "The castle?"

"Yep," he said. "Remember the castle?"

She grew quiet and shook her head slowly back and forth. "I don't like this place."

"I know, baby," he said, "but we're only going to be here for a little while. We're not coming to stay like last time. We're visiting. I'll get you a candy bar out of the vending machine, okay?"

"Ohhhh candy," she said and clapped her hands again.

Andrew called Olivia from the parking lot and told her he was running a little late but was just around the corner and she should let the guy he was relieving go ahead and leave. He didn't need any more prying eyes than necessary. Once he saw Paul, the day shift guy who was always in a rush to get home to his boyfriend, rush out of the hospital and drive away, Andrew knew it was safe to go inside – or as safe as it was ever going to be.

When he walked in with Alex trailing behind him, Olivia's jaw dropped. She looked up at the camera and back at Andrew who rolled his eyes and shrugged his shoulders.

She crossed the dark atrium floor quickly and grabbed hold of his arm. "Are you out of your mind? You are so gonna get fired for this one."

"I didn't know what else to do," he admitted. "You have no fucking clue what I've been through."

She studied his face for a second then grabbed his left hand and lifted it to examine his arm. "Why are you all scratched up?"

He winced as she touched a tender spot. "I got thrown through a window."

She laughed, scrunched up a corner of her mouth, and continued to examine his cuts. "Seriously. You look like a bunch of tiny ninjas threw ninja stars at you."

He shrugged her off and touched a hand to his head where he felt a bit of pain. He wasn't sure if it was from a cut or a headache coming on.

"So, what happened?" she asked again.

"Liv, I wasn't kidding. I got thrown through a fucking window."

"Holy shit," she said and seemed to dwell on it as if trying to figure out how that would've happened to him. He'd passed her by the time she turned around and asked, "Gore?"

"No," he said. "Your buddy, Father Dennis."

"Not funny," she replied.

"I wasn't joking."

Olivia looked at Alex who was focused on her handheld video game. "So, she…" Olivia started to say but then let the words trail off.

Alex glanced back at her for a second and passed her a little girl's wave and smile. "Hi Livia."

"Hi, Alex. You wanna go have a seat in my chair and play your game where it's more comfortable?"

"Really?" Alex asked.

"You bet," Olivia said. "Go ahead."

Alex gasped, excited to sit in the big girl chair, and then ran to it, plopped down, and gave it a couple of spins before settling back into her video game.

"So weird," Olivia whispered, her eyes still glued on Alex. Then she leaned closer to Andrew and whispered, "I can't believe you fuck her. Do you guys play, like, hide the soldier or, like, peek-a-boo with it?"

"Liv," Andrew said, "that's sick."

"Seriously," Olivia said. "You went from me to her? You kinky son of a bitch."

"You know I don't when she's like that."

"Right, Ruby."

"Exactly."

Olivia shook her head and turned her attention back to Andrew.

She looked down at his arm and said, "Joking aside, she fucked you up. This isn't good, Drew. I don't like it. I mean call it what you want, but this is fucking spousal abuse."

"It's not."

"Whatever. What happened?"

"You won't believe me when I tell you."

"Try me."

"Remember that priest personality of hers I told you about?"

"Yeah."

"I don't know what's going on, but it attacked her and me."

"You mean she attacked you?"

"No, like it was out of her body. Like its own entity."

Olivia laughed. "That's not possible, Drew."

"I know. That's what I said, but it happened."

"No," she insisted. "That's not possible."

"Liv, it threw me through a damn window. I'd say it's pretty fucking possible."

"So, *she* threw you through a window. I mean they say sometimes they can have superhuman strength and—"

"No, when I woke up, she was like she is now. She was Alex and she was asleep on the floor. That priest was on top of her, like a demon thing with a long tongue. It was licking her face. When I told it to get off her, it pounced on me. It wasn't her. It was something else."

Olivia rubbed at her arms and pursed her lips.

"This isn't funny," she said. "I mean if this is your idea of a joke—"

"I promise it's not."

"I know I've been mean and I've said some mean things. I've joked around. I've—"

"It's not a joke. That's why I brought her here. The other night Mr. Grainger, The Quiet Man, he said something to me. Right after Old Lynne did this," he pointed at his bandaged ear, "to me, he warned me. Told me it wanted her. I didn't know what he meant at the time, but I think he was talking about that priest."

"So, you want to see The Quiet Man," Olivia said.

"Will you go with me?" he asked.

"I don't know, Drew."

"Scared?"

"Yeah, this time I'm kind of scared."

"Never thought I'd see the day Olivia was scared."

She laughed. "Me neither."

A few minutes later, Andrew and Olivia walked down the hall to Mr. Grainger's room with Alex walking behind them, still focused on her video game. About halfway down the hall, Peter came out of his room and tucked Alex away. He was now in control of Beth's body. It was evident by his footsteps. Where Alex's sneakers had made short, tiny squeaks against the tile floor, Peter's were larger, harder thuds.

"I told you this would suck," he suddenly said from behind.

Andrew turned around and told him, "Keep playing your game and we'll find you something to do in a little while."

"Any cute girls in here?" he asked.

"Play your game," Andrew repeated.

Olivia looked left at Andrew out of the corner of her eye and softly said, "Peter?"

Andrew nodded. "Yep."

"Olivia would be cute if she wasn't such a..." Peter let his words trail off.

"Such a what?" Olivia asked, turning around to face the teenage boy in Andrew's wife's body.

"What?" Peter asked.

"Finish what you were going to say," Olivia demanded.

"Seriously," Andrew said, "are you going to stand here right now and argue with a teenager?"

Olivia turned around, laughed, and facepalmed herself. "You're right. I can't believe I just did that."

"Welcome to my world," Andrew whispered. "That's me. Literally. Every. Single. Day."

The hallway lights blinked. Andrew and Olivia stopped walking. Peter bumped into them from behind. The lights blinked again.

"They need to fix these lights," Olivia said.

"That would be nice," Andrew agreed.

The lights blinked a few more times and then stayed on. Andrew felt his heartbeat speed up as they reached The Quiet Man's room. A quick glance through the small window in his door showed him sitting on his bed, with perfect posture, staring straight at the wall across from his bed.

Olivia opened his door. "Mr. Grainger, do you mind some company?"

Silently, he turned his head to look over at them. His face remained stoic as he nodded only once. Then he looked past Andrew and Olivia and saw Peter. His eyes opened wider, and his head jiggled from left to right in a frantic shaking of his head. He raised one arm and pointed at Peter.

"Not her," he said.

"Okay," Olivia said, "calm down."

"Not her," he repeated.

"Okay, okay," Olivia said, "Drew, want me to keep her in the hallway."

Andrew looked at Peter and said, "Hey, buddy, do you mind hanging out in the hall with Olivia for a minute or two?"

Peter shrugged his shoulders and said, "Whatever. Guess it doesn't really matter. Whatever gets us out of here quicker."

"This will get us out of here quicker," Andrew said.

"Then yeah," Peter agreed.

Olivia put a hand on Peter's shoulder and ushered him out of the room.

"Okay, she's gone," Andrew said as he moved to stand in front of The Quiet Man. "Why are you afraid of her?"

The Quiet Man didn't answer at first. He simply craned his neck as if making sure Peter was out of earshot.

"Mr. Grainger," Andrew said. "What is it about my wife that scares you?"

"He is with her," The Quiet Man leaned forward and whispered, glancing left and right as if afraid he might be heard.

"Who is he?"

"The priest, but he is not one."

"Not what? Not a priest?"

He nodded.

"And you say he's with her?" Andrew asked. "Like with her now?"

He nodded again. "Always with her. Always was. But... but it's different now."

"Different how?"

"Before he only watched. He wanted her but he only watched. He stood in the corner. Always standing. Always watching. In every room she entered."

"How do you know these things?"

"He told me. Like he told the old lady."

"What lady?" Andrew asked.

The Quiet Man put his hands up over his head and threw them back like a big whoosh of wind. Like wild hair.

"Old Lynne?" Andrew asked.

He nodded.

"The priest that isn't a priest told us everything. He showed us things he wanted to do to her. Sick, evil, vile things." The Quiet Man closed his eyes and his lips quivered. A tear ran from each of his eyes as he suffered memories of what the evil priest showed him. "He comes from a terrible place. A place of so much suffering. He showed me things because of the man I used to be. Because of the things I did. But I ain't that man no more. I don't do those bad things. My killin' is done."

Andrew had never heard any stories about Mr. Grainger, The Quiet Man, having a violent past, but that didn't mean there wasn't one. It occurred to him that maybe he was quiet for a reason. His silence might have been his own doing. He didn't talk because he didn't want to. He suffered in silence because he felt he deserved to.

"The things he wants to do to her, Andrew," The Quiet Man continued, "nobody should have to see. Nobody should have to endure. You have to save her."

"Mr. Grainger—"

"The priest that isn't a priest stood and watched always. He watched you and her when you did things. Dirty things in beds and in closets. He wants to hurt you for those things. She's his and you took her from him. And he's going to hurt you for it."

The thought of that creepy old priest standing in the corner or squeezed into the janitor's closet with them while he made love to Beth in here – had sex with Ruby – it made him cringe, brought goosebumps to his arms.

"Why would he want to hurt Beth?" Andrew asked. "There has to be a reason."

"He wants to hurt her for what was done to him," The Quiet Man added.

"What was done to him?" Andrew asked.

The lights in the room blinked.

Mr. Grainger's eyes shot open wide. "Uh oh."

"What is it?" Andrew asked.

"Uh oh," he repeated.

The lights blinked again.

The Quiet Man pursed his lips and tears ran down his eyes. His cheeks trembled. "I don't wanna die."

"You're not going to die," Andrew said.

"We're all going to die," he said. "He's here." His head jerked left, and both his arms shot up as he grabbed hold of Andrew's forearms and dug his fingernails into them, locking eyes with him, and added, "He's here… and he's not standing in the corner anymore."

The lights flickered off and on, reminding Andrew of the strobe light in the condo building the night before.

Out in the hall, the sound of all the rooms unlocking sounded off one by one.

Click.

Click.

Click.

Click.

Lunatic laughter.

And screams.

Wails of agony.

Andrew raced for the door and as he reached to open it, he heard what sounded like a punch to the gut and air leaving the mouth of the man behind him. It was a long guttural sigh that seeped from somewhere deep inside the old man.

When Andrew looked back, The Quiet Man's stomach had sunken in as if a giant weight bore down on it. The stomach popped back out as if the weight was released but then sunk in again. In and out, in and out, like a transparent beast was hopping up and down on him or kicking him wildly in the gut.

The Quiet Man tried desperately to breathe, but he couldn't grab hold of a breath. His fingers went to his mouth and clawed at his lips where he tried frantically to pull his tongue out of his way or anything else that might be obstructing his airway, but nothing worked.

Andrew ran to him and tried to help. He thought he might be seizing at first, so he pulled out his wallet and was about to stick it in his mouth to keep his tongue down but suddenly blood shot from the old man's mouth. A geyser of blood. It spouted forth from his throat as the invisible demon continued to shove inward on his gut, pushing his innards out his mouth.

The Quiet Man coughed again, and more crimson liquid splattered onto his lips and chin. His eyes went bloodshot, fully red, like all his blood was boiling over and searching for ways to escape his body. It trickled out his nose and leaked from the corners of his eyes. He coughed blood once more and then pitched forward and fell face first onto the floor.

Andrew backed away and stood staring at the man he'd been talking to only moments before. An invisible culprit had murdered Mr. Grainger right in front of him. Andrew's mouth opened to call out, to curse, to taunt the malevolent force in priest's clothing, but fear grabbed hold of his words. If *it* could do *that* to The Quiet Man, what would stop it from doing the same to him?

Loud raspy breathing filled the air and the temperature dropped suddenly. Andrew saw his own breath blowing out in gasps. He wanted to turn and flee but he couldn't get his feet to move. All he could do was stare down at the lifeless, bloody body of Mr. Grainger.

It's still in this room with me.

Andrew clenched his fists and trembled. Hairs on the back of his neck stood up and he feared if he turned around now, he'd be face to face with the priest. To stand here staring seemed like certain death, but to turn around meant facing the unknown and he knew whatever was in this room with him wouldn't let him leave so easily. Not after he'd come here seeking answers. Not when the one man to give him the information he sought was now lying in a pool of blood.

These were his thoughts when his next breath exited his body and his frosty billow of breath suddenly stopped and spread to the sides as if blown against a presence standing only a few inches from his face.

His response was immediate. Like a kneejerk reaction, he swung out with his fist in a right hook meant to knock the head off whatever invisible being was in front of him. His punch came with so much force it would have buckled even the sturdiest of men, but it met nothing but air and threw Andrew off balance, sending him into a spin that nearly had him crashing to the floor.

Laughter filled the air, taunting him, and Andrew knew brawling with an unseen force was going to get him nowhere but crumpled up on the floor dead like The Quiet Man. He turned to flee, fearing he'd feel a sudden jerk from a sharp claw ripping out his spine.

But no attack came.

He exited the room so fast he nearly barreled over Olivia. She yelped and threw her arms up, startled by his sudden appearance. Andrew kicked the door shut behind him.

"Don't go in there!" he yelled.

"Andrew," Olivia squeaked out.

Peter stood next to her, also staring down the hall at the patients who'd all left their rooms and spilled out into the hallway. All of them clawed at their own faces. Their eyes, like The Quiet Man's, were completely red, filled with blood.

Bloody tears streamed down their cheeks and chin, ran over their necks and onto their hospital uniforms. They bumped into each other and ran into the walls and doors. So confused. So hurt.

Charlie Dap wore his pajamas and one of his spit-shined dress shoes, like he'd been in the process of trying them on when his door popped open and the pain kicked in. Now, he raked at his face and stepped gingerly down the hallway in a lopsided fashion. Up on the heel of his shoe. Down on the sock of the other foot. His moans broke Andrew's heart.

"What is happening?" the voice of an old lady begged to know. "What is happening here? Why is this happening? What is happening?"

It was Agatha Halstead, the romance reader. She sat on the floor outside her room, hugging her legs with one arm and pulling at the strands of hair that had fallen from her bun with her free hand. Blood trickled down her cheeks and she continued asking why this was happening.

Andrew knew all these people's faces and all their names. They were all innocent old men and women for the most part. So what if Toad Phillips like to make ribbit sounds or if Adrian Lockheed liked to eat with his toes? They didn't deserve this.

"Please!" someone cried out from within the crowd of roaming patients.

It's my fault. I brought her here. He wants her. We should have stayed home. We should have never come—

"What the fuck is going on?" Olivia asked, tearing Andrew from his thoughts.

"It's him," Alex's little voice announced.

No longer Peter, the teenager had hidden in his room, leaving his little sister to come out and face the monster. Somehow, she seemed bravest of all the personalities.

Hoarse laughter echoed down the length of the hallway.

Olivia grabbed Andrew's arm. "Drew."

Silence. Then more laughter. The lights blinked and then went completely out.

Now, in pitch blackness, all they could hear was the screaming of the patients and their cries for help.

Guards ran in from different areas. Their voices rang out and flashlight beams danced across the walls and into their eyes as the unaware members of security searched for meaning in a dark sea of crazy.

"What the fuck is this?" a man yelled. Then it sounded like he too howled in pain.

"We need back up on the first fl—ah!"

"Olivia!" Andrew yelled. "Alex! Both of you, hold onto my hands."

"I'm not going anywhere," Olivia replied.

"Daddy?" Alex called out.

"I'm right here, baby," he said as he grabbed her hand.

He slid his fingers through hers, but something didn't feel right. There in the darkness, as his hand joined hers, he thought Beth's fingers seemed to go on too long. They were too frail, too dry, too coarse, and ended in nails too sharp.

"Thank you, Daddy," the hoarse, garbled voice of Father Dennis said as the hand snapped shut around Andrew's and squeezed with a strength Beth could never possess.

Andrew's knees wobbled and the bones in his hand threatened to snap. He yelled in pain and his legs went limp. Andrew fell to his knees with watery eyes under the weight of Father Dennis's strength.

"Kill them all," Father Dennis ordered.

The lights flickered, and the naked form of Old Lynne came into view, on all fours, her bare, pale tits dangling as she sat back on her haunches and put her hairy, nappy mound on display. She snarled at the ceiling and sniffed at the air. Her body slick, damp with sweat, and bone white, like a fucked-up feline on the hunt. Her wiry hair reflected the flickering glow of the neon lights overhead.

Nearby, Lady Anne, the patient who thought of herself as royalty, crossed the hall blindly and muttered, "Help me. Please."

Old Lynne sniffed once her way, then turned toward her, sprung off her heels, and galloped a few steps before launching herself onto the woman and tearing her teeth into her throat. Lady Anne screamed but her cries for help died quickly as she choked on her own blood. Old Lynne yanked her mouth away and blood spurted all over the walls. Between the feral woman's teeth hung bits of flesh.

She looked over at Andrew and growled, blood running down her chin. Old Lynne giggled and blood bubbled up between her teeth. Then her eyes moved to Olivia and then down to Beth who'd tripped and was sitting on her ass a few feet away.

As Andrew looked at Beth, he saw the demon over his shoulder, what was once Father Dennis was now a thin-skinned monster with bluish veins, a long pointy nose, beady black eyes, sharp and jagged teeth, and thin, stringy grey hair dangling from his black hat. This was him in pure demon form and he was worse than anything Andrew could have ever imagined.

"Why, Andrew," he said. "Lovebug." He opened his mouth and let his long purple tongue slither out and with it, a giant cockroach fell onto Andrew's lap.

Andrew slapped at the roach, smacking it away from him, and yelled, "Olivia, take Beth and run!"

He no longer cared which of his wife's personalities was in control. They were all his wife, and he wanted her safe. That was all that mattered.

Andrew climbed to his feet as quickly as his aching body would allow and tried to yank his arm free from the demon's grasp, but the evil one was faster than he was and was stronger. As soon as his shoes touched the floor, the creature jerked Andrew's arm up and launched him toward the ceiling where he caught him by the neck and wrapped his long, bony fingers around his throat.

Dangling there above the floor, Andrew fought to free himself from Father Dennis's grasp, but the creature had a tight clutch around his throat and squeezed harder the more he fought.

"I could kill you easily like I did that weak coward you called The Quiet Man," the demon hissed. "You know why I don't?"

Andrew kicked at the demon, thrashing wildly, and trying to do damage but nearly passing out as the evil priest dug its claws into his skin. At any second, a slight pull in opposite directions could rip his throat open.

"Fuck you," Andrew managed to wheeze out.

Faces of Beth

The demon laughed. "I haven't killed you because I want you to suffer seeing the things I'm going to do to Beth."

With that, the evil creature roared and shoved him into the ceiling, driving his back into the tiles above, bashing his skull against the metal plumbing overhead before yanking him down and slamming him against the hard floor.

It all happened in one swift movement, but to Andrew, the pain seemed to go on forever. He felt himself lifted and flung back down to the floor. Then he was there on his stomach trying to make sense of it all.

Through blurred vision, he caught a glimpse of Olivia running with her hand clasped around Beth's. The demon bent over and licked Andrew's face. His tongue was like sandpaper as the rough strip ground against his flesh and threatened to tear off his skin. Andrew cried out in pain.

The fresh stench of urine and shit was strong in the hallway. Andrew didn't stay down for long, and when he finally climbed to his feet, the lights were on again. They were no longer flickering. Dead bodies littered the floor in front of and behind him. Most were patients and some were guards. It was clear from the foul odor that many had soiled themselves during the attack.

Ripped open intestines, probably at the hands of Old Lynne, added to the reek.

Where is that old bitch anyway?

He hoped she was dead and that his wife and Olivia had managed to escape before she or the demon in priest's clothes had reached them. Andrew said a silent prayer that they were still alive. He prayed Beth and Olivia had found a hiding spot and were still there now or that they'd escaped the building.

Maneuvering around the bodies was impossible, so Andrew was forced to step over them. Leroy Slouch, a patient who'd always been kind to him, now watched the ceiling with a broken, purple neck and eyes that would never again see the living world. Andrew tried to avoid his gaze but felt his death stare as he walked into its lifeless path.

I know. It's my fault, Leroy. I'm sorry.

If Andrew hadn't come here, none of these people would be dead, and for what? What information had he gathered? None really. He hadn't learned anything from The Quiet Man other than the fact that the demon had been with Beth all along. That he'd been watching the whole time, hiding in the corners of the rooms.

Whatever the fuck that meant!

Had he been at Andrew's house all this time too? Hiding in the corner of every room she entered? Was he standing in the living room when Andrew talked to Peter, watching in the restaurant when he and Alex ate breakfast, peeking in the bathroom when he fucked Ruby in the shower?

Could he have done this all along? Could he have slaughtered them all? If so, why did he wait?

Looking around at the dead patients, Andrew hoped all this was caught on the cameras. Surely all this would be recorded. They would see Old Lynne biting and tearing her way up and down the hallway. They would see the priest killing and everyone bleeding out of their fucking eyes.

They would see everyone going completely fucking insane.

"Beth!" Andrew yelled, knowing it was probably a dumb move.

He took a few steps and stumbled. His knees, hips, back, and jaw ached. The demon priest had fucked him up. Andrew looked above him and saw the missing ceiling panels where he'd been hoisted and body slammed as if he'd tried to battle the Undertaker at *WrestleMania*.

A quick glance behind him showed where all the debris had landed and reminded him why every bone in his body hurt.

"Beth!" he called once more, looking at each body lying on the floor ahead of him and behind him, making sure she wasn't one of them. She wasn't.

It dawned on him that this could be a trap. Calling out to her could be dangerous. If she was hunkered down somewhere, and she came out of hiding because of him, the demon might find her, but he hadn't been thinking straight. He'd only wanted to find his wife.

But why? You couldn't protect her before. Do you think you'd be able to protect her now? Would anything be different this time?

"Andrew?" It was Olivia's voice.

It wasn't Beth, but at least it was someone he knew. If Olivia had made it, maybe Beth had too.

Maybe Beth was still alive.

"Andrew!" It was Olivia again.

"Andrew!" this time it was Beth.

They were calling to him from the next hallway.

Andrew limped down the hall, stepping over dead bodies as quickly as he could. A few of the patients were still alive. Some whimpered and cried, but even the ones alive were in bad shape. They probably wouldn't make it through the night. Most had been ripped open either at the throat or the stomach by what looked like a rabid dog.

Old Lynne.

She'd been dangerous from the start. Andrew had always known it. That's why he'd been so afraid of her. As if simply thinking of her was enough to summon her, he heard her bare feet padding down the tiled hall and her hands slapping the floor.

Fuck. Where is she?

Even with the lights on, everything was always so damn dark in here. It was the middle of the afternoon, yet it seemed like night. He'd forgotten it was broad daylight outside.

Where are you, you bitch?

Andrew looked around, searching for something – anything – that might serve as a weapon. The only thing in sight was a plant. A fake tropical palm tree. He'd walked by it a thousand times before. It stood high, nearly six feet tall, and at its base was a pot. It was plastic so it couldn't be *that* heavy.

The charging feet grew closer.

He only needed to make it out of the hallway and into the atrium before Old Lynne pounced on him. If she got to his back and ripped into his neck the way she had all those other people in the hall, he was done for. She would surely kill him with one bite, and he didn't have a whole lot of strength left to fight her off.

He still had a good thirty feet or so to go.

Limping as quickly as he could, he moved down the hall at what felt like a snail's pace, hearing her raspy breath growing closer and closer.

"Andrew!" Beth yelled again.

"Andrew, hurry!" Olivia called out.

He was sure they were in the rec room.

Twenty feet to go.

Old Lynne's hands and feet slapped the floor, and her growls grew louder. She laughed as she approached, knowing she would finally sink her teeth into the orderly she loved to fuck with night in and night out. This was the moment she'd been waiting for. This was when she'd finally taste his meat.

Ten feet.

"Argh!" she screamed.

Andrew reached for the plant, grabbed it at about the halfway point, and lifted it as he swung his body. The old woman was flying through the air when he spun around to face her.

Her arms were outstretched, bloody fingernails poised and ready to rip out his eyeballs…

Teeth barred and bloodied…

Eyes as black as the demon father's…

Grey hair blown back in the breeze…

And tits dangling down…

When the potted end of the plant met the side of her face, it bashed her skull in so hard her body flew to the right, smacked against the corkboard that announced the week's meals, and sent her crashing to the floor where her dead stare remained fixed on Andrew even when her soul left this world.

"Andrew!" Beth yelled from directly behind him.

Andrew turned to find his wife standing there. He wrapped his arms around her and squeezed her so tightly he thought he might crush her.

"I thought I might've lost you," he said.

"No," she said, "Olivia took me into the rec room."

"Yeah, we hid," Olivia said from behind her, and he'd never been so happy to see his friend again either. "My God, your face."

Olivia reached out and touched Andrew's cheek. As her fingers touched his skin, something changed in Beth.

"Take your hands off my husband," she said, and suddenly lifted Olivia up by her throat, the same way Father Dennis had thrown Andrew around so easily. Long nails grew out of Beth's fingertips, and they punctured Olivia's skin, causing blood to run down her neck. Then she ripped sideways, tearing into her throat as she flung the woman against the wall and onto the floor.

"Beth!" Andrew yelled. "No!"

As he ran to stop her, Beth backhanded him and sent him flying against the wall. Andrew's body flopped onto the floor, and he lay there sprawled out and half unconscious. His eyes bounced heavily and as they blurred over, he watched Beth turn into the priest and walk toward the door.

17

When Andrew woke at Myles-Bend, he wasn't sure if he'd been out for seconds, minutes, or hours. It was dark in the atrium, but the lights were always dim there. The cops hadn't arrived yet, so he couldn't have been out long. Murmurs of complaint and whines of pain echoed down the halls where patients who'd survived the massacre were barely clinging to life.

Olivia.

Andrew looked toward his friend's fallen body. It remained in the place where it had collapsed.

Beth was gone. He'd watched her walk out of the building after turning into Father Dennis. He'd never seen the demon priest in his wife's body before the moment he revealed himself and attacked Olivia. Before that, Andrew had only assumed he was one of her personalities. Now, it seemed, he was part of her or using her as some kind of vessel.

What was it The Quiet Man had said? *Always with her.* The priest who wasn't a priest was always with Beth.

And during Gore's ramblings the other night, he'd said something that made sense now too. Gore said he might have stained her, might have made her body a receptacle of evil, a canister that could carry wickedness, he might have opened their home to something truly sinister.

Fuck. Gore, what have you done?

Drool dripped from Andrew's lips as he crawled across the floor and made his way to his friend's unmoving body.

"Olivia," he called out to her as he approached. He didn't expect an answer but felt the need to say her name.

"An... drew," came a whispered reply.

"Olivia?" Andrew got to his hands and knees and then forced himself up to his feet as he moved across the atrium and toward the sound of her weak voice.

She lay on her back, staring up at the ceiling with tears running down her eyes and collecting in her ears. Blood leaked from her lips and ran from her throat.

Unsure of the injuries she'd sustained, Andrew was careful not to lift her.

"Liv," he said, "for fuck's sake, Liv."

"Not... Beth," she squeaked out. "Old priest."

She knew. She understood it wasn't Beth who'd done this to her and for that he was thankful. His sweet wife wasn't capable of something like this. But she'd been Beth only moments before. This demon had latched onto her. He was with her now wherever she was.

On the far side of the building, not near the main entrance where he'd entered earlier with Alex but over where the security staff rallied, he heard the squawk of a radio. "10-4. Sending backup. Don't enter 'til arrival."

"Roger that. What's the ETA?"

"Five. Maybe less."

Cops were in the building. If they hadn't already set up a perimeter outside, they would soon. He needed to leave before it was too late.

"Liv, I have to go, okay?" he said.

She tried to shake her head "no" but could barely move.

"I have to find Beth before she or he hurts more people. The cops are here. If they find me, they won't let me leave."

She stared at him and could barely keep her eyes open. Her bottom lip quivered. He leaned over and kissed her forehead. "I'm sorry."

Then he called out once, loud enough that he knew the cops would hear, "Help! There's one alive in here but she's badly hurt! Help!"

With that, he ran for the door and prayed they'd find Olivia soon.

Andrew hoped Beth had gone home. It was the only place that made sense. She wouldn't go to her family, and she had no real friends. Their home together was the only place she felt safe. As he parked his car at the curb and looked up at the broken master bedroom window, the one he was thrown through earlier that morning, he couldn't help chuckling at the irony of this being Beth's safe haven.

A bed sheet was pinned there now. Paloma's work. More for privacy than for any kind of protection, and the gesture brought him a moment of comfort, a brief optimism thinking she'd taken the time, after surely being shaken up herself, to do him this favor. She was a sweet woman. There was still *good* in this world. Yet Paloma didn't deserve to go through all this.

He wondered what she told her family when she called them. Did she whisper tales of working for the psycho lady and her weakling husband or did she speak of them with pride? Did she pity them and ask for prayers or talk of saving up enough money so she could get the hell out of here? Andrew only hoped she considered them family and spoke of them in such a way.

Andrew stepped up the front walkway and glanced around the neighborhood. It felt oddly normal, like his neighbors had already forgotten what occurred here this morning.

This morning. Wow.

The day had flown by quickly and dusk would be setting in soon. Not that time of day mattered anymore. Father Dennis, or the demon playing that role, had proven he could attack at any time. Yet night was unwelcome. Andrew didn't look forward to the surprises darkness might bring.

He approached his front door cautiously, mindful of the fact the mailman was only a few doors down, making his rounds like he normally did. One neighbor a few houses down had his garage door open like usual, and classic rock played at a low volume. He'd be in there somewhere tinkering with his car. To everyone else, this was like any other day.

Andrew's hand trembled as he placed it on the doorknob and slowly gave it a turn. He hoped he'd push it open to find Peter playing one of his video games on the couch and Paloma busy in the kitchen preparing dinner, but he wouldn't have blamed her for running away the moment they'd left the house.

Finally, he turned the knob and pushed open the door, watching the thin wedge of darkness swing open wide to reveal the dark entryway of his home. Alex didn't greet him with, "Daddy!" Peter didn't call out, "Did you bring pizza?" No sound came to him from inside the house and neither did the delicious aroma of a freshly cooked meal.

Paloma wasn't preparing dinner. There was no fresh earthy scent of cilantro or the citrusy tang of lemon being squeezed into a chicken and rice dish. Meat wasn't sizzling in a pan. None of his favorite mealtime offerings teased his senses.

Instead, he was met with the acrid odor of shit. Like someone had squatted on the kitchen floor and relieved themselves or had taken a giant dump on the couch and rubbed it into the seat cushions. The foul stench assaulted him the moment he closed the door behind him. With it came the buzzing of flies.

Inside the house was pitch dark with the blinds closed to the outside world. Andrew reached for the wall and felt around for the entry hall light switch. For a second, he thought the power might be out but realized that couldn't be the case when he saw the flickering white light coming from the living room. His fingers found the switch and he flicked on the light, casting an orange glow down over him. Now, he was illuminated while the rest of the house was not.

"Paloma," Andrew called out.

Not too loud though. If she was around, she would be close enough to hear. If not, he feared alerting anyone or any*thing* that might be lurking deeper in the house's gut.

At what point did my home become a living thing? When did it become the demon's accomplice? This is OUR home. OUR safe place.

Andrew decided right then he would not fear Father Dennis in his home. This was his house. He owned it.

"This is my home," he announced. "Mine and Beth's. Any evil spirit here is not welcome. You can leave now."

He wasn't sure why he said it or where the words came from. He must have heard them spoken in a horror movie where the simple verbal banishing of evil from one's home would see it forced out, never to return, but the sinister chuckle that reverberated through the house told him it wasn't going to work here.

What started as a low murmur picked up in intensity and volume until it was all-out laughter that bounced off the walls and came at him from all directions. One second it was a low and gravelly cough-like sputter and the next it was a high-pitched shriek. It went back and forth between the two pitches until it drove Andrew to put his hands over his ears.

And that God-awful stench was enough to make him want to vomit.

Andrew stumbled into the kitchen because it was the closest room to him, and he thought grabbing a knife to protect himself would be a good idea. As soon as he rounded the corner and turned on the light, he froze and stood staring at the scene in front of him, fighting the trembling that started in his legs and worked its way up his spine and into his arms.

There, hanging in the center of the kitchen by her throat, was the woman he'd hired to help take care of his family.

A twisted-up bed sheet was wrapped around her throat and tied to one of the wooden beams in the ceiling. Her normally caramel-colored skin was now purple, and her tongue lolled out of her mouth, swollen and ready to burst.

The worst was her eyes. One was bulging out of the socket. The other had a spoon driven into it, like she'd been in the process of trying to scoop out one eye when she'd hanged herself. The sharpest point of the utensil had broken through the gelatinous part of the eyeball and blood and mucus was now crusted around it. Flies landed on the spoon, flew away, and then landed on her eye.

Beneath her feet and toppled over onto its side was one of the dining room chairs.

A puddle of piss and shit had formed near one of the chair's legs. Streams of muck had run down the old lady's leg and onto the floor, explaining the odor in the house.

"Andrew?" a voice called out.

It wasn't the sweet childlike voice of Alex, and it wasn't the soft voice of Beth. Ruby had no reason to come out at a time like this. There was nothing sexual about this situation. She wasn't going to get her rocks off right now. It was Peter. He was in the living room.

"Peter?" Andrew replied as he grabbed the largest of the kitchen knives and cautiously made his way to the living room where the entire space flickered with the white static of a TV channel not set to anything.

The volume was down so all was silent except Peter's terror-filled whisper as he choked out one word, barely audible it was so soft. "Andrew."

He stood at the center of the living room, between the couch and the TV. It was Beth, of course, but Peter was out of his room and had taken over her body. It was clear by the way he stood with his shoulders slightly hunched. His mouth was open as if he'd been stopped in mid-sentence.

His face remained straight, staring at the wall between the living room and the kitchen, the wall over the dining room table where a painting of an Italian vineyard hung. His chin was pointed in that direction, but his eyes shifted nervously toward Andrew, seeking help, but Andrew didn't understand why.

The boy was standing alone in the living room. Andrew looked left to see if anyone was in the entry hallway. Nobody was there. He spun around to make sure nobody was approaching from behind him. No one was.

He looked back at the painting over the dining room table and at the table itself. Nothing.

"Peter," Andrew said, as he took a step forward.

"Stop," Peter warned him.

Andrew halted.

Peter's hands trembled as he raised one and pointed a palm at Andrew as if the hand gesture would ensure he wouldn't move. "He's here," he whispered.

"The priest?" Andrew asked.

Saying those two words seemed to scare Peter even more. Tears formed in his eyes and a couple spilled over and down his cheeks as his head jerked up and down just barely, in his attempt to secretly nod.

"Where is he?" Andrew asked, once again scanning the room and the area around them.

He remembered what The Quiet Man had said about the demon sticking to the corners of the room, so he looked there in the shadows, but he didn't see anything.

With the light off and no furniture in the corners, Andrew's imagination wreaked havoc on him. He imagined the priest squatting down in one of the corners, using the shadowy darkness like a blanket, watching them, and waiting for his moment to attack.

He glanced once more behind him, at the far corner behind the couch, and saw nothing.

"Peter, where is he, man? You're freaking me out."

"Behind... me," Peter said.

Andrew didn't see anything behind Peter. He was standing only a couple feet away from the boy.

But then a shadow emerged.

Rising from the floor as if levitating from an invisible puddle in the carpet, Father Dennis's tall, skinny frame lifted slowly. The wide, round brim of his hat stuck out from the sides of Peter's legs as it moved up his calves, his knees, thighs, butt, back, shoulders, head, and then higher until the old man was towering over him.

Andrew was close enough to reach out and touch him, but he too was frozen. The pasty, veiny face of the priest who was not a priest

Faces of Beth

turned his head and the sound it made was like a wooden doll so brand new it wasn't used to maneuvering yet. The creak and crack his bones made nearly made Andrew piss himself.

"Peter," Andrew managed through a breathy voice. "Peter, run!"

It was too late.

The old priest brought one of his long, bony fingers around to the front of Peter's throat. His fingernail was several inches long, jagged, and sharp. With one swift movement, he swiped his nail across Peter's throat.

"No!" Andrew yelled as he ran to his wife.

Beth's eyes went wide, and she fell to the floor.

Andrew swung the knife he'd brought from the kitchen, but Father Dennis disappeared into thin air and the knife blade went unanswered.

Andrew dropped the knife to the floor and fell to the carpet where he scooped his wife's body up and pulled her into his lap. He cradled her there and sobbed into her face, forehead to forehead.

"I'm so sorry," he cried. "Beth, I'm so sorry."

He cried like never before and didn't care that his tears fell on her or that his slobber and snot mixed together and ran down his own face. His wife was dead, and it was his fault for not getting to her faster. If he'd only moved more quickly. If he'd only reacted as soon as he saw how terrified Peter was.

Andrew kicked out and felt his foot thump against something.

He stared through his tears and saw a second body. His foot nudged it, the shoe of a body that wasn't his wife.

Using his shirt sleeve, he wiped at his eyes, mouth, and nose, and when his vision finally cleared, he saw a teenage boy lying on the carpet. The boy had frosted blond hair, wore a T-shirt with some rock band logo, blue jeans, and tennis shoes. His throat was slit open, and blood soaked the carpet where he lay.

"What the fuck?" Andrew muttered.

"Andrew?" came the voice of Beth.

He stared down at his wife whose head was cradled in his lap and saw her staring up at him through the flickering of the TV light. He couldn't believe it. He lifted her chin and touched her neck. No cut. Not even a scratch. Beth was fine.

"How is that possible? I saw him—"

"Andrew, what's going on?" Beth asked, and it was Beth, not one of her personalities. This was his wife, his actual wife staring back at him.

"Baby," he said, "Oh, my God. Baby."

She was confused, as she should have been, but when she glanced down at her feet and saw the teenage boy lying on the carpet, she freaked out and pushed away from Andrew's arms. She screamed.

"Andrew! What is, who is—"

"I don't know," he replied.

She leaned closer to the figure lying across from them and then gasped and covered her mouth with her hands. "Peter," she mumbled through shaking fingers.

He'd been thinking it, but it didn't make sense. She had dissociative identity disorder, multiple personalities, but they were all inside her head. They weren't physical beings. They weren't alive. How could one be dead on the floor in front of them?

"This is what you imagined him to look like?" he asked, not knowing any other way to put it.

"This *is* what he looked like," she corrected him. "He wasn't an imaginary friend."

But then, as if he was in fact imaginary, Peter's body began to dissolve. It evaporated. His body, his clothes, and his blood slowly dematerialized as if it had never existed.

"Drew—" Beth started.

"I see it too," he assured her.

All they could do was watch as Peter was erased from their world.

"Is he like," Andrew tried to think of the correct way to phrase his question. "Is he back inside you? Like one of your personalities again?"

Beth looked him in his eyes, and he could see so much confusion there as she shrugged her shoulders and said, "I don't know. I don't think so."

Andrew knew the truth. Peter was gone. The priest killed him, and he was gone forever.

"Baby," Andrew said, taking one of her hands in his, "I don't understand what's going on, but we need to get out of here. We're not safe here."

She stared at him for what seemed like forever. She bit her bottom lip and her eyes glossed over, but she didn't cry. "I understand. We have to go."

18

Beth seemed to be in shock. She wasn't saying much of anything. The fact she was still Beth surprised him. Usually, when things got stressful, she let one of the others out of their rooms. Andrew wondered if, after what happened to Peter, the others were afraid to come out. Was the Father Dennis *thing* capable of killing them all?

"I don't know where to take you," he said aloud as he drove down the highway.

The sun was setting over the horizon. Darkness had already begun to wrap itself around the sky. They needed a place to stay for the night. He had no family to burden with his troubles and he didn't trust Beth's.

He had a feeling the cops would be looking for him if they weren't already. After what happened at Myles-Bend and now at his home, he wasn't sure where to go or what to do. If Olivia lived, she'd tell them the truth, but the chances of that were—

No, don't go there. Get out of your head.

If the cops went to his house, they'd find Paloma hanging in his kitchen. Would they blame him? Would they think he'd killed her? He could spend the rest of his life in prison! And how would he explain what happened to Paloma's family? How would he even get in touch with her family?

Faces of Beth

"Beth, I know you don't want to talk about these things, but I need to know why this... this thing is following you. In the hospital, Mr. Grainger said it was always with you. That it was in the corners of the room, always following you."

"Stop it," Beth said.

"If that's true, that means it was with us always. It was watching when we thought we were alone. It watched us make love."

"Stop it."

"Why would it do that and why would it attack now, after all this time?"

"Stop it!" Beth screamed and tried to unlock the passenger door.

Andrew's instinct to reach out and stop her caused him to swerve the car to his right. The car coming up next to them let out a series of honks. "Shit!" Andrew cursed under his breath as he straightened the wheel.

"Watch the road, asshole!" the driver yelled out his window as he sped past.

Usually, other drivers' road rage would upset him, but right now, his only concern was his wife's safety. He instinctively held a hand up as if to say, "thanks for the warning." Then he looked over at Beth and said, "What are you doing?"

"You're not listening to me," she cried. "Let me out of the car."

Andrew carefully pulled the car onto the side of the highway. He grabbed hold of Beth's arm before she could get out.

"Let me go," she whined.

"Beth, please."

"Just let me go. If I go... If I get out now and never come back, all this will go away for you. You should have never been with me, Andrew. I told you that. I've told you that a hundred times. I'm no good for you. I'm not good for anyone. It's why I checked myself into the hospital in the first place. But you couldn't leave well enough alone."

Her words hurt, but she was right. She had tried to warn him years ago that she'd checked herself in for a reason. That she wasn't as innocent as she seemed and that a relationship with her would mean a relationship with all of *them*. That she'd buried things from her past that even she wasn't able to remember and sometimes memories bubbled up as if trying to break through the surface from deep down in the darkest trenches of her soul.

She'd warned him and he hadn't listened. He hadn't wanted to. He never would. Even now, he couldn't imagine a life without her. She was right. She could get out of this car and most of his problems would fade away, but he didn't care about that. He was in love with her. She was his wife, and if she got out of the car, he was going to chase her down and drag her back.

"You don't get to do that," he told her. "Not after all we've done together to build the life we have. We make it work. *I* make it work. Because I love you. And I'm gonna be honest with you, Beth. I'm scared. I'm terrified something's going to happen to you, but even more than that, I'm pissed off and want to figure out how to stop this fucking thing, this pariah that's latched onto our relationship and decided to suck the life from it."

She let go of the door handle and fell toward him. Andrew caught her and wrapped her in his arms. He held her there on the side of the highway and kissed the top of her head.

"I'm sorry," she said. "I don't know why I'm like this."

"It's okay, baby," he promised. "I kinda like you."

"No. No, you can't. I'm a mess."

"I met you like this though. I mean, who knows, maybe without all these problems you'd be a total bitch."

She laughed into his shoulder. "Maybe."

"You definitely might be more boring."

She laughed.

"Now, we really need to get off this highway. If the cops are looking for us, pulling over like this is going to make it mighty easy for them to find us."

"Where can we go?"

Andrew looked off in the distance and saw the bright red neon sign of a popular hotel chain. It was as good a place as any. At least there they could rest and get something to eat.

"A hotel I guess," he said. "For now. Until we can figure out something else."

Andrew drove to a hotel that was special to them, one they'd visited on their wedding night and had frequented the few times he'd taken her for a night out of the house. Sometimes it was nice to get away for the weekend, even if it was only downtown. Plus, this place had self-parking, in a garage, so he didn't have to worry about his license plate being recognized on the street.

The hotel staff was as gracious as always and being in the heart of the city, they were used to clients not wanting to use a credit card. Again, just in case the cops were looking for him, Andrew needed to buy them a little more time to figure things out. Not that prostitution was running rampant, but many business owners and high-profile guests brought escorts or dates who weren't their significant others to the hotel for private meetings and secret rendezvous.

Paying with cash and getting a room for the night wasn't a problem. Andrew did have to deal with one nosey older couple who passed him dirty looks and sidelong glances at Beth as if she was the secret he was trying to keep. It didn't dawn on Andrew until he saw the older woman's look of disgust that he'd gotten his ass kicked back at Myles-Bend and must look a fright.

In the old couple's eyes, he was probably some pimp, drug dealer, or other lowlife who'd gotten himself into trouble and was dragging his lady into a room for the night.

He decided to be the bigger man and pass them a "You two have a good night" as he and Beth made their way to the elevator. The couple didn't respond, but then again, Andrew hadn't expected them to.

It surprised even him that he was still able to remember pleasantries given the shit he'd been through today. And *they* couldn't find it in themselves to respond. He chuckled to himself. If they only knew why he was so battered and bruised.

But I'm sure they've *had a rough day.*

"I'm hungry," Beth said, putting her head against his shoulder as they made their way up in the elevator. "Starving actually."

It felt so good having her by his side. He savored the feel of her arms wrapped around his and her cheek against his shoulder. If only she'd remain like this. He felt the tiniest seed of hope form inside him that maybe Peter's demise had scared the others away and now he'd finally be left alone with the woman he loved.

Did he mean that though? Wouldn't he miss Alex and her innocent laugh? The way she told him anything he asked? She didn't hold back information the way the others did. She didn't see the wrong in telling the absolute truth, even if it could hurt his feelings.

Would making love to Beth be the same without the sexual openness of Ruby? Wouldn't he miss dirty talk and oral sex without having to beg for it?

Or how about Gore? No, fuck Gore. If he never had to clean a bloody doorknob again and never had to listen to his angry grunts or frustrated sighs, he'd be fine with that.

If he had to choose from any of this, the answer would always be *just* Beth. He would take her any way he could have her. If he could have her full-time, that would be the best thing possible. If he had to put up with the others when they came around, he would do that too. As long as it brought him back to moments like now when he could be alone with his wife.

"I love you, Beth," he said. "I need you to know that."

She looked up at him and squinted from the lights above. "I know you do. And I love you too. You know that, right?"

He nodded and smiled. "I do."

The lights inside the elevator flickered and Andrew felt his heart drop. Beth held onto his arm tighter. When he glanced down at her, she was looking back at him and in the blinking light, he swore he saw her skeleton through her skin as if he'd gained X-ray vision and each time the lights came on, he was peering through her flesh and straight at her bone. She smiled at him, and he watched her teeth part into a sinister grin.

Instinctively, he pushed her away from him and stepped back.

"Andrew?" she asked, frightened by his reaction. He could hear the fear in her voice, but he couldn't stop the terror creeping up his spine.

Was it his imagination? He rubbed at his eyes. He hadn't slept much. She looked normal when the lights popped on.

This was his wife, but he'd seen what else seemed to live within her, and he'd seen what that monster could do. If Father Dennis, or the demon calling itself that, released itself from her body right here inside this elevator, whoever stepped into it next might walk into a bloodbath – with *his* blood splattered all over the walls.

"Andrew," Beth said.

The lights flickered again and there it was, that skeletal smile. That grin from inside her body while on the outside she appeared worried. Something inside her was enjoying his fear, and he wondered if it was the Father Dennis demon playing tricks on him, reminding him he was near, making sure he understood the power it held over him and the situation. He, it, could pounce at any time.

Andrew fell to the floor and scooted on his ass to the corner of the small box carrying them higher into the building. It seemed to be moving upward at a snail's pace.

When will this fucking door open?

"Andrew," Beth repeated, and this time there was something different in her voice. "Andrew, what's wrong with the lights? Andrew, where are you, Lover?"

Lover?

The elevator let out an audible *ding* and the lights popped on at the same time as the doors swung open. Standing in front of him, with her seductive stare, was Ruby. She stepped toward him and put a foot between his legs, making sure the toe of her shoe nudged his balls and wiggled up and down against his cock. She held out a hand to help him up.

"What are you doing down there, baby?" she asked.

Her face was normal. It was the Ruby he'd made love to a hundred times. He took her hand and climbed to his feet, knowing this night was about to take a turn for the better.

If he could get the creeping dread to go away.

His loving wife was there inside that body, but he feared evil was in there somewhere too.

19

"Mmm, fear is an aphrodisiac," Ruby moaned as she pushed Andrew against their hotel room door and kissed him hard while fumbling with the front of his pants, "and there's no reason to fear me. You only have to fuck me." Their mouths collided once again. "You want to take me from behind tonight, baby? I think you need to. You need to pound it out of you."

Being with Ruby was like being in one of those dream worlds that made no fucking sense at all. One second, you're running for your life, trying to flee demonic monsters with ten-foot arms who seem to run five times faster than you, and then all of a sudden you're in a red room with naked women grabbing at your balls and shoving tits in your mouth.

It made no damn sense, but Andrew was aroused nonetheless and couldn't stop Ruby's advances. She reached into his zipper, grabbed hold of him, and gave him a squeeze.

Andrew pulled her hand away. "Ruby, wait. We need to get inside."

He'd almost added "where it's safe" but there was no safe place, was there?

"You're no fun," Ruby whined as he turned and used the card to open the digital lock.

The light on the card reader changed from red to green and then clicked, allowing him to push open the door. Ruby shoved her way past him and threw herself onto the bed like she'd had too much to drink. "Woop," she called out, followed by laughter.

Andrew wished the scenario were different and he could join her in lighthearted fun. He wanted nothing more than to plop down onto the bed with her and kiss her as they both shed their clothes in wild abandon, but he couldn't shake the sense that they weren't alone.

He glanced around, remembering what The Quiet Man had told him at Myles-Bend before collapsing to the floor in a puddle of his own blood.

The demon was always there in the corner of the room.

No sinister being occupied the corners of this room. At least none he could see, but that didn't mean one wasn't there. He'd never seen the demon in the hospital or at their home. Andrew had never even felt its presence all those times they'd been spied on when they thought they were alone.

Ruby wasted no time as she kicked off her pants, removed her shirt, and unclasped her bra, dropping all to the floor. She bit her bottom lip and winked at Andrew before sliding back further onto the mattress. Gravity grabbed hold of her beautiful breasts as she lay back on the bed. Andrew's eyes were drawn to her pale skin, those dark nipples, and the softness of her curves. He'd held her breasts, had cupped them in his hands, had traced those nipples with his tongue and pursed them between his lips. He was becoming aroused even though he knew he shouldn't be at a time like this.

This was wrong. They needed to come up with a plan. *He* needed to figure out what to do next. Fucking Ruby wasn't the answer.

"Ruby," he said, "I don't think you understand the situation. Peter's dead."

Ruby rolled her eyes. "You're such a buzzkill. A party pooper."

"Ruby—"

"I know. I get it, but honestly, what else are you going to do at a time like this? Are you going to save the world tonight, lover? I doubt it. I don't know about you. Maybe it's my limited way of thinking or my immature mindset, but if I'm going to go out, I want to go out one way and one way only—fucking."

If Ruby had been created for any reason at all, Beth had made her to handle sexual situations. It seemed she wasn't meant to deal with other matters.

Yet Paloma was dead, hanging in his kitchen. Olivia might be dead. Peter, who'd never truly been alive, had he? Well, he was dead, too. So much death. So much pain. So much suffering. And he was fucking terrified of the Father Dennis thing—of what he'd seen in the elevator.

Seeing Ruby on the bed was still turning him on. It was like he needed her to get his mind off everything else. He needed to fuck all these other feelings away if for no other reason than he didn't know what else to do. Maybe making love to Ruby would free his mind of all this other clutter. Of all this madness. Maybe it would rid him of the fear he felt whenever he thought of all that had happened today.

Maybe she's right. Maybe fear is an aphrodisiac.

Plus, it was hard to argue with her logic. If he was going to die, making love to his wife would be the way he'd choose to go.

Ruby used one finger to gesture for him to come to her while she used the other to push the fabric of her powder blue panties into the cleft between her pussy lips. It was "come here" with one finger and "play here" with the other.

Andrew flipped off the main light, leaving only the dim lamp by the door on.

He stepped closer to her knowing he should shower first. It had been a long day, they'd both gone through some shit, and he would feel much better being with her after rinsing the sweat, blood, fear, and frustration from the day down the bathtub drain. Ruby would have none of that though. He knew because he'd tried to put her on pause many times in the past. She wasn't one to wait when she wanted something. When she wanted him.

When he reached the bed, she sat up and looked him in his eyes as she unfastened the front of his pants and pulled them down. He was fully erect. Ruby always got him that way in a matter of seconds. Her eyes never left his as she took him in her mouth.

Andrew closed his eyes and did his best to forget the skeletal grin he'd seen inside the elevator, but when her teeth slid over him even slightly, he cried out in fear thinking demonic chompers were going to bite off the tip of his cock.

Ruby seemed amused by his outburst and massaged his balls to calm his nerves.

Before he knew it, he'd flipped her over and was taking her from behind, in what he saw as the safest position possible, as he did what she mentioned earlier and pounded her, taking all his sadness, fear, and rage out on her. She gripped the sheet, slapped the mattress, and thrust back onto him as she too gave him everything she had until they were both weak, trembling, and collapsing onto the bed together in an exhausted heap of slick body parts.

Maybe it was being out of the house and inside a hotel room that gave them both a sense of freedom to be as loud as they wanted to be. Perhaps it was the sense of danger they both felt. It could have been a simple act of desperation, a need to feel something good when everything felt so wrong lately. Whatever it was, the sex was better than ever, and Andrew held her there in his arms and would have been content to stay that way forever.

As he lay there spooning her from behind, smiling as his nose brushed against her neck, he said, "Ruby, I—"

He stopped. He'd almost told her he loved her, but this was Ruby, and even though she was in Beth's body, it seemed wrong. Those words were reserved for his wife. It didn't matter if she had a handful of personalities or a hundred. She'd always come back to being Beth at some point, and *she* and only *she* deserved those words.

"What is it, baby?" she asked.

"Never mind."

"Tell me."

"It's nothing."

She pushed him onto his back and climbed onto him. Her naked body lay on top of his, sweaty and warm. He loved the feeling and wondered how long they could remain like this. Usually, he would be quick to get out of bed in case she switched to one of the others.

"You love me, don't you?" Ruby asked.

"I..." he didn't know how to answer this question. Not from her.

"It's okay, you don't have to answer that. I know you really love *her*. I'm here for moments like this. Moments when you need to be treated like a real man. I take care of you. She gets the love from you. I can accept that."

There was sadness in her voice, and Andrew wished he could take it away. He could say the words. He could assure her he loved her. Beth would never know, right?

How would she know? If they're never in the same place at the same time, how would Beth know?

The same way Ruby knew so much about Beth, he assumed. It would be wrong to lead Ruby on. Sex was one thing. She was right. They took care of each other's needs in that way. It wasn't like he forced her into it. It was the opposite in fact. She was the one to come on to him. She seduced him every time she was around.

"Yeah, it's her you love," Ruby added after the long silence Andrew hadn't meant to let linger.

"I'm sorry," he said. "I love our time spent together."

She laughed. "Me too. At least there's that."

"Yeah."

"She's a good girl," Ruby said.

"She is."

"Make sure you take care of her no matter what, okay?"

"Always," he said, thinking about her words and realizing they sounded so final. Like she was saying farewell. They were words meant to be said at an airport when getting on a plane and about to wave goodbye to your loved ones.

"Andrew," she said, "can you kiss me?"

Her body rested on his and he lifted his head up to meet her face. Their kiss was soft, deep, and loving.

"Take care of her," she said.

Then she screamed as her body was jerked off him and violently thrown across the room. In the dim light, he saw Ruby launched through the air. Her body crashed against the TV atop the dresser and tumbled to the floor.

Andrew leapt out of bed, flipped on the main light, and watched in naked awe as the demon priest stood at the center of the room with Ruby – Beth – dangling in front of him. He'd lifted her up by her throat and held her there as if she were weightless.

It was the same exact way he'd handled Andrew at Myles-Bend, and Andrew's hands instinctively went up to his own throat where he could still feel the creature's claws there digging into his flesh.

"Let her go!" Andrew demanded.

The demon priest chuckled.

Ruby slapped lightly at his arms, trying to fight, but her strength was already gone.

With his wife's body dangling before him, Andrew was forced back into the situation he'd experienced at his house when Peter was killed. He was too far to reach out and touch them, but he couldn't just stand there and watch. This time, he didn't hesitate. He ran at the demon, but the creature was quick and with both hands, he ripped outward and tore Beth's neck completely open as easily as one might tear his own shirt off his chest.

Blood splattered Andrew's face and chest, drizzling him in Beth's warmth as he slid forward with all his rage aimed at the priest. The demon disappeared in a black ashen cloud, dropping the body, as Andrew dove at him.

Andrew had already taken flight, planning to tackle the demon priest, but all that was in front of him now was his wife's naked, blood-soaked body. He slammed into her as she fell and charged through the scattered black ashy remains of the demon.

Beth's body landed on the floor. Andrew ran headfirst into the wall below the window. He collapsed onto the carpet and stared through blurred vision at the lifeless body next to him.

He fought through his daze and crawled toward his wife, wiping at the tears forming at his eyes until he realized there were two bodies on the floor, like back at his house. Hope overcame him as he moved faster, reaching for her, and slapping at her body.

"Beth." She didn't move, but he saw her, and he knew he wasn't imagining it. He slapped at her arm until he was close enough to grab hold of it and squeeze it. "Beth."

Beth lay there unfazed. Her neck was fine. No blood. She was already coming out of it, blinking rapidly, trying to make sense of where she was.

Andrew buried his face in her chest and cried. He slid his face up to meet hers and kissed her lips. "Thank God."

"Drew," she replied weakly. "What happened?"

He looked past her and got a closer view of the woman lying dead on the floor. This one did have her throat ripped open. She looked nothing like Beth. She was a very attractive blonde woman, kind of trashy looking with black highlights in her hair. She wore a lot of makeup.

She, like Beth, was naked, and her body was like a stripper's. She had big, fake tits, a toned stomach, and a tiny waist. She was the kind of girl who'd have a million followers on social media, the one guys would line up to see at a strip club.

Andrew looked once more at her throat and was sorry he couldn't stop it in time.

The woman's throat was ripped completely open. The skin hung free, like jacket flaps on an unzipped coat leaving everything on the inside exposed.

Stuck to her sweaty, bloody chest was a gold nameplate encrusted with diamonds. It read: Ruby.

This is Ruby.

Again, he didn't understand how it was possible for her to have an actual body. She wasn't real. She was a piece of Beth and Beth was here next to him completely unscathed.

"Ruby," he said, reaching out to touch the girl's hand. "I'm so sorry."

All she wanted was for me to tell her I loved her.

"You didn't deserve this," he told her. "I'm going to figure out how to kill this fucker."

It wasn't I love you, but it would have to be good enough.

"Daddy?" came a little girl's voice next to him.

Andrew glanced over at Beth to see her hunched over with her arms crossed in front of her chest, looking worried and bashful at the same time.

"What's going on?" Alex asked. "Where are all my clothes? And… and… and what happened to Ruby?"

20

Nowhere was safe. The demon priest was taking out Beth's others one by one. First Peter and then Ruby. Only Alex and Gore remained before Andrew was sure he'd go after Beth herself. It made sense in a way. The doctors said Beth created these personalities to shield her from trauma, to protect her from having to face memories of things that happened in the past, and to prevent her from confronting new threats when they arose.

If her personalities were in fact layers of protection she'd created, walls she'd built around herself, then the demon was breaking down each of them so he, or *it,* could finally be in control of her.

Andrew couldn't help thinking of the insect world and the way worker bees or soldier ants protected their queen. Like the dream he'd had about the ants. What was it Beth had told him in the dream?

"Unlike humans," she'd said, *"ants are all on the same wavelength. They help one another. They have many friends ready to attack. They are all ready to fight to the death for one another. To stop evil."*

Beth had built an army to block her, and the demon was knocking the pieces off her chessboard.

Once Andrew put his clothes on and had Alex dressed with her shoes tied, he set her on the bed and tried to come up with a plan. The hotel was clearly a bad idea. Every place seemed like it was. Again, the thought of turning himself, themselves, into the police came to mind, but then he imagined little Alex sitting in a jail cell when the priest came for her. Nobody would be there to protect her.

Like you're doing a great job protecting them anyway.

After the intense lovemaking session he'd had with Ruby, it was weird seeing Alex here in front of him. She never came out at night. It wasn't her time. She was Beth's morning face and even she seemed to feel out of her element. She chewed on her bottom lip nervously and stared up at the ceiling.

"I don't like it here," she said.

"I know you don't," Andrew replied, "but I really don't know where else we can go right now."

"I want to go home."

"Home isn't a good idea."

"But why?"

"It just isn't."

With her seated on the bed, Andrew had to keep stepping in front of her, putting his hand in front of her eyes, and saying, "Baby, don't look at Ruby." Finally, he came to his senses and ripped the comforter off the bed, but as he was about to drape it over Ruby's dead body, it began to dematerialize.

Andrew tossed the comforter aside and squatted next to Ruby. He reached out and tried to touch her thigh one final time. He wasn't sure if it was more for himself or for her. He thought it might be for both, to remind himself she was real and to let her know he did care for her, but it was of no use anyway. His hand passed right through her body. She was nothing more than a ghost traveling away from this world.

"Fucking hell," Andrew muttered.

"The bad thing got her," Alex said.

It made no sense lying to her. The priest could show up again at any moment, and Alex should know she was in danger.

"Yes," he said.

"He got Ruby and Peter?" her voice dropping to a whisper.

"Yes."

He didn't understand why the priest didn't pop up right now and kill Alex too and then take care of Gore so he could have Beth all to himself. *Gore. Why isn't Gore coming out? Is he afraid?* Gore was the only one who might stand a chance against him. If what Gore said the other night was true, he was the reason this was happening.

"Alex," Andrew said, "I need Gore to come out of his room and talk to me. Can you do that? Can you get him?"

She stared at him and then scrunched up her mouth and nose like she smelled something rotten and shook her head. It was a bad idea. She didn't like it.

"Huh uh," she said. "No way."

"Alex. Please."

"Nope. Nope. Nope."

"Alex, I need you to do this right now."

She furrowed her brow and crossed her arms in front of her chest defiantly. It would be an adorable gesture coming from his wife if they were in any other situation, but right now he needed her to comply with his request.

"Alex, I'm not asking. I'm telling you to do this. Tell Gore to come out of his room, right now."

Alex's face went from angry to sad as she lowered her eyes to her lap and said, "Fine. I'll tell him. But he's gonna be mad at me."

She closed her eyes and squeezed them shut as she smooshed her face up and concentrated. She shook her head. Her lips moved but no sound came out. She talked internally, thrashing her head around as a struggle ensued inside her. Finally, she opened her eyes and said, "He won't do it."

Of course, this wouldn't be easy. "Ask him why."

She screwed her eyes shut again and then opened them and said, "You were there. You saw. That night Gore killed those people." Her eyes went wide as she said it, the way an unaware child's would when hearing shocking news for the first time. She closed her eyes, moving her mouth as she spoke with Gore internally again, and then opened her eyes and said, "The innocent should never die. The demon was waiting for that. That impure act gave him more power than he'd ever had over Beth. Over us. And now."

Alex put a finger to her own lips and loudly said, "Shh. No. No more. No, no, no more. I don't want to hear this. Daddy, I don't want to talk about this anymore."

"Tell Gore to come out then," Andrew told her.

She tried once more but it resulted in another shake of her head. "He won't. Please, Daddy. Can we stop now? I don't like this."

"We can stop," Andrew said, reaching out to Alex and pulling her into his arms.

She hugged him tightly.

"I'm scared," she whispered. "Sister Saint Andrews was right. He's a bad man."

Sister Saint Andrews?

"Alex, what do you mean by that?"

"What do I mean by what?"

Andrew pulled away from her and looked her in her eyes.

"Sister Saint Andrews?" he asked.

"I don't know. The lady in the pajamas. She told us he was a bad man. She said that he... that he... um..." She put her tongue between her lips and thought hard. "He didn't have holes. He wasn't holy." She giggled. "She stopped him the last time. Helped Gore stop him."

"Wasn't holy," Andrew repeated. "Sister Saint Andrews."

He pulled out his phone and searched the nearby area for Saint Andrews. Beth had mentioned spending some time at a live-in school for girls when she was younger. Her dad was a businessman who traveled quite often, and her mother was a drunk unable to take care of her on her own, so she spent a great deal of time in and out of boarding schools and private schools. One of them was local. He supposed it could've been a Catholic school. He'd never asked.

He found it.

Saint Andrews School for Girls.

It closed in 2001 after a fire consumed most of the second floor. Now it was only a church. It had to be the place.

"Come on," he told Alex, taking her by the hand and leading her toward the door.

"Where are we going?" she asked.

"To see the woman in the funny pajamas."

Andrew parked his car at the curb and peeked at his sleeping wife in the backseat. She'd been Alex when she passed out. The whole drive over, he kept looking into the rearview mirror, terrified he'd see the demonic face of Father Dennis grinning back at him. It seemed inevitable. Yet here they were. They'd made it to the church and Beth was sound asleep.

With her eyes closed and her lips parted only enough to let her breath escape, she looked so peaceful. He'd always envied how tranquil she seemed when she slept. For all the madness her body put her through, at least when she drifted off to sleep, it allowed her to dive in deeply and shed the day's difficulties.

Then, even when she woke, she started the day as a child. Alex's playful innocence allowed her to step into each new dawn with a fresh curiosity and juvenile wonder, gradually becoming older and wiser as the day progressed. He'd never thought about it before, but it did seem that in her mind's attempt to protect itself through the creation of different personalities it also used them to prepare her for each day. From child to teenager to reality to slut to badass vigilante killer who emerged during the darkest part of the night.

And Father Dennis?

He wasn't one of them. He couldn't be. He was something different. She didn't create him. Something else did. Something evil. Something that might've been born right here in this church.

How does something evil grow inside a place so holy?

Andrew quietly got out of the car and stood in the open doorway, staring over the vehicle's roof and through the chain-link fence, at the church he supposed his wife once called home. It wasn't much to look at now. It was clear the place had been fixed up only enough to serve its purpose after the fire took out the second floor.

Now, what was once a fairly large school was reduced to a small rectangular building that probably served as apartments for the priests and nuns still living there. At the building's center, the roof shot upward into a tall point, the church's steeple, where a large cross looked down over a small garden and what was probably the children's playground once upon a time.

Andrew imagined there had probably been slides, swing sets, and maybe even monkey bars when Beth was a student here. Now, there was only a freshly cut lawn, two benches, and a fountain with a statue of the Virgin Mary at its center pouring water into it from a bowl tucked under her arm.

Sometimes churches gave Andrew the creeps. Not all of them, but some filled him with dread rather than the uplifting peace and serenity everyone else seemed to experience. This church, and maybe it was because he knew something bad happened to his wife here, seemed ominous. Here he was assuming Beth attended classes here. It made sense. He supposed he would find out once he shook her awake.

Andrew couldn't shake the feeling the church was alive and staring back at him. He tore his eyes away from the church and glanced at the neighborhood around him. It was quiet. Behind him, across the street from the church, was an empty park that was clearly neglected. Garbage was strewn all about and someone desperately needed to rake the leaves.

The homes around the church had the glow of lights behind drapes and curtains, but any nightlife took place behind closed doors. Nobody walked the sidewalks or sat on porches gossiping. It reminded Andrew of his great grandparents' neighborhood he used to visit as a kid. It was full of old folks. Like everyone in the area had moved there all at once in their late twenties to early thirties, claimed all the property, and then sat on it and refused to let anyone younger move in.

Mass at church must have been full of folks with white hair, bald heads, wrinkles, and liver spots.

This was the kind of place where most of the inhabitants would die all around the same time and then their younger family members would move in or the properties would be sold and a whirlwind of upgrades would take place, whipping this place into shape and turning it into a modern mecca with trendy upscale shops, fine dining establishments, and condos.

Then this church, which had probably been here for ages, would have to modernize—or move. Developers wouldn't stand for this stain on the block. They'd probably knock down the church and build a 24-hour gym.

Why exercise the soul when you can strengthen the body? Only one looks great in selfies.

Andrew closed his eyes and massaged his temples. He was losing focus, thinking about things that had nothing to do with his situation. The truth was, he was afraid. Looking through the fence and at the church's front doors once more, he realized he was scared of the place. Not because it was a church, and he was some filthy heathen. He thought of himself as a decent man, but he was terrified of what could have happened in there to make Beth turn out the way she had.

He leaned down to peer into the back seat. Beth was still asleep. He hated waking her, but this wasn't something he could do alone, and he wouldn't let her out of his sight even if it were.

"Baby, it's time to wake up."

She mumbled something in protest.

"Beth, baby. We're here."

It was clear right away, by the way she rubbed at her eyes with two closed fists, that Alex was still in control. She dropped her hands into her lap, frowned, and looked back at him with only her right eye open. "Daddy?"

"Alex, we're here."

She turned her head to look out the window. When she saw the church, her head began to slowly move from side to side as she shook her head in protest. "No," she whispered.

"We're going to see the lady in the funny pajamas."

"They all wear funny pajamas here."

So, this is the place.

He was right. Beth had attended classes here. Relief washed over him that he might get some answers but at the same time, he loathed what he might learn. Did he really want the truth about Father Dennis? Or about his wife's connection to the demon?

This might lead you to the only way to defeat him before you lose your wife forever.

Andrew focused on the present and tried to keep the conversation lighthearted by answering Alex with, "Well, you like pajamas, right?"

"Only my unicorn ones."

"Let's pretend everyone's wearing unicorn ones."

She smiled. "Even me and you?"

"Sure, kid."

"Okay, but you promise you won't leave us here like Beth's daddy?"

"I promise I won't leave you here. I'm never leaving you anywhere."

She pursed her lips and looked once more out the window before taking a deep breath, swallowing hard, and replying, "Well, okay then."

Alex scooted toward the driver's side of the back seat where Andrew took her by the hand and helped her out of the car.

Andrew glanced once more down the street as they made their way around the car and toward the church. Not a single car moved from its parking spot. Inside all those houses he imagined people watching reruns of old shows like *Gunsmoke* or maybe even 80s sitcoms like *Night Court* or *WKRP in Cincinnati*. No, people were probably sitting on their couches eating microwavable TV dinners on foldable dining trays while watching *Wheel of Fortune, Jeopardy*, or other gameshows old people liked.

What will Beth and I watch at their age? What will a judgmental asshole like me guess about us when we're in our seventies or eighties?

Because they would grow to be that old together. He had to believe that. Tonight was only a steppingstone. It was another test to their marriage, another hurdle for them to get over. Once they survived this, because they would, how different would life be without Peter or

Ruby? Would that mean more rotations for Alex and Gore? Or was he wrong about the other two and they weren't really dead? Was it possible it had been in his imagination?

With his free left hand, because he held onto Alex's with his right, he rubbed at his left temple. He felt like he was going crazy. So many absurd things had happened today. The events at Myles-Bend had definitely occurred, but the dead teenage boy and the sexy lifeless blonde, both evaporating into thin air – that shit was insane. It defied all logic. They weren't *real* people.

He'd just lifted the latch that allowed them access to the garden and the walkway to the church doors when his cell phone buzzed in his pocket.

"Hold on," he told Alex as he pulled out his phone and checked the screen. He didn't recognize the number. He hit the button to answer it, held it to his ear, said hello, and felt his heart drop at the dry, frigid tone of the person on the other end.

"Andrew Mason?" the voice asked.

"Yes."

"Husband of Bethany Mason?"

"Yes."

"I'm glad I was able to reach you. I've tried calling a few times. Left a couple of messages. This is Detective Pierce with—"

Andrew hung up his phone, dropped it on the ground by his feet, and smashed it with the heel of his shoe. He didn't know if it would do anything to prevent the cops from tracking him, but he'd seen it done in action movies and thought if there was even a chance it would work, it would be worth it. He would deal with the cops later. Right now, he needed to save his wife, and the police would only get in the way.

"Uh oh," Alex said. "You broke your phone."

"Yeah, it was junk anyway. I needed a new one."

With that, he pulled her toward the big double doors that led inside the main church. He was about to grab hold of the handle and enter when Alex tugged on his finger and said, "Not in there."

"Huh?"

"That's the church."

"Yeah, that's where we're going."

She shook her head and pointed at a door off to the left. It led into what looked like the apartment complex part of the building.

"Over here then," he said as he listened to her and approached the other door.

As he grew closer, he saw there was a small plastic strip near the top that read: Office.

He reached for the knob, but it was locked.

"Great."

"It's always locked," she said.

Alex, for being the child of Beth's personalities, was proving to be most helpful. Peter had always been pretty much useless caught up in his video games, Ruby only desired sex, and Gore was an asshole who only wanted to go out late at night and hurt people. Andrew was lucky to have Alex with him right now.

He didn't think to check the time before smashing his phone, but he guessed it was sometime around eight o'clock. The night was still young and maybe someone would answer if he knocked. So, he did. Light knocking got him nowhere, but once he began to pound on the door, he heard movement on the other side and an old man's voice said, "I'm coming. I'm coming. Hold your horses. I'm coming."

The door popped open and there stood a short old man with a ring of white hair on his head. He wore a normal house robe that was much too large for his body. A crossword puzzle book was crammed into one of the front exterior pockets. He squinted in the light shining down from above the door.

"I'm sorry, but we are closed at this hour," he said.

"I understand," Andrew replied, "but this isn't a normal circumstance. My wife, Beth, um… this is Beth here with me. She attended the school that was once here. We are having some… uh… some trouble and I was wondering if maybe one of the nuns who was here at the time might still be around."

The old priest stared at Andrew with his eyes still squinted and his mouth open, tongue sticking half out of his mouth, like he was trying to understand what Andrew was saying by tasting his words on the air.

Finally, he slammed his mouth shut, sucked on his teeth with a loud smack, and said, "That was a long time ago. And as I said, we're closed. Maybe if you come back tomorrow, we can—"

"We might not be alive tomorrow," Andrew interrupted him. "This is a serious situation, Father. I'm sorry. I'm assuming you're a priest."

"I am."

"I'm afraid we're in danger."

The priest stepped through the door and looked out into the garden, left then right, then looked past them and out into the street. He cocked his head to the side and returned his gaze to Andrew before letting his eyes fall on Beth, or Alex, who had her shoulders hunched and was staring at the floor.

"Come in," he said. "I'm Father Frederick. Come inside the doorway here, but only inside the doorway. I still don't know about this, and I can't have you wandering the halls."

They stepped into the warm dim glow of the doorway. Father Frederick closed and locked the door behind them.

"Do you happen to remember the sister's name who was here when you attended the school?" the priest asked Alex.

When Alex didn't answer, Andrew rubbed a thumb against her palm and said, "It's okay, baby. I know you're afraid, but you can talk to him. He's trying to help us."

Alex shook her head and kept her eyes at the floor.

"You can look at him," Andrew told her.

She shook her head. "The father told us we don't look at him. We never look at him. Our eyes belong on the floor. And our mouths wherever we're told to put them."

The priest's eyes opened wide, and wrinkles formed across his brow.

A chill ran down Andrew's spine. He'd never heard the story of what happened here, but that was almost enough.

"I can assure you that is not something we—" Father Frederick began when Andrew let his anger take over.

"What exactly went on at this school?" Andrew asked, his inquiry aimed at the priest.

Of course, it wasn't Father Frederick's fault, but he couldn't help feeling like the man was associated with a corrupt system that had hurt his wife. His instinct was to protect his wife, so he stepped in front of her as if to shield her from harm.

"Oh, my child," Father Frederick said, shaking his head, sadness written on his face. He put a hand on Andrew's shoulder and gently moved him to the side so he could address Alex. "I'm sorry for anything you have suffered here. You must have been here toward the end when Father Dennis oversaw things."

The mention of the demon priest's name was enough to make Andrew wince. Like his name being spoken out loud might summon him to the church.

Alex nodded but only barely. It was more like a slight tremor, a quick jerk of her head.

"Only one of our nuns was here at that time. Sister Mary Francis assisted Sister Antoinette in managing the younger children of the school. I believe all the girls from second grade under. Sister Antoinette passed away a few years back, but Sister Mary Francis is still here. She lost her vision in the fire that consumed most of the school, but she has a sharp memory. She would be the person to talk to."

"I know it's late," Andrew said, "but do you think we could talk to her?"

Father Frederick looked at Alex who was still peering at her feet. He shook his head slowly, not saying no, but showing his disgust for the suffering the girl had gone through because of a history at his church.

"You know what they say about bad apples," the priest said. "The world has rotten fruit strewn about. In police departments, in schools, in our military, in government offices and all forms of politics, and every single other place there is. If you look hard enough, you will always find abhorrent, evil, vile entities the *enemy* has sent to infiltrate places we think of as safe-havens. Satan is a tricky fella. He creates some of the best masks, the most amazing costumes, and keeps his demons smiling with the most outstanding special effects, so good we can't see it for what it is even while our people are in constant agony, and the demons are laughing. And, so, it happened here as well. Father Dennis was a black mark on the Catholic church. He wore his mask, danced his jig, all while the children suffered. I hope you can understand that."

Andrew nodded.

"Good," the priest said. "I will see if Sister Mary Francis is up to speaking right now."

21

Ten minutes later, Andrew and Alex sat in chairs across from Sister Mary Francis who was still dressed in her nun's habit. Either she hadn't changed clothes for the evening, or she'd redressed for them. Andrew wasn't sure what nuns wore to bed. Did they sleep in their habits, or did they change into robes or pajamas as Father Frederick had for the night?

The old lady's face was pale, and she had scarred skin around her eyes, forehead, and nose. Her eyes were milky white. She was blind, Andrew knew, but it still felt as though she were constantly staring directly into his eyes. She smiled from time to time and Andrew got the feeling she was a pleasant person, a sweet lady, but could be tough when necessary. When the school was open, she must have ruled with an iron fist and pampered with a feathered glove.

Andrew sat quietly, looking around the office. Bookshelves lined the left wall with several Bibles, a large variety of encyclopedias, and other random texts. Framed diplomas, certificates of completion, and awards hung on the walls for several different priests and nuns. Most of the furniture was old, oak, dark, and the office smelled of cinnamon.

This was exactly the kind of place Andrew could imagine being summoned for getting in trouble in class. He'd heard tales of nuns hitting kids' knuckles with rulers. His grandmother used to tell him stories of when she'd gone to Catholic school and had been disciplined in such ways. It was the ruler or the paddle. This was the kind of office where such disciplinary measures would be carried out.

"Sitting here, I kind of feel like I'm in trouble," Andrew said with a snicker.

Nobody else laughed. Alex's fingernails scraped nervously at her wooden armrest.

"I'm sorry Sister Antoinette is not here to share this moment with us," Sister Mary Francis said. "She was there from the beginning, the beginning being when he first came to the school and first began leading the sermons. This was before Bethany came to study with us."

Alex kept her face lowered, her eyes in her lap.

"Do you remember much about your time here with us?" the nun asked, her question obviously directed at Beth, even though her eyes remained straight down the middle of them both. When Andrew's wife didn't answer, Sister Mary Francis added, "It is okay to speak to me."

"No, ma'am," Alex replied. "I... I don't want to talk."

Andrew wasn't used to hearing Alex so serious. So shy. She usually used the word "nope" more than "no." She was clearly under the impression she needed to behave herself in the nun's presence. Order and obedience had been established with Sister Mary Francis. This wasn't fear like it had been out in the hallway with Father Frederick. Alex was afraid of priests and for obvious reason.

He wondered if this was the nun Father Dennis kept insisting he ask Gore about. Was this the nun he mentioned repeatedly?

But why? It's clear Alex isn't afraid of her.

"Her voice," the nun said. "It's so childlike. Does she always speak like this?"

Andrew wasn't sure how much to tell her. He was still untrusting of this place but knew if anybody might be able to help, it was this church. If they'd been the start of it all, maybe they could end it.

He must have let the silence linger too long because she added, "I ask because I've also studied quite a bit of child psychology during my years here and—"

"She has dissociative identity disorder," Andrew informed her.

Sister Mary Francis stopped talking. In her silence, Andrew once again felt like a child about to be scolded for interrupting the teacher. He felt a strong urge to apologize.

"I'm sorry for interrupting," he said.

"No need to apologize. That is good information to have. I'm thinking. I do recall this child, and it's my turn to apologize as I know it might sound cold, but I obviously remember Bethany because of the events that led to the fire." She passed an open palm across her face, letting her fingertips touch her closed eyelids. "A fire that took my eyes and has led to a lot of therapy of my own. So, the events themselves are still quite fresh in my mind. But some of the details of the children involved evade my memory. I remember Bethany clearly. She was a sweet child. So young and so innocent. Absolutely stunning. I'm afraid it was that pure beauty and innocence that seemed to call to the evil entity stalking our halls."

Is she blaming Beth's beauty and innocence for what happened to her?

"You see," she continued, "evil is drawn to the divine. It has a lust, if you will, a desire to destroy the exquisite, the most immaculate of God's creations. Bethany was a child like no other. She sang like an angel. Did she ever tell you she was in the choir even at such a young age?"

Andrew glanced over at Alex. A smile had formed at her lips. She was proud of the things Sister Mary Francis was saying about her.

"How old was she when this all happened?" the nun asked herself, sifting through her mental Rolodex for the answer. "I believe she was in kindergarten, maybe the first grade."

"She was six," Alex said, "like me."

"Six, like you," Sister Mary Francis agreed. "Yes, I suppose that makes perfect sense. That was when you were born, right little one?"

Alex shrugged.

"How many personalities does she have now?"

Andrew chuckled, not in amusement, but in a bit of disbelief as he thought of how he should answer the question. "Well, that's a tough one. I thought it was originally five."

"Please explain," the nun said.

"Well, Alex, who's here now. The six-year-old. Peter, a teenage boy. Ruby, kind of the um..." he was too embarrassed to flat out say the slutty one, so he went with, "the promiscuous one, Gore the aggressive one, and I thought Father Dennis was another."

Sister Mary Francis's smile faded. Her lips were a flat line. Her face showed no emotion at all when she said, "Please explain further."

"That's why we're here," Andrew said.

"I thought you were simply here seeking a reason for her condition, answers to questions because of the trauma she's experiencing due to the dissociative—"

"No, that's not it at all," Andrew said. "We've been dealing with that our whole relationship. I've come to deal with it by considering her personalities family members. You know, Alex is the daughter, Peter the son, Ruby the sister-in-law, Gore the brother-in-law, and I thought Father Dennis was the grandfather. I know it's strange, but it's my own way of keeping myself sane about it all. When each one comes out of his or her room and takes over, I simply pretend I'm dealing with that family member until Beth is back in place."

"I understand, and I think it's a very mature way of dealing with it. I commend you, Andrew. It sounds like you love Bethany very much. But I'm concerned about this Father Dennis personality."

"He's not a personality at all, Sister. At first, I thought he was. He was only coming out when it was his turn, or at least that's what I thought, you see – the others – they all take turns. It's a pretty consistent rotation. Alex, Peter, Beth, Ruby, Gore, Father Dennis. But then the old man became violent. He would throw me across the room and demanded I asked Beth about the nun."

"The nun?"

"The nun. So, I thought maybe something happened with a nun, like maybe it was a nun who..." Andrew turned to Alex and said, "Honey, close your ears for a second." Alex did as she was told and Andrew leaned in closer to Sister Mary Francis as he whispered, "I thought maybe a nun had molested her here. It's the only thing that seemed horrible enough to fracture her mind the way it is. I mean I'm no psychiatrist, but I work at a hospital, at Myles-Bend, and I know how this stuff works. It's usually something pretty damn – I'm sorry – pretty darn serious to mess someone up the way Beth's been traumatized."

"Maybe if I explain what happened here," the nun replied, "it'll help shed some light on things. One specific nun does come to mind. A nun who wasn't a nun at all. Pure evil is sometimes too cunning, too manipulative for the human mind to fathom."

A nun who wasn't a nun at all. Andrew thought of The Quiet Man's words. *The priest who is not a priest.*

Sister Mary Francis put both hands to her eyelids as she told the story.

"Father Dennis came to us when the church was in dire need of direction. We were struggling with the girls' school and the head priest before him, Father Christopher, was old and very sick most of the time. So, we saw Father Dennis's arrival as a blessing. He was kind, he always wore a bright smile, and he was so full of energy and light. You would think the man never slept. He bounced around constantly.

"He was a scholarly man, too. That is, he would read not only the Holy Bible but other texts. He once explained to me that it was important to understand the words of other men in order to battle the wits of wise men. One book, in particular, he gained a special interest in. He became quite fond of a black book that appeared similar to a Bible with its silk pages and tiny words. It had no title though. None that I could see. It seemed the longer he studied this book, the more he lost that energy and light I spoke of. He stayed up late, slept in, stumbled in tardy to his sermons.

"His skin became paler, dark rings formed around his eyes, his clothes were wrinkled, and his breath was foul enough that others began to complain about it.

"Father Dennis had changed. First, it seemed to be only his appearance and his hygiene. Then he started making odd remarks in the hallways, sexual innuendos if you will. He would say things to the

nuns that would make their faces beet red and would have them coming to Sister Antoinette and Sister Pamela. They tried, together, to have a talk with him, but he convinced them he had no devious intentions and the nuns had simply misunderstood.

"He was our priest. It wasn't yet to the point we would report him to the bishop. To do that is a big deal and would cause problems in our parish. We all understood we needed to give him a chance and we hoped now that he was aware that he was making people uncomfortable, maybe he would refrain from these strange behaviors.

"It only got worse. One of the sisters who reported him, Sister Evelyn, mysteriously fell down the stairs one evening when going to check the children. She broke her arm and her collarbone. Too frightened to talk about it, she left the church after that, but not before telling her best friend, me, that Father Dennis pushed her down the stairs. If she'd told me sooner, perhaps I could have done something that would have stopped the fire, but she told me much too late.

"While the nuns grew more and more suspicious of Father Dennis, everyone else thought he was a saint gifted with the powers of God. He began to speak in tongues during his sermons. I have heard many people speak in tongues over the years, but I promise you, I had never before then and have never until this day heard anything like what Father Dennis was speaking. It wasn't the word of God. This was something that sounded like it came from the pits of hell. And while he did it, people would drop to their knees in the pews and raise their hands to him. Tithes rose during his sermons, people flocked to the church to see him.

"Teenagers even attended mass, and we'd always had problems getting teenagers through our doors. This was when things got worse still. Father Dennis began to tell dirty, filthy, sexual jokes in the middle of mass. Some of the older members of the church were disgusted and left but the teenagers laughed hysterically. They told their friends and soon even more teenagers attended. The more arrivals, the dirtier the jokes.

"It was at this time Father Dennis began to pay special attention to the children in the choir. He would call them out by name and mention how pretty their hair was or how soft their skin was or how big their eyes were. For Bethany, it was always her lips. He would comment during his sermons about how one must have lips of a goddess to produce the voice of an angel. We, the nuns, were disgusted by this.

"Father Dennis started spending his afternoons walking through the halls of the school. This was an all-girls school, mind you. He had no business in these halls. If they were in the classrooms, and if he were a normal priest, sure, he could come visit and talk to them about God and about manners and such. But he wasn't a normal priest, and he didn't only visit during class time.

"He liked to walk the halls when the girls were eating their supper. He would sit with them and say strange things to them. They weren't allowed to look at him unless he told them to. He would feed some of them who were old enough to feed themselves. He would touch their hands.

"Other times he would walk the halls when he knew it was bath time for the girls. Sister Antoinette and Sister Pamela both warned him that the hour between 6:00 p.m. and 7:00 p.m. was off-limits to everyone because the girls were having their baths and getting ready for bed. He would still arrive, whistling as he made his way down the hall, peering into every door and window until he found Bethany.

"It seemed to mostly be her. She'd caught his eye. He was smitten. Obsessed was a better word. She would disappear on the playground and then we'd see Father Dennis open one of the doors and let her out to rejoin us. She would throw the scraps from her lunch tray away and on her way to the bathroom, she'd go missing. We'd find her sitting on his lap as he showed her pictures in his black book.

"Nobody knows exactly what happened or what he did to her, but we all had our suspicions. Bruises appeared on her sometimes. She began to change, too. She would hum a song and for a while, we couldn't figure out what it was. One of the older nuns who'd lived a different life in the 80s recognized it as Madonna's—"

"'Like a Prayer'," Andrew interrupted her story.

"Yes," Sister Mary Francis agreed.

"Unbelievable. She still hums that today. I asked her about it, and she said she's always liked that song."

Sister Mary Francis closed her eyes and rolled her shoulders. "It still gives me the chills."

"I'm sorry for interrupting," Andrew said. "Please keep going with the story."

"Little Bethany would hum that song on the playground and at bedtime. She started having a bit of a temper and even bit one of the other girls for trying to play with her doll. She didn't sleep much. She would wake up screaming. Nightmares plagued her. We did our best to keep her away from Father Dennis, but it seemed he always found a way. This time, Sister Antoinette and Sister Pamela did report him to the bishop. He didn't seem to believe them. They went higher, to the archbishop, and were reprimanded for going above the bishop's head. It seemed nobody would listen to them. Everyone who knew Father Dennis loved him and refused to believe the stories.

"Meanwhile, Father Dennis's skin grew paler, he lost so much weight he was practically skin and bones. You would think he was dying of a disease. Sister Pamela had the lock changed and made a new rule that only nuns were allowed on the school side of the church. No males at all. Period.

"All the sisters were put on rotation to walk the halls and act as security, to safeguard the children at night as they slept, but during lunches, dinner, and bath time, the halls were quite busy with nuns moving about as they assisted the children. With so many of the sisters on hand, there was no fear Father Dennis would slip by. There didn't seem to be a need to pay more attention to Bethany than to anybody else since all hands were on deck, as they say, and the deck was void of any male presence.

"That was what we thought. Until, once again, Bethany went missing. I was on the night shift rotation that evening, and I noticed she was not in her bed when it came time to tuck her in.

"Of course, we searched every floor of the school until we noticed the main door had been manipulated. A piece of cardboard had been placed in the lock to stop it from clicking shut. Nobody would know unless they exited the school and none of us would have a need to leave that time of evening.

"I should have taken Sister Pamela with me. I should have taken all the others actually. I went straight to Father Dennis's room and what I found there still chills me to my bones. His door was unlocked, that was how smug, how sure of himself he was. How unafraid of all of us he was.

"I heard his deep voice singing before I ever reached for that door, and she was humming along with him. That song. 'Like a Prayer' as you said before. It still haunts me. When I opened the door, the first thing I noticed was little Bethany. I cannot see with my eyes now, but I see this vision all the time."

Sister Mary Francis put a hand to her mouth and cried. Tears flowed down over her cheeks as she continued her story.

"I'm sorry. I haven't spoken of this in a long time. Father Dennis's room was lit up with candles. He liked his candles. They were everywhere. And in their orange glow I... I saw little Bethany. Only six years old. She stood there completely naked with her hands down at her sides, her legs spread open, and her eyes lowered to the ground with so much shame on her face.

"As I glanced over her body to see if she'd been injured, I saw blood dripping from her right hand. A long gash ran across her palm.

"The moment she saw me, she threw an arm over her chest, the blood slathered hand smearing her flesh with red, and closed her legs, cupping her left hand over her to hide her private parts, what I myself had taught her was her special, private place that should never be touched until she was one day married and in love.

"'I didn't want to,' Bethany cried. 'I didn't want him to touch me. I didn't want to touch the book.'

"Bethany's body began to twitch. It was the strangest thing. If you'd asked me then, I would have had no idea what was happening. But now, I do believe this was the moment that, as you say, her mind fractured. I think this was what broke her. She twitched and she looked lost.

"A hiss came from my right, yanking my attention away from her.

Somehow, I'd been so appalled by what I'd seen, I missed the fact that standing only a few feet to my right, where he'd been making this little girl model naked for him, was Father Dennis. Only he was dressed in a nun's habit. His face was pale, the rings under his eyes were so much darker, and his skin was ashy. It was brittle and flaking away.

"Father Dennis turned toward me and every prayer I'd ever learned left my mind. Terror filled my heart. In his right hand was the black, dark bible of his, opened to a page with one dainty red handprint. He'd used Bethany's hand in his book. Her blood.

"He glared at me and yelled one word. 'You!' He took two steps closer to me and as unbelievable as this will sound, a long and purple tongue slithered out of his mouth the way a snake would dart from its hole. It lashed out at me, and I fell backward in my attempt to dodge it. I stumbled right out of his room and into the hallway.

"The door slammed shut in front of me. My prayers came back to me. I leapt to my feet and ran at the door, slamming my fist against it as I recited prayers I was ashamed I'd forgotten in the face of evil. I clutched my rosary in my left hand and banged on the door with my right. Screams emitted from inside the room. Male and female. A war waged on the other side and all I could do was listen to this six-year-old angel fight off a demon that had slithered its way through our door.

"Finally, one of my prayers worked and the door opened on a scene I still can't believe to this day. That little girl was on top of Father Dennis, still in his nun's habit, and she was growling at him as she smashed her fists against his face, throat, and chest. Blood from her cut right hand splattered his face and flung across the room as she battered him with all the might her tiny body had.

"Father Dennis was laughing at her, but she kept fighting with the strength of a grown man. The priest couldn't physically knock her off him. She had pinned him to the floor and was beating him uncontrollably.

"A strange wind kicked up during their battle. It blew the books off Father Dennis's shelves and threw papers around the room. Some of the candles went out, casting shadows over most of the room, but one of the candles tipped over and the flame went wild. It raced over the pages of a book left on the priest's desk. It ran down the side of the desk and crawled over Father Dennis's habit. That nun's habit he should have never been wearing was suddenly ablaze.

"Father Dennis cackled, screaming as the flames lit up his head and hair. I ran into the room just in time to yank little Bethany off him and shoved her into the hallway, but as I turned to flee with her, Father Dennis wrapped one burning arm around my face and set my veil on fire."

Sister Mary Francis lowered her face to her desk. Even minus sight, her eyes seemed to drop in shame or in defeat.

"I was able to escape him and slam the door shut behind me, locking him inside, even as my scalp and upper portion of my face burned and melted. I would never see again, but I could hear the sounds of him howling in pain and screaming in agony as he burned on the other side of that door.

"That's the story of how the school went down in flames. We were able to get all the kids out. Father Dennis died that night. He burned alive."

Sister Mary Francis paused, then touched her hands together softly.

"Now, you understand what happened here," she said. "Of course, the church was rebuilt, the part that burned down, but we never rebuilt the school. That's why the back part of the building is shaped oddly. We refused to build on what we considered tainted ground. And back behind the church is the cemetery so we, unfortunately, did not have enough land to continue on with the school."

Andrew listened to the entire story. The tale was more twisted than he'd imagined. The disgusting son of a bitch had dressed like a nun to lure a child out of her secure surroundings and into his lair where he stripped her naked and was about to do God knows what to her if not for Sister Mary Francis stepping in and saving her.

Who knew what unimaginable things he'd already done to her all those other times he'd been able to whisk her away from the nuns and hide her in his office? That secret was forever locked deep inside her in a place even she could never break into. Only that demon priest who wasn't a priest knew what he'd accomplished so many years ago, and only he knew what he still had in store for her.

"You're quiet," Sister Mary Francis said.

"I don't know what to say," Andrew admitted. "It all sounds so—"

"Unbelievable?" she asked.

"Yeah, but then again, everything I've seen seems unreal so this... this is just another layer of insanity to pile on the rest."

They all remained silent for a minute. Alex chewed on one fingernail and as she did, Andrew reached out to her and took her other hand, opening up her fingers, and revealing the scar on her palm. The scar he'd asked her about and she'd said she couldn't remember where it came from.

"He did this to her," Andrew said, running his fingers over the rough surface of her skin. "She still has the scar on her palm."

"I am sorry," the nun replied. "I believe he left us all with scars."

She'd lost her sight. That was one hell of a scar.

"I've seen him," Andrew said. "In my house and where I work and—"

"Maybe the shock was too much," Sister Mary Francis replied. "Maybe she created a personality to match his to, I don't know, scare away anyone else who might try to touch her inappropriately?"

"I'm her husband."

"You're Beth's husband, but not Alex's or any of the other personas."

He thought about this for a moment and almost accepted it before quickly snapping out of it and shaking his head. "No. No, I've seen him."

"I'm sure you have, Andrew. Like you're seeing Alex right now and—"

"No, you're not listening. I've actually seen him. He isn't one of her personalities. He leaves her body. I've seen him, a physical manifestation of him, side by side with Beth. I once saw him on top of Alex as she slept, with his demon tongue licking her face."

"I'm afraid that is impossible."

"Sister, the church performs exorcisms. I'm sure there has been much more that has happened that's fallen outside the realm of possibility."

She nodded. "Perhaps, but this. He was a real man. A member of this church. Evil, yes, but real. I do believe Father Dennis became possessed during his time here. Something in that black book. He must have become obsessed with something he was studying and perhaps it became obsessed with him. I suppose if he made some kind of pact with… I don't know, Andrew. This all just seems so—"

The lights in the room flickered.

Alex looked up at the lamp to her right.

They flickered again and she shifted her gaze to the lamp on the left.

"Uh oh," Alex whispered. "I think he's here."

"Who's here?" Sister Mary Francis asked.

Andrew thought it was a dumb question, but then again, she hadn't yet seen the demon priest, not since her run-in with him all those years ago when he was still in human form. Not that she would see him now with her eyesight gone.

It was his wide-brimmed hat that came into view first, rising from behind her seat, in stark contrast to her tan veil. His black sleeves might have remained hidden behind her broad shoulders if he didn't have them out to his sides with his palms raised to the sky as if calling down lightning from above. His jagged fingernails curled inward, making a clacking sound as his knuckles popped and cracked in defiance.

His purple tongue split down the middle as it unfurled around the right side of her face, slithering away from him like a serpent.

Sister Mary Francis froze in place, her lifeless eyes glancing right even though they'd never see the evil lingering there. She seemed to sense it.

Then he stood upright, towering over her, glaring down at her with a sneer that put his full hatred on display. Black veins pulsed over his pale white cheeks and as he sucked his tongue back into his mouth, his throat moved with a giant gulp that made it look like it might burst to make room for it. His gritted teeth chipped and crumbled a bit, shards of white enamel spilling out with his thick mucusy spittle.

The nun sitting in front of him sat rigid at first, fear written on her face, but then it was like she realized once again she was in the house of God. Her shoulders relaxed and she smiled.

"Good evening, Dennis," she said.

"Youuuuuuuu biiiiiiiitch," he growled.

One clawed hand came up, and it was clear to Andrew he was about to attack. He'd seen it twice this evening, and he wasn't about to let her fall victim to the same trick.

"Sister!" Andrew yelled. "Duck!"

He jumped out of his chair, ran at the desk, and leapt over as the nun leaned forward. Andrew sailed through the air with his fist raised, ready to pummel the demon priest where he stood, but right when his fist should have connected with the creature's bony chin, the demon disappeared. Andrew smashed into the wooden cabinet behind the nun. Framed documents fell from the wall and shattered on the floor.

"Gotcha, bitch," Father Dennis announced, and Andrew knew even before he rose to his feet what he was going to see.

As he gripped the desk and pulled himself up to his knees, he saw Alex's broken body fall to the ground, not as Beth, but as a six-year-old with ribbons keeping her brown hair in pigtails. She wore blue jean overalls, a pink T-shirt, and her face hung to the side.

Lifeless.

Tongue lolling out of her mouth.

Her neck snapped.

Eyes that were once so full of life now reduced to brown voids, blank circular pools that spent their last seconds wondering why. Just why. Frozen now in that state of fear and bewilderment.

Alex was dead.

Not Alex. No, not Alex. I didn't even get the chance to say goodbye.

Beth's sleeping body sat slumped over in the chair and Father Dennis was once again gone.

22

"No," Andrew said, dropping to his knees to stroke little Alex's forehead.

He felt an overwhelming need to push her bangs away from her eyes. Over the years, he'd stared at his wife's face as she acted out the whims of a child whenever Alexandra was out of her room and in control of Beth's body. But if he'd ever closed his eyes and tried to picture the body that would match the voice, the attitude, and the energy that was Alex, this would be it.

"What has happened?" Sister Mary Francis asked, still seated at her desk.

Andrew looked back at her with tears welling up in his eyes. He wished she could see the havoc caused by the old priest who'd once walked these grounds. The old bastard now destroying the world around him.

"She's dead," Andrew answered.

He gently lay the child down on the ground and stood to be near his wife who was still passed out in her chair.

"Who is dead?" the nun asked. "Bethany?" When he didn't answer quickly enough, she asked again, "Is Bethany dead?"

Andrew watched his wife's chest rise and fall with her breath.

"She's not dead. That's the thing. The demon, Father Dennis, kills her over and over again. He slashes her throat, chokes her to death, breaks her neck. But each time he does it, he kills the personality in control of her."

"I don't understand."

"You're not the only one. The weirdest fucking part – shit, I'm sorry. My language. You know what, fuck it. We've got bigger problems, Sister. The weirdest fucking part is when he kills the personality, they die and become real."

"What do you mean they become real?"

"It's like they fall out of her body as a real person. First, it was Peter. The teenage boy. When Father Dennis killed Beth with him inside her, she collapsed on my living room floor, but when she fell, an actual teenage boy fell to the floor too, outside her body. The same thing happened in the hotel room when Father Dennis killed Beth again with Ruby in control. And now, this time, with Alex. Sister, come here. I know you can't see, but maybe you can feel."

Sister Mary Francis stood from her desk and reached out. Andrew took her by the hand and helped her walk around to where Alex's body lay on the floor.

"Can you get to your knees?" he asked.

"Getting down is never the problem. But getting up, I will need your help with that."

She carefully dropped to her knees, and Andrew took her right hand and led her to Beth's leg.

"This is Beth," he told her. "You can feel she's asleep in this chair. She collapsed in it when Father Dennis dropped her."

The nun ran her fingers up Beth's calf and thigh until she felt her ribs and arm and then touched her face. "She is still very beautiful."

"She is," he agreed. "Now, remember Alex was in control of her when we were talking?"

"Yes, of course."

Andrew took her hand and led her down to Alex's forehead. That's where he let go.

"Father Dennis snapped Beth's neck with Alex in control," he informed her, "and I don't know how to tell you this, but there is a dead six-year-old lying on your office floor."

Sister Mary Francis traced over Alex's face with the fingertips of her right hand. Her left hand went to her mouth where she cupped it and stifled a cry.

"I know," Andrew said, "but she'll disappear soon. It happens every time."

"Disappear?" The nun's hand was still on Alex's leg when the child began to dematerialize. "Oh," she called out as her hand passed through the leg. "What is... what is happening?"

"Like that," Andrew told her. "Her body is disappearing right now. She's vanishing."

The nun's blind eyes were on the spot where Alex had been only seconds before. She brought them up to meet Andrew's face but never quite settled on him. It seemed she was peering at something over his shoulder.

"Sister," he said.

She adjusted her face, so it seemed she was now looking at him.

"Where is the demon now?" she asked.

Andrew understood she was talking about the Father Dennis *thing*. He shrugged, forgetting for a second she couldn't see his gesture. "I don't know," he said. "He always disappears after he kills one of her personalities. But he'll be back. He wants her for himself. I came here because I thought you might be able to help me stop him."

"You can't stop him," a deep, throaty growl came from Beth's body.

Andrew knew that voice. It was Gore. Finally, he'd come out.

"It's about damn time you showed up," Andrew said.

"Who's here?" Sister Mary Francis asked.

"The last of Beth's personalities. His name's Gore. He's—"

"I'm the one who caused this," Gore growled. "You two idiots know nothing. The priest was grooming Beth all those years ago. He was preparing her for this moment. His dark bible called for the blood of a child, one who'd grow into a human host for what you're calling a demon. The priest knew he'd die. He needed to die, but his plan was to possess the child. He cut her palm and put her blood in the book. Signed her soul away. She was to be his puppet. But *we* stepped in. He couldn't take over her body as long as we kept her pure. Kept her from doing anything evil."

"But you were evil, you fucking lunatic!" Andrew yelled. "You went out at night and killed—"

"I fought evil," Gore argued. "I saved lives. I stopped the innocent from being hurt. Everyone I killed was under the charge of a demon. They were murderers and rapists. Until the night you were with me, and that young girl died on accident. She was innocent. That should have never happened."

"That let him in," Andrew said, finally understanding.

"Beth," Gore continued, "because of me, was no longer innocent."

"So, if you hadn't been out there trying to save the fucking world!" Andrew yelled.

Gore lowered his head. "You saw the people I saved. You saw them in that apartment. Imagine all the ones you did not see. I got my first taste of blood when I saved Beth from the priest that day of the fire. I beat him until my fists, Beth's fists, were bloody."

"That was you," Sister Mary Francis said. "The one growling and hissing and snarling. Like an animal."

"That was the day I was born," Gore said. "Beth snapped, and she created me to protect her. The priest had no idea how strong she was when he picked her. Her beauty was one thing, but her strength was something else. Peter was smart, he could figure shit out. Like in the games he played. Ruby was conniving, and a bit of a tease. She could get us into situations the rest of us could not. Like in a relationship with Andrew here who could help protect us. Especially in that hospital."

Andrew felt his heart sink. Was that all he was? Was he only another level of protection?

"Are you saying Beth never loved me?" Andrew asked.

"Oh, fuck off," Gore replied. "Of course, she did. You know she did. Even Ruby loved you. We all – they all do." Gore's face lowered in what appeared to be a moment of sadness. Of vulnerability. "They all did. Alex was the one with the biggest heart. She had the childlike wonder, the imagination. And me, I'm the strength."

"Then why haven't you been fighting?" Andrew asked. "You're hiding like a little bitch while everyone else is dying."

He wasn't sure if he should challenge Gore like this, but he needed someone to fight, and so far, he was doing it alone. And he was losing.

"Because he's too strong," Gore admitted. "With each one of us he's killed, the stronger he's become, and now it's only me. Then he will have full control of Beth."

"How do we stop him?" Andrew asked.

"I don't know," Gore said. "Maybe if we had his dark bible we could—"

"We do have his dark bible," Sister Mary Francis interrupted.

"You have it?" Andrew asked. "Where?"

"If you have it, that should help," Gore said. "I'm leaving now."

"Gore," Andrew said, "we need your help. Beth needs your help."

"I am sorry, Andrew," he replied, "but I can't win this one, and you saw what happened to the others. If I come out, I'll die."

It was clear when he returned to his room because Beth's shoulders relaxed, and she fell back into her seat. Her eyes opened groggily, and she rubbed at them, like she was coming out of a nap.

"Andrew," she said when she saw him. "Baby, where are we? And why is it so cold? I'm freezing."

She shivered and wrapped her arms around herself. Andrew immediately took off his hoodie sweatshirt and helped her pull it over her shoulders.

"Better?" he asked.

"No," she said, "but I'm sure it'll help."

She looked around the room and her eyes came back to the nun. "Where are we?"

Andrew took both her hands in his and rubbed her knuckles with his thumbs. He had a lot of explaining to do. He didn't know if she could sense that Ruby and Alex were both gone. Either way, she needed to understand what was happening. This was a fight she needed to be involved in. Especially if Gore wasn't going to be of any help.

23

The dark bible was locked in a glass box with a cross, a rosary, and a Holy Bible resting on top of it. Standing on each side of the box was a bronze statue of an angel wearing armor and wielding a giant sword. Andrew didn't know enough about religion to know which angels they were supposed to be, but he did recall God having soldier angels.

The dark book itself looked similar to the Holy Bible, only it had no text on it at all. The edges were torn and frayed, but it was in fairly good condition considering it had been in a room engulfed in flames.

"It is protected here," Sister Mary Francis informed them. "He cannot enter here and even if he could, he cannot get through the barriers protecting it. This is a holy place."

"Isn't this whole building a holy place?" Andrew asked. "Wasn't it a holy place when he took my wife up to his room and smeared her blood in the book to begin with?"

Sister Mary Francis was silent.

"Wasn't it a holy place when you nuns were forced to fend for yourselves against a madman stalking the halls in search of little girls?"

"Every day I think about this," she replied, "in some way, shape, or form. I ask God how HE could allow this to happen under HIS roof. I have chosen to believe God allows small slivers of evil to be seen in places deemed holy in order to remind us that it does in fact exist. It is easy for us hiding behind these walls to pretend Satan's evildoings outside aren't real or aren't as bad as people make them out to be. You've heard the saying 'practice what you preach.' Well, maybe God sometimes forces us to practice instead of only preaching. What happened to Bethany was horrible, but it did bring the nuns together and showed us that true evil is out there and it's capable of taking even the most renowned priests, if given an ounce of wiggle room. Do you understand?"

Andrew shook his head. "I don't care what the lesson is, Sister. I only want my wife to be safe. So, if this, all that's happened to my wife and me, is another way of showing you what true evil can do, let's remind Satan what good can do."

Sister Mary Francis smiled. Beth did too.

"I want this to be over," Beth said. "I'm tired. Like really tired."

Andrew put an arm around her and held her close. "I know you are, baby." He looked down once more at the black book in the glass case. "So, this is it, huh? This is what started it all?"

"It should have burned all those years ago," Sister Mary Francis said. "We found it outside on the ground, beneath Father Dennis's room's small window. He'd tried to climb out himself, but he was too big and couldn't do it in time. He burned alive while barely half out of the room. But he did manage to fling the book out ahead of himself."

"And you said my blood is in there?" Beth asked. "That's what ties him to me?"

"That's what Gore said," Andrew replied.

"So, we burn the book," Beth said. "If it burned when he did, none of this would have happened. So, let's burn it."

Sister Mary Francis held her hands in prayer and touched her fingers to the bridge of her nose. "I don't know about this."

"It's clear he didn't want this book to burn," Andrew reminded her. "He threw it out ahead of himself. So, let's send the book back to whatever hell he got it from."

"I'm afraid this is something I must get permission for," Sister Mary Francis said. "I do not even have the key. It's kept by Father—"

Andrew didn't wait for her to finish. They'd been through enough already. He grabbed one of the statues guarding the box and lifted it above his head.

"Andrew!" Beth yelled, interrupting the nun.

"Wait, what are you doing?" Sister Mary Francis yelped and flailed her hands, blindly reaching out to the box, swiping at the contents atop it, and snatching up the rosary, cross, and Bible. "This is guarded and sacred—"

Andrew waited for her to move and then brought the statue down hard and smashed through the top of the box. Glass shattered and rained down over the dark bible. He reached in carefully and grabbed the book, bringing it close to his mouth to blow the dust and tiny shards of glass off it.

"Andrew, you can't—" the nun started.

"Where are his ashes?" Andrew asked.

"My God," Beth said, staring numbly at the shattered box when Andrew grabbed her by the hand and led her out of the room and back into the main office.

"His ashes are where they fell," Sister Mary Francis informed him. "I mean the debris was carried away to tidy up the property. His remains were dust along with the part of the building that went down in flames. Most of it was carried away."

"Show me where it happened," Andrew demanded as he walked to her desk, snatched up a book of matches used to light candles, and walked out of her office and back into the corridor.

"You can't just go anywhere you please in here," she called out after him. "Andrew, I'm a blind woman. You're moving too quickly for me to follow."

"Do you remember where it happened?" Andrew asked Beth as he continued out of the building.

"No," she said. "I don't remember any of it. Please, slow down. You're scaring me."

He refused to move any slower. He was a man on a mission, and he knew Father Dennis would be returning soon since he now held the man's prized dark bible under his arm. Any second now, he'd pop up and fling Andrew through a fucking window or toss him across the hall.

"Does Gore know?" he asked. "Ask Gore where it happened."

"I... I don't know how," she said. "I don't know how to do that. Please. Andrew, you're hurting my wrist."

Fire burned inside him. He wanted to kill Father Dennis, or whatever you did to demons, send him back to hell, maybe? Olivia, Paloma, Peter, Ruby, and Alex all demanded it. They deserved revenge for the way he slaughtered each of them. It seemed everyone was terrified of the priest who came and went at will.

The priest who'd spied on his relationship with Beth all her time at Myles-Bend.

The priest who'd occupied her body like one of her personalities.

The priest who'd visited their bedroom in the middle of the night and who'd thrown Andrew against a wall. Out a fucking window, too.

"Andrew, go out the front door and turn right!" Sister Mary Francis's voice called out to him. "You'll see the still-charred-earth when you round the corner of the new building. That's where it happened!"

"What's going on?" a woman's voice asked from somewhere behind him.

"Is everything okay out here?" another woman asked.

"Excuse me, do you know what time in the evening it is?" a man's voice called out. "Have some respect for people trying to get some rest."

Members of the church were coming out of their rooms to see what all the shouting was about. Andrew didn't have time to look behind him to assure them everything was okay. Everything was not okay.

"Sisters," Sister Mary Francis said somewhere in the hallway behind him. "Get dressed and meet me outside. All of you. The time has come. Father Dennis is back, and I will need all of your help this time."

Andrew found his way to the front doors, unlocked them, and pushed his way out and into the garden, half expecting to see Father Dennis waiting for him outside. He flinched as he pushed his way through, making sure Beth stayed behind him in case he was right, but there was no demon priest waiting on the other side.

Wind blew through the trees, the fountain burbled, and the rest of the world remained silent. He'd considered having Beth remain inside the church, but he didn't see how she'd be any safer there. She'd been inside as a child, and nobody had been able to protect her from the evil son of a bitch and what he'd done to her then. She'd been inside when the attack on Alex occurred. It was clear she wasn't safe anywhere.

At least if she remained by his side, he knew *he* would die trying to protect her. He couldn't say the same for anybody else.

That's an unfair thought. Sister Mary Francis lost her eyes and nearly her life trying to rescue Beth.

If she'd done her job correctly, she wouldn't have had to. The priest should have never been able to get his hands on her in the first place.

Perhaps he was being unfair still. What would he have done differently? They'd locked the place down and denied any males entrance to the school area where the children were housed. And the sick son of a bitch had dressed like a nun to get his hands on Beth. The mere thought of it gave him the chills. He'd seen the priest, and he couldn't imagine bumping into him dressed in a nun's habit.

Get out of your head. You're not afraid of him. He should be afraid of you. You have his book. You have matches. You're going to set this unholy fucking text on fire.

"Andrew, let's go back inside," Beth begged him. "I don't want to be out here. I don't want to see him. Please, I don't want to see him. I think I remember what he looks like, and I don't want to see him."

She was practically dragging her feet the way a child would, forcing him to pull her across the lawn.

He stopped and wrapped his arms around his wife. "I know you're scared, baby. I'm scared too, but he's been in our home. He killed Paloma."

"Paloma?" Her mouth opened wide, and she blinked a few times, shock taking over her face. She'd had no idea.

She'd been with him in the house after Peter's death, but he hadn't told her about Paloma. She was like a member of the family. Hearing of her death was like hearing of an aunt's death or a grandmother's, someone who lived with them and took care of them and spent all the holidays and special occasions with them.

Andrew nodded. "Yes. He killed Paloma. This has to stop."

She batted her eyes, coming back to reality. If there had been any other personalities left, one would have come out right now to save her from the shock she was experiencing, but they were all dead except one, and he wanted nothing to do with helping Beth right now. It was time for her to learn to take care of herself. She could no longer hide behind shutters. The windows were open. She needed to see it all so she could fight and get past it.

"We have to do this," he told her.

"And if it doesn't work?"

"Then at least we fought together."

She nodded.

Andrew pulled her in close again and kissed her forehead once before planting a kiss on her lips. "I love you, Beth."

"I love you, Andrew."

Andrew turned and pulled her toward the corner of the building, like Sister Mary Francis instructed.

"Father Dennis!" Andrew yelled. "I've got your book you fucking lunatic, and I know what you did to Beth! Come out and face me like a man. None of that appearing and disappearing pussy shit you keep pulling. Good and evil. Right here, right now."

An overhead security light at each corner illuminated the church grounds but only about twenty feet or so away from the building. Everything beyond that was dark.

Andrew led Beth around the corner and saw the spot Sister Mary Francis had told him about. The ground was still scorched earth. Nothing had been built over it. The soil was dead but only so much of it was visible for the rest was plunged into darkness beyond where the security lights could reach.

They walked cautiously to the back corner where Andrew peered around to the rear of the building. To their left was the large, rectangular patch of dead earth that had once been the school and to their right, way on the other side of the church, was the cemetery.

The church backed up to a wooded area and most of that was shrouded in darkness.

"I don't like this, Andrew," Beth complained. "It's too dark."

She was right. The priest who wasn't a priest could be standing so close to them and they wouldn't even see him. He could be standing in the darkness where the security lights couldn't reach. He could be watching from the shadowy tree line. He was probably staring at them right now.

Like he used to stand in the corners of the rooms.

Andrew held Beth close as he turned in all directions to make sure the priest wasn't anywhere near. He kicked at the ground. "So, this is where you burned, huh? You sick, pedophilic, Satanic piece of shit!"

Still, nothing.

"Maybe we should go back inside," Beth suggested.

Andrew pulled out the book of matches, lit one, and held it up close to the book. "Guess I'll have to do this without you then."

The flame touched the silky pages and caught but just barely. Fire lit up the side and burned softly. It didn't go up quite the way Andrew expected. In fact, it was close to burning out as a gentle breeze blew around them.

"It's not working," Beth said.

Andrew lit another match and was about to touch it to the side of the book when a voice from behind made him jump.

"You are right." the gravelly, demonic voice of Father Dennis said.

Andrew let go of Beth and turned around to see the tall figure of the priest standing over him, at least two feet taller than he was. His wide brimmed hat kept most of his face in darkness, but his purple tongue snaked out and slithered through the air.

"This is where I burned," Father Dennis added, as he lashed out with a speed Andrew couldn't match and swatted him away with a backhand that was so strong it sent him spinning through the air, "and it's where you die."

The book flew from Andrew's grasp. It hit the ground before he did and bounced a few times then skidded to a halt at Beth's feet. She leaned over to pick it up.

"Don't touch it, Beth!" Andrew yelled at her as he crawled to his hands and knees.

"Please, touch it, Beth," Father Dennis said with a chuckle, stepping slowly toward her. "Touch it like you touched it so many times before."

Hearing the sexual connotation only fueled Andrew's anger. He charged at Father Dennis and swung his right fist at him as the priest was about to reach for Beth. The fist went through the demon's body, like he was only an apparition. Andrew swung his left fist and the same happened.

"You're a fucking coward!" Andrew roared. "Fight me! Stop pulling this phantom shit!"

Father Dennis cackled with laughter as he stood still and let Andrew swing in frustration with each fist going unanswered. He couldn't land a punch.

Then, as Andrew grew tired, Father Dennis grabbed hold of the front of his shirt, lifted him up, and tossed him into the air again. This time Andrew flew even farther than he had the last time.

"Andrew!" Beth yelled.

She ran at Father Dennis and swung the book at him in an upward arch. Unlike Andrew's punches, the book connected with him, hitting him hard on the chin and sending the monster stumbling backward. He scrambled a few steps on his heels, nearly fell over, but then dropped to one knee, steadied himself, and stood once again.

He dusted himself off. "Try that again, you little bitch."

"You're not so tough after all, are you?" Beth asked. "Picking on children and women."

She lifted the book and was about to hit him with it again when he swung outward and slapped the book, causing it to slam backward into her face. The strike caught her off guard and knocked her back. She hit the ground hard and smacked her head on a rock.

"Beth!" Andrew yelled, leaping to his feet and running toward her.

He reached her and slid his arms beneath her, cradling her, no longer giving a shit where the monster was. He only cared that his wife was okay.

Father Dennis chuckled. His shoes thudded across the scorched earth as he took short, heavy steps toward Andrew and Beth. He whistled a tune, and Andrew knew it well, it was the one Beth sang so often. 'Like a Prayer' by Madonna.

"Do you know this song?" Father Dennis asked.

Andrew ignored him and pushed away the rock Beth's head had landed on. His thumb came back bloody. "Beth, Beth, please wake up. Please, baby. Tell me you're okay."

"Little Bethany used to sing it to me," Father Dennis continued. "She would look right at me, and she would smile. With those lips of hers. She would smile and sing with all her heart. I couldn't wait to soil that heart. To connect it with the darkness. To climb inside that body of hers and do such nasty things with it. I still have those plans, Andrew. Your wife's signature is in my book. She's mine. I've been killing off her personalities one by one."

Andrew lay his wife down softly on the ground and reached for the rock beside her head.

"I have something to confess, Father," he said.

"I don't take confession anymore, Andrew," Father Dennis said as he came closer, "but what the hell. What is your confession, my son?"

Andrew scooped up the black book on the ground next to his wife along with the rock next to her head and leapt to his feet. "I'm not one of her fucking personalities!" As he yelled it, he slammed the book into Father Dennis's face and brought the rock around at the same time, cracking his skull with it.

The demon howled in pain and stumbled backward. Andrew didn't wait. At the first sign of weakness, he leapt at the demon again and was racing toward him when Father Dennis began to laugh hysterically. Andrew was only a foot away and was about to attack when the demon lashed out again, grabbed him by his throat, hoisted him up in the air, and slammed him face and stomach first into the scorched earth.

"I will bury you here," Father Dennis hissed.

The book flew from Andrew's hands and bounced off the ground.

Andrew's arms flailed as he coughed with his face in the dirt, sending up plumes of dust and wisps of dirt as he fought to breathe with the demon's nails digging into his neck and holding him down. Black, scorched dirt. The ashy remains of burnt grass and a destroyed church entered his nostrils and passed his lips. He coughed again, choking, struggling for fresh air. He was drowning on dry land.

This can't be how you die.

"You let him go!" came a familiar voice. It sounded like Sister Mary Francis.

"By the power of Christ, you will let that man be!" came a man's voice that sounded like Father Frederick.

"Back to hell with you!" came another woman's voice.

The grip on his neck was loosening. Andrew pushed back and was still met with resistance, but he was able to turn his head enough to gasp for breath. Air filled his lungs and stung at first, but he wasn't dead, and that meant he was still in the fight.

"This is where it ends, Dennis!"

"Back to hell with you!"

Prayers went up, different ones from different people. From what Andrew could see through blurry eyes, at least ten to fifteen nuns, with a couple of priests, stood around him in a circle, shaking fists with rosaries wrapped around them and splashing holy water at him.

Father Dennis backed away from Andrew, crouched down, and covered his head, like a child trying to protect himself from schoolyard bullies.

Andrew crawled away from him, searching for the dark bible. He saw it and scurried toward it. He was on his hands and knees, about to reach it when he felt a clawed hand at his ankle. He glanced behind him to see Father Dennis's long, bony, clawed hand holding his leg. The demon grinned at him with gnarled, jagged teeth and then twisted his hand.

The crack in Andrew's ankle sent scorching pain up his entire leg and into the rest of his body. It was like liquid heat, hot lava, ran through his limbs. He cried out in agony.

Behind him, Father Dennis rose to his feet with bent knees and clawed hands reaching for the sky. He screamed out loud like a banshee and then swung his arms out and around wildly as if he were swatting at a swarm of angry bees. Gusts of wind emitted from him and blew toward the nuns and priests who fought to stay on their feet at first, but the demon's power was too strong, and the wind launched the nuns and priests clean off their feet.

One priest smacked against the building at his back.

A nun flipped through the air and flopped across the ground like a dead fish.

Sister Mary Francis dropped to her knees to keep from being thrown. Some of the others did the same but weren't so lucky. All the members of the clergy were scattered and disposed of, unable to hurt Father Dennis. He seemed indestructible.

"We need to burn the book!" Sister Mary Francis yelled.

Father Dennis heard her and marched over to where Andrew had been crawling only moments before and snatched up the dark bible. Then he walked to Beth, who was still out cold, grabbed her by the hair, and lifted her unconscious body up like a ragdoll. He tossed her over his shoulder and walked toward the graveyard.

"Beth!" Andrew yelled. "He's taking her to the cemetery!"

Andrew climbed to his feet and tried to follow, but as soon as he put weight on his broken ankle, he fell to his knees again. Left to cry out for his wife, Andrew was nearly hopeless. He tried once more and hopped after them, but he couldn't move quickly enough.

"Fuck!" he yelled as he fell to the ground.

Father Dennis was about fifty feet ahead of him and was going to disappear with his wife when Andrew yelled out the only thing that came to mind. "I don't need your book! I only need this page!"

Father Dennis stopped. Beth was still out cold on his shoulder when he turned around to face him.

"I only need the page with Beth's handprint!" Andrew yelled. "And I've got it."

He pulled out the book of matches and lit one.

"No!" Father Dennis yelled.

In his panicked state, the demon didn't stop to look through his book. If he had, he would have seen the page was right where it should have been. Andrew had nothing. But it was enough to force the bastard to put Beth down on the ground and come back to her husband. That was all Andrew wanted. He didn't care about his own life. He only wanted to give Beth a few more minutes to survive.

Beth, please wake up. Wake up and run. Just wake up and go. Run away from here! Face him another day. Please, God. Please keep my wife safe from harm.

Father Dennis stalked after him while behind him he could hear the rumblings of the priests and nuns recomposing themselves and bringing up the rear. It didn't seem there was much they could do, but Andrew would be happy to have witnesses. He didn't want to die alone. Maybe they could at least whisk Beth away to safety.

"Where is it?" Father Dennis asked as he moved swiftly toward Andrew.

"Like I'm going to tell you," Andrew replied.

"Oh, boy, a broken ankle is nothing. Wait until you feel what I break next. Maybe I'll start with your femur. I'll pick your bones apart the same way I picked apart Beth's little guardians. Her friends. Her personalities."

"Hey!" came a deep growl Andrew knew well. It came from the other side of the demon, back where he'd left Beth. "About those guardians. You missed one."

Beth had risen to her feet and was stepping toward them, moving into the light only long enough for Andrew to see her pull the hood of her sweater over her head, the sweater he'd given her because she was cold. She stood with her fists clenched and her chest heaving up and down.

"I already whooped your ass once, a long time ago," Gore said. "'Bout time I did it again."

24

Andrew nearly fell to the ground and thanked God. Gore was finally stepping out to fight for Beth. It was the reason he was created. He was her only guardian left.

Father Dennis stood between them. He glanced back at Andrew and then looked once more at Gore, trying to decide which of the two was most important to attack. He needed to get that page of his book from Andrew, but he also needed to kill Gore if he had any hope of possessing Beth's body.

It seemed like he might choose to come after Andrew first. He, or the page of the book he thought Andrew had, was the immediate threat. If that page was burned, this was all over for the priest. Just as Andrew was sure he was about to fight to the death, Father Dennis did something unexpected. He looked down at the book in his hand, flipped it open, and turned to the page Andrew claimed to have.

"Fuck," Andrew mumbled under his breath.

Father Dennis slapped an open palm against the page in question, which would have landed his own large, bony handprint right on top of six-year-old Bethany's tiny bloody palm print. Then he turned toward Gore and moved that way.

Gore turned and walked away from Father Dennis, clearly leading him away from Andrew. Even now, he was doing what Beth would have wanted. He was trying to save Andrew's life. He knew what was in Beth's heart, and she loved her husband. All her personalities, her guardians, knew that.

"Beth," he said as he slapped a hand against the grass.

He wouldn't be able to stop Gore from leading the demon priest away. They were going to battle, but it wouldn't be here where Andrew could get hurt.

"We have to follow them!" he yelled back at the two priests and the nuns limping toward him.

Father Frederick was the first to reach him. He had his arm linked through Sister Mary Francis's.

"What is happening?" he asked.

"It's Beth, my wife. She has other personalities. It's a long story. One of them is trying to protect me. He's challenging the demon to a fight."

"Oh, no," Sister Mary Francis said. "Sister Fay, gather the others. We must go to the cemetery now. That's where they're headed."

One of the nuns, Sister Fay, returned to the rest of the crowd and barked orders at them.

"My ankle's broken," Andrew said. "Can you help me get there?"

"Maybe it's best if you let us handle—" Father Frederick started to argue when Andrew shut him down.

"This is my wife fighting *your* demon," Andrew reminded him. "Help me get to them. I will not let her do this alone."

With the help of Father Frederick and a strong nun, Andrew was able to hobble toward the battle about to rage in the cemetery.

The Father Dennis *thing* looked back over his shoulder as the crowd made its way among the tombstones and surrounded him. "You've all come to witness the transformation."

"There won't be a transformation tonight, priest," Gore called out. "For that, you'll need to get through me."

Father Dennis leaned his head back and laughed. Then he leapt forward, ripped a gravestone out of the ground, and swiftly threw it at Gore.

The violent vigilante in Beth's body didn't spin or dodge. He ran straight at the gravestone, cocked back his fist, and slammed it forward, tearing his knuckles through the concrete pillar. It exploded like it had been hit with a stick of dynamite.

Andrew's jaw dropped.

He'd seen this personality in action. He knew he could fight, could protect himself, and could kill easily and without remorse, but he'd never known him to have supernatural powers quite like this.

Gore's fist came out of it bloodied, but relatively undamaged.

"Whoa-hoa!" Father Dennis cheered, antagonizing Gore. "You're much stronger than this weakling." He jabbed a thumb at Andrew.

"Why don't you let him hold your book for you?" Gore suggested.

Father Dennis cackled again. "Perhaps not."

"Fine," Gore said, "I'll give it to him."

This time it was the hooded figure in Beth's body who attacked. He ran at Father Dennis, jumped onto a nearby gravestone, and brought a superman punch down against the demon priest's chin.

Andrew wondered why Gore was able to hit the priest and he hadn't been able to unless he was brandishing the dark book. Did it have something to do with the fact they both operated in worlds that weren't necessarily based in reality? Or was Father Dennis simply willing to fight fair after being called out?

The strike to his chin only made the priest stagger back but he lashed out with his right hand quickly and slashed his nails across Gore's chest. Andrew flinched at the thought of what that might do to Beth's breasts. Would this injure her, or would it be like when the priest killed her other personalities and Beth remained unfazed?

Gore leapt back with the demon's forward slash. The claws did rip through the sweatshirt but didn't seem to hurt the vigilante. Instead of doubling up in pain, he spun into the attack and landed a spinning back-fist against Father Dennis's right temple.

"Unf," the priest grunted.

Gore spun the other way and did the same with his other fist, swinging a back-fist at the other side of the priest's face, but this time the priest expected it, caught his wrist, and yanked Gore by his arm, tossing him across the cemetery where his body slammed into a headstone and the young man went down hard.

Father Dennis stalked after him, creeping through the headstones, toward the spot where Beth's body landed. Gore must have crawled away and come around behind the priest because just as the demon pounced on where he thought the young man would be, Gore leapt out of the shadows with a headstone of his own and slammed it down against the back of Father Dennis's head.

The concrete slab shattered against the demon's head and the evil priest fell in a cloud of dust and crumbling debris. He hit the ground hard on his stomach with his arms outstretched and dropped his black book. It landed on the grass next to him.

Gore stood over the sinister being for a moment and when he was sure he wasn't going to get up, he kicked the book away from the priest's reach. Then he walked over to it, bent to pick it up, and tossed it toward the crowd of nuns. "You know what to do with this!"

If Gore had a fault, it was his arrogance. He was too cocky for his own good and that led to only a few seconds of turning his back on Father Dennis, but that was all the time it took.

The demon priest silently stood from his spot on the ground.

"Behind you!" Andrew yelled.

It was too late.

Father Dennis grabbed Gore by the back of his neck and dug his claws in. He shoved his other hand into the vigilante's back, gripping his spine.

Gore's face twisted in pain. His mouth opened but no words came out. His eyes twitched and his lips quivered. It was the only time Andrew had ever seen him terrified. At that moment, his warrior spirit died, and Andrew glimpsed the panicked face of a young man realizing his own end.

Below him was a broken cross-shaped headstone. The tip had been chipped away and what was left was a sharp, spear-shaped edge jutting up to the sky.

The demon priest held Gore there for only a second, but that second seemed to go on forever before Father Dennis slammed him down on the sharp point. The stone impaled Gore's body, shoving through his back until the bloody edge came out the front of his chest.

"Beth!" Andrew screamed. "No! No, Beth! Gore!"

A gasp shot out of Gore's mouth as blood erupted past his lips and burbled over his chin. A look of confusion came over him. It wasn't supposed to end like this. He was winning. He had the upper hand.

"Guess there will be a transformation after all," Father Dennis said.

Gore sputtered and spat more blood as he tried to talk.

"What?" Father Dennis asked. "I believe our hero has last words."

He leaned forward and Gore spread his legs wide to kick Father Dennis's legs apart and knock him off balance, then he wrapped his arms around the priest's body, roared, and with one quick jerk, he used all the power he had left to pull him onto the jagged stone cross with him, impaling him, too.

Face to face, Gore spit blood right into Father Dennis's eyes as he yelled, "I said, 'burn it!'"

Father Dennis struggled to free himself, but Gore held him in place, hugging him tightly to his body.

Andrew crawled toward his wife, toward Gore. He pulled himself to his feet where he hopped toward them.

"Andrew stay back!" Father Frederick ordered, but his voice was dull and far away. It sounded like it was underwater.

Father Frederick and one of the nuns placed the black bible on top of a slab of stone. All the nuns surrounded it. They each took a match and struck it while reciting the Prayer to Saint Michael, calling on the holy archangel to assist in the battle against evil.

They spoke in unison. They spoke with strength and determination, and they did not stop. When they finished, they repeated it.

Andrew could hear them behind him chanting. He knew they were about to light the dark bible on fire, but he crawled to her anyway. Beth was there pinned to the demon priest, stuck staring at his face, holding him there while the ritual behind him continued.

He was only ten to fifteen feet away when he heard their final words.

"Carry our prayers up to God's throne, that the mercy of the Lord

may quickly come and lay hold of the beast, the serpent of old, Satan and his demons, casting him in chains into the abyss, so that he can no longer seduce the nations."

They must have set their matches to the book because suddenly Father Dennis was ablaze, and with his body connected to Gore, Andrew was forced to watch his wife's body burst into flames with him.

"No!" Andrew screamed. "No, Beth!"

Shrieks emitted from the demon priest. His face transformed into something that wasn't human at all. It became the charred, blackened beast Andrew imagined all along lurking beneath the false skin, that priestly façade he'd hidden beneath all this time. Now, he writhed in pain as the flames melted the flesh from his nonexistent bones.

Gore was surprisingly silent, and Andrew hoped he couldn't feel any pain.

More than anything, he prayed his wife would be okay. He'd seen it happen several times now with her other personalities, but one could never be sure.

"Beth," he whispered.

"Andrew," Father Frederick said, "please don't get any closer. We don't need you to burn too. The book is gone. The demon is gone."

"Gore is gone," Andrew said.

From where he now stood, he could see the crispy remains of the young vigilante, but with the hood over his head and his scalp burning, he couldn't make out his features. He was sure, like the others, he wouldn't look anything like Beth. He would have his own persona, his own face, his own entire wardrobe – all of it.

"Thank you for everything, Gore," Andrew said. "Thank you for saving us."

"Andrew, look," Father Frederick said.

Before he glanced to his right and saw her, he heard Beth's cough. Her body rolled out from behind a nearby gravestone. She was dressed the same way she'd been earlier, minus his hoodie sweatshirt. She crawled across the ground, coughing, and hacking up soot.

"Beth," he said.

"Andrew," she replied.

He collapsed to his knees and crawled toward her where he wrapped her in his arms and lay there holding her. He was with his wife. With the *real* Beth. He was her only protector now, her only guardian. He looked forward to it. To every day they'd share together.

"Thank you, God," he whispered, lying there in the mud in a Catholic church cemetery. "Thank you for Peter and Ruby and Alex and most of all for Gore."

25

Things were hectic for a while. There was an investigation at Myles-Bend. All the security cameras went ballistic during the attack. Most showed no clear image at all, but a few were sharp enough to show Old Lynne attacking a few of the patients and one of the guards. There were no answers as to why the doors were unlocked and all the patients were free to roam the halls.

Olivia lived but never returned to the job. After recovering from surgery on her throat, she suffered nightmares, panic attacks, and would require years of therapy due to PTSD. Andrew promised to call and check on her often.

Andrew was fired from the job when camera footage showed him bring an ex-patient into the building. The only working footage was from prior to the attacks, from inside the atrium, when they first arrived. That was enough to lead to his dismissal. He claimed he rushed his wife out of the building once Old Lynne started attacking people in the halls.

Paloma's death was ruled a suicide. With no note left behind, an immigration case worker stated cases like this happened because of the depression of missing family back home. Since they lived illegally in the United States, they were afraid to travel because they wouldn't be able to come back into the country if they left. So, they suffered silently, missing their children and grandchildren. Usually, the fact they were sending money to their loved ones was enough to keep doing what they were doing but occasionally, the sadness was too much.

Andrew lied and said he didn't know Paloma was here illegally. He told the police the truth about meeting her when she was a janitor at Myles-Bend and that he knew when she left that job, she needed work and a place to stay, he needed help around the house, so they made a deal for her to live with him. They bought it and didn't ask as many questions as he thought they would.

In the end, everything blew over much easier than Andrew expected. Andrew and Beth considered selling their house. It held so many bad memories, but they decided it was also the place containing all their good ones. It had been their home since the beginning of their relationship and had been Andrew's childhood home.

Father Dennis was gone. His presence was neither seen nor felt since the unholy black bible was burned in the cemetery.

Like all Beth's other personalities, the demon had disappeared.

"I never realized I could feel him," Beth told Andrew one morning over breakfast on the back porch.

"What do you mean?" Andrew asked.

"I think he'd been haunting me so long I didn't know what my own body felt like without him hovering over me. I always felt drained. Tired. Weak. Now, it's different. My eyes feel more open, the air when I breathe feels so much cleaner, and I feel much more energized. I feel lighter. He's really gone, Drew."

Andrew loved seeing her like this. Of course, he'd seen her smile before, but she'd been doing it so much more often now and when she laughed, she did it with her whole body. She was so full of life. She slept through the whole night now, they cuddled more, and they'd made love several times since the demon left. Their life wasn't perfect, but it was a work in progress.

"You also weren't getting much sleep constantly cycling through the others," Andrew reminded her. "Gore was going out late at night, Alex was getting up early, Peter was frying your eyes staring at video games all day, Ruby was..." Andrew scooped up a fork full of eggs to try and hide his lack of explanation for what Ruby was doing.

Beth looked back at him and only nodded her head in agreement. As Andrew looked at his beautiful wife, he thought about Ruby, and he knew it was only right to be honest with Beth. If they were going to start this life over and do this right, she should be able to decide if what he did hurt her or not. There should be no secrets.

He set his fork down on his plate and closed his eyes for a second before opening them and looking her in the eyes. "Beth, there's something I need to tell you about Ruby."

"I know what Ruby was doing," she said, her eyes falling on her plate. "What you two were doing."

There was silence between them.

Finally, she spoke. "I don't blame you. It was me. My body. And she seduced you, even back at the hospital. I lied to you before."

"You lied to me?"

"Yes, well, kind of. You asked me once before if I saw the things the others did when they were in control of my body. If I remembered things. I said no. It was the easiest answer, I guess. The truth is most of the time when one of my other personalities was in control of me, I had no awareness and no memory afterward either. But sometimes I was semi-conscious. It was rare but sometimes I was there, kind of like taking a backseat in your own body."

Andrew's heart sank. He wondered if she was there during any of the times he and Ruby had sex. Was she there, semi-aware, witnessing the lovemaking?

"Don't worry," she said, as if reading his thoughts. "I was never there when you two – did it." She looked off to the side and for a moment Andrew thought she might cry. "Thank God for that," she added, "but I felt the soreness after, when I was back in my body. A woman knows. I can't blame you though. Who could? I mean it's your wife's body. Your wife who didn't want to make love to you and then suddenly is all over you?" She laughed. "If roles were reversed, I would have done it too."

"So, you would have still thought I was hot, even if a more dominating and flirtatious version of me came after you in this body?" Andrew asked.

Beth laughed again. "Totally." She took a sip of her orange juice and then added, "Really, I owe a lot to Ruby. We might not even be together if she hadn't intervened. I remember talking to you that first time alone, outside, at the hospital. I was too shy. Too damaged. Nothing would have happened. Then I blacked out. Next thing I knew, we were pretty much in a relationship."

"Yeah," Andrew agreed, "Ruby wasn't shy at all that day." He reached across the table and took Beth's hand in his. He caressed her knuckles with his thumb. "I need you to know something though. None of that stuff with her mattered. It's you I love. It's you I've always loved."

"I know."

"Ruby knew that too. I told her. She was sad but she understood."

"Do you miss her?"

"I miss them all in their own way." He laughed. "It's so weird because at first, it was so hard to wrap my head around. You as all these alters, these others, it was mind-boggling."

"I bet. I'm really sorry for what I put you through."

"You never have to apologize for any of it. For anything. I got used to it and they really did become like family members, so in a weird way I do kind of miss them, but through all that time, since the day I met you, I've always wished I had you and only you. That's been my wish since day one. That I didn't have to share my time. That I could have you 'round the clock."

Beth smiled and got up from her chair. She walked over to Andrew and leaned down to kiss his head.

"You've got me 'round the clock now," she said.

"I do," he said, looking up at her.

As he looked up at her face, his gaze passed her hands which he couldn't help but notice were rubbing her belly.

"But you might have to share that time again soon," Beth said.

"What do you mean?" he asked.

"I know the doctors said I wasn't able to get pregnant. But... I don't know if it had something to do with, you know, all that happened or what, but... I'm pregnant, baby."

"Beth, this isn't funny."

"I'm not joking."

"You're not joking?"

He slid his chair back and stood up. She was shaking her head.

"Wait," he said, "you're really not joking?"

"I'm not joking."

He rushed at her, took her face in both his hands, and kissed her hard. At that moment, for the first time in their marriage, Andrew knew everything was going to be okay. He had no doubts. Magic had finally entered their lives. This wasn't a hurdle they needed to get over. This was a blessing.

No matter what challenges they might face ahead, they had a baby coming, and they would finally have a *real* family. A promise he made to Beth came back to him. It was one he remembered reciting all those nights ago when he waited for Gore to come back from doing whatever it was Gore did at night. He was so angry he had to wait up for him. But he'd promised Beth this one thing and now, with their baby on the way, he understood its importance more than ever.

Family is family. Remember that. No matter how crazy things get. Family is family.

Andrew now understood it was much more than that. Family was indeed family, but family wasn't only the people you were forced to share ties with by blood. Family could also be the ones you chose or the ones who filled gaps in your life you didn't even know were there.

They could be the little girl who smiled back at you over pancakes as she stabbed her fork at the fruit face on her plate. They could be the teenage boy who invited you to play video games with him. They could be the young woman who never let you feel unappreciated. They could even be the asshole you always disagreed with who you know would always be there to defend you no matter what.

Before Beth and all the personalities she brought with her, Andrew had been alone. He thought he'd been okay. The truth was, he was only making his way through life one day at a time. They all gave his life meaning. They might have been difficult, and they might have brought new challenges every day, but he realized now whether they were real people or not, they were still his family.

"We have another chance at a family," Andrew said as he took Beth's hand and kissed her knuckles.

"Another chance?" she asked.

He nodded. "Yeah. Another chance."

She wrinkled her brow. She might not understand right now. If he had to, he'd explain it to her later, but he was grateful they had a baby on the way. This time he would appreciate little Alex.

The End

NEWSLETTER SIGN-UP

If you're not already a subscriber and you want to keep up with all things Carver Pike, sign up for Carver's Horrific Sunday Paper and get my monthly (or not-so monthly) newsletters straight to your inbox. I promise I'm not a pest, but I'll let you know about new releases, upcoming projects, freebies, events, and all kinds of other cool info. Just go to https://carverpike.substack.com/ or click HERE if you're reading this on ebook and want to go directly to it.

ABOUT THE AUTHOR

My name is Carver Pike. Since as far back as I can remember, I've been fascinated by everything horror. I'd sit cross-legged in front of the TV and watch The Texas Chainsaw Massacre while devouring a bowl of Kaboom cereal. I always wished the ghost at the end of each episode of Scooby-Doo wouldn't be just another man behind the mask. I wanted real ghastly ghouls, dastardly demons, and malevolent monsters.

At some point, I knew I couldn't sit back and keep watching this horror world from the stands. I wanted to be in the game. So, now I wield this virtual pen and sling ink onto this page with the hopes of someday being a major player. I want to create those worlds you visit, feed that fear that keeps you up late at night, and entertain you in ways only the greatest storytellers can.

I'm currently living in West Virginia where there is plenty of spooky stuff to write about. When I'm not writing, I'm usually watching horror movies, reading a good book, or interacting with readers on social media.

Hopefully, we'll form a great author-reader relationship and you'll come to trust that Carver Pike will always keep you entertained.

Check out http://www.CarverPike.com for more info.

ALSO BY CARVER PIKE

Be advised, some of the other works by Carver Pike are graphic in nature and should only be read by a mature audience. Make sure you read the blurb first to see if a book is for you.

The Edge of Reflection Series

Twisted Mirrors

Figments of Fear

Seed of Sin

The Fractured Fallen

Diablo Snuff Series

A Foreign Evil: Diablo Snuff 1

Passion & Pain: A Diablo Snuff Side Story

The Grindhouse: Diablo Snuff 2

Slaughter Box: A Diablo Snuff Story

The Maddening: Diablo Snuff 3

Grad Night

Redgrave

Shadow Puppets: Scarecrows of Minnow Ranch

Scalp

Faces of Beth

The Collective Series (a 10-episode multi-author series)

We All Fall Down: Quills and Daggers 2 (Episode 10)

Discovering Ivory in a Charcoal Cave: A Poetic Journey to Beat Depression

Printed in Great Britain
by Amazon